the making of isaac hunt

the making of isaac hunt

LINDA LEIGH HARGROVE

MOODY PUBLISHERS
CHICAGO

© 2007 by
LINDA LEIGH HARGROVE

Editor: Lisa Crayton
Cover Design: Linda Leigh Hargrove
Cover Image: istockphoto.com
Cover Photography: Kendra Cleavenger
Interior Design: Ragont Design

Library of Congress Cataloging-in-Publication Data

Hargrove, Linda Leigh.
  The making of Isaac Hunt / Linda Leigh Hargrove.
    p. cm.
  ISBN 978-0-8024-6269-5
    1. African Americans—Fiction. 2. Passing (Identity)—Fiction.
  3. Race relations—Fiction. 4. Domestic fiction. I. Title.

PS3608.A735M35 2007
813'.6—dc22

                                                    2007005330

ISBN: 0-8024-6269-3
ISBN-13: 978-0-8024-6269-5

1 3 5 7 9 10 8 6 4 2

Printed in the United States of America

To my three sons

on an ordinary afternoon in late October I discovered the truth about me. Like fire, that single truth stirred a hunger and created a hurt, but in the end it opened the door to a wholeness beyond my wildest dreams. All in all, I don't regret embracing that truth. I only regret the time I wasted in running from the freedom that came with it.

I planned to drive to Richmond that Sunday afternoon a few hours ahead of my parents. I told them I wanted to visit old school friends before our weekly visit to the rest home where Granddaddy stayed.

"I know it's kind of a last-minute thing," I said, hoping it didn't sound like another one of my lame stories. "But I haven't seen any of them in a couple of years."

"Oh?" Mom said, dragging the word out. She stared at me with those big brown eyes over her half-glasses and brought her Eartha Kitt-like voice up a half dozen notches. "Sounds interesting, Isaac," she added like she expected to be invited along. Then she winked and said, "Give Senator Holloman's daughter our love."

"Behave yourself," Dad said. "Your mother and I will meet you outside your granddaddy's room around two. Don't go trampling in bothering him before we get there. He needs his rest."

He gave my blond hair a once-over, and grunted. "You need a haircut. How can you even see to drive?" He went back to rummaging through his briefcase. Apparently, making preparations for upcoming meetings at the Fourth Circuit Court of Appeals took front seat to his concern over his only son's dishonesty.

Later, I sat in the Alzheimer's wing outside my grandfather's room for over an hour waiting for the woman I had lied for. A single white rose in my lap.

Her name was Rose. She had eyes the color of milk chocolate, skin like the choicest cream, and the pinkest lips. She was real and easy to be with. Every third Sunday for more than three months she'd dodge work at the front desk and meet me on the bench outside Granddaddy's room. We had a special spot in the woods.

I closed my eyes and leaned my head back against the mud-colored cinderblock wall and pressed the rose to my lips. Then I placed the rose on the seat beside me and linked my hands behind my head.

Someone was walking toward me. The footsteps were muffled and slow. I kept my eyes closed, faking sleep. The footsteps stopped and someone poked me in the chest.

"Wake up, Isaac," came the whisper.

Another poke to the chest. "Isaac."

"Good afternoon, Mr. Patterson," I said without opening my eyes.

He snorted and moved in closer. I felt his warm breath on my cheek. "We've been waiting all day, kid."

He had been eating raw onions again. I coughed. "I'm not doing it anymore. That's what I told you last time, Mr. Patterson." I looked up into his blue-gray eyes. "It's over. Remember?"

He stuck out his bottom lip and gave me a squinty-eyed frown.

I shook the hair out of my eyes and looked at him hard. "I'm not doing it anymore." I waved my arms like an umpire calling a man out. "No more."

"What do you mean, you're not doing it no more. Kid, it was your idea."

"Well, it was a bad idea. And I don't want to do it anymore. Besides, they know."

Mr. Patterson sat down beside me and placed his silver cane across his lap. He stroked it with the heel of his hand. His age spots looked like coffee stains on white china. "They don't know a thing we don't let them know."

He looked at me sideways and winked. "You know what I mean, bro."

I couldn't help but laugh. Little white men with canes should only say the word *bro* if they want to be laughed at. "They know." I winked hard and tipped my head toward the surveillance camera down the hall.

"Playing checkers," he whispered. "That's all they think we've been doing. Nobody has to know it's anything more."

The squeak of a wheel cut Mr. Patterson short. He was looking over my shoulder with wide eyes. The scent of cheap aftershave rose around me.

"Yes, Isaac. It's just a friendly game of checkers," said the voice behind me.

I turned and nodded to the thin clean-shaven man in a wheelchair. "Good afternoon, Mr. Smith. Getting a little exercise?" I forced a smile. Sweat glistened on the loose skin of his neck. There was a bead of sweat on his upper lip that made his face look dirty. His eyes, as pale as mine, sparkled irony.

He pulled at his black leather biking gloves. For a few seconds I couldn't take my eyes off them. That's when I noticed what he had tucked in the folds of the blanket spread across his legs—an envelope marked I. Hunt.

Mr. Smith finished looking me up and down then nodded. "Mr. Hunt." Then he gave Mr. Patterson a smile that did nothing to warm the air and barked, "Bye, George Patterson."

Mr. Patterson stood and gulped. "Afternoon, Mick," he said and left.

Mr. Smith stared at me some more. I stared back some more.

"You're quite the young entrepreneur for a shaggy-headed college student, Isaac Ulysses Hunt." He jerked his head toward my grandfather's door. "Old Ulysses would be proud."

I glared at his white face then clenched my teeth and looked away.

He wheeled himself closer to me and lowered his voice. "They don't know. That note you received came from me."

I looked at him. He was a thin, pasty old man. His Aqua Velva or whatever it was stung my eyes. The insulated shirt he wore only concentrated the aroma. His blue eyes were set back under a heavy brow with wild salt-and-pepper eyebrows. He narrowed those eyes and smiled at me. I looked away.

"That's a very nice rose you have."

"What do you want from me?"

"Want?"

"Yeah. This is where you ask me for that little favor so you can keep my little secret."

He sighed. "If I wanted to blackmail you I would have done it a long time ago. Besides it was kind of interesting watching you operate. Getting all these old white folk to trust you with their money. It beat bingo and reruns of *Diagnosis Murder*, that's for sure. What'd you do with the money?"

I stared at him. *That's for me to know and you to find out.* My turn to narrow my eyes and smile.

His smile faded. "Doesn't matter, I guess. Push me."

"I'm waiting for someone."

"Rose? She's not coming."

I frowned.

He glanced down the hall past me. "I'll tell you outside. Just push me, Isaac. Too many eyes here."

I laid the rose across the back of his headrest and I pushed.

Mr. Smith directed me toward a back entrance and down a wide leaf-littered path to a clearing with stone benches overlooking a small pond. Dry leaves rattled in the breeze. A few squirrels frolicked on a log nearby. I knew the spot well. It felt empty without Rose.

Mr. Smith shifted in his chair and reached under his blanket. He pulled out a half empty bottle of whiskey.

"Here, hold this."

I took the bottle and sat on the bench beside his chair.

He reached under his blanket again and pulled out two crinkled paper cups. He handed me one and took the bottle back. His clammy white fingers brushed mine. I flinched.

"Hold your cup closer."

And you're against me gambling? I almost said. I rolled my eyes and placed the empty cup on the bench beside me.

"I take it you don't care to drink with me then."

Mr. Smith shrugged and screwed the cap back on the bottle before tucking it under his blanket again.

"I need to get back. My parents should be here soon." Upsetting my parents was only a distant thought; I still had Rose on the brain.

"She's not coming back, Isaac. Rose, I mean."

"You're repeating yourself. How do you know that anyway?"

He slumped and looked out over the pond. "Yesterday, Rose and I sat here and we talked about you."

I frowned at him.

"Rose was my daughter."

I couldn't help but gape.

He shrugged and with a smirk said, "She got her mother's looks."

Mr. Smith shifted in his chair and gulped the rest of the whiskey in his cup. He poured himself another and continued. "She's a bright girl most of the time but put her in the same room with a handsome face and a single white rose and she turns into a naïve flighty little thing. I asked her what she knew about you. Your work. Your family. She said she thought you were in finance and came to visit your mother every month." He looked at me.

I winced. "We haven't exactly talked about—"

"She said she thought your mother was the widow Inez Hunt, a white woman who lives across the hall from me."

I winced again.

"Then she went on and on about you. Your clothes. Your car. Your looks. 'He has the most exquisite coloring, Daddy.' That's what she said."

Exquisite? She was one for strange words.

He shook his head. "That's when I knew I had to tell her my little secret. Though I knew as soon as I opened my mouth that she'd do the same thing her mother did ten years ago. Leave me."

He hung his head and stayed quiet for several minutes. He coughed and ran the back of his hand across his top lip. I stood up. Rose was a wash, and I didn't want to hear the rest of what this old white man had to suggest about me. "Mr. Smith, I—"

"You know what passing means, Isaac? Passing for white, I mean."

A stiff breeze blew between us. I pulled the collar of my

peacoat in tighter and leaned over him. "I'm not trying to pass, Mr. Smith."

He tucked his cup and bottle away and stuffed his hands under the blanket. "My daddy was about like your folks. Real fair. My mother she could have passed. But she didn't. She was a proud woman. Proud to be black. When I was seventeen, they were both killed in a car accident. Daddy's brother took me in. I graduated high school. Enlisted in the army. Did nine months in Korea. That's where I was wounded." He pointed at his legs. "And that's where I discovered the benefits of passing. I came back. Conveniently forgot my uncle's address. Fell in love with a white woman. Married her on her daddy's front porch overlooking the Chesapeake. Had our lovely Rose. Made a nice living passing for white.

"My sweet Leslie thought the sun and moon rose and set at my command 'til the day my uncle shows up and I have to tell her my little secret. She took Rose and left. All these years I thought she'd told Rose. Yesterday, when I realized Rose didn't know—"

He shook his head and ran a shaky hand through his thinning hair. "You know what your granddaddy told me one day? He said, 'A lie is a lie is a lie. No matter how pretty you tell it or how long you live it, it's still a lie and in the end when it's brought to light, it breeds misery.' Right out of the blue. That's what he said. I was sitting in his room playing old Al Green and he kinda woke up and came to his senses just for a few seconds."

He glanced at me and stopped short. I was trying hard not to roll my eyes. I'd heard that lie line many times from my grandfather. It was as tired as Mr. Smith's blanket.

" 'I'm not black, daddy.' That's what my Rose said before she left me."

He stretched out a hand, palm down, and looked at it. His hand started to tremble and he caught his breath. Tears dropped into his lap. I looked away then turned to go.

"Isaac. Wait."

He handed me the envelope. "From Rose."

I took it and stood there for a few seconds looking at that wilted rose and the shrinking old man. I remember thinking as I shifted on my cold feet that this talk had really been more for him than for me. It was obvious he didn't care any more for me than the man in the moon but he needed to say these things to unload some guilt. He was old and guilt ridden. I knew the truth about who I was. I wasn't living a lie, I told myself.

Man, I couldn't have been more wrong.

⌒

"Where's Betty's boy?" came the scream a second time. It was my grandfather's voice a few thousand decibels louder than anything I had heard coming out of him in a coon's age, as he would say. And it was certainly louder than anyone at Glenbrook Rehabilitation Center would appreciate.

I chuckled and said something about his medication needing adjusting as I entered Granddaddy's room. My parents weren't amused. Dad was hovering over his father's bed. Mom was standing near the door wringing her hands.

When I walked in she pushed me back and pointed to the bench outside the room. "Sit."

"I want to see Betty's boy!" Another yell. "Can't a dying man have a last request?"

Last request?

I pushed past my mother. "No, Mama. I want to talk with Granddad."

"Isaac—" my father started, then muttered, "Chloe, honey, stop him."

Granddaddy's eyes widened. He smiled and stretched his yellow-brown arms toward me. "There's Betty's boy. Come give me a hug, Isaac."

I studied the old man from where I stood. His light brown eyes didn't look like they had three months ago—wild and glassy like those of an animal in pain. During that visit, he'd talked endlessly to an invisible person named Mimi. The woman, I found out later, had been his secretary for a few months during his many years at the Department of Justice in D.C. Their affair had lasted for several years.

"Guilt will do that to a man in his last days," Ricky Hunt, my father the wise judge, had pronounced on the ride back to Raleigh.

Granddaddy had on one of those 9/11 T-shirts with a large bald eagle and flag enfolding the Twin Towers, and the words "In God We Trust" across the top. I stared at it for a few seconds, not sure what to make of the words. *God and Granddaddy?* I chalked it up to another slip in reality for him.

I glanced behind me to where my parents stood—their eyes stretched wide. Dad shifted toward me a bit but stopped short when his foot hit the corner of a bulging duffel bag propped against the wall.

My mind went briefly to Mr. Smith out there crying in

the woods. Racked with guilt and regrets. Weighed down with the burden of lying all his life.

What kind of burdens were weighing on my grandfather, I wondered?

I stepped closer to the bed. His blue bathrobe, the one I had given him when I was twelve, was stretched over his thighs. I placed my hand on the worn terry cloth and leaned in. "Who's Betty, Granddaddy?"

"Your mama, Betty Douglas. She lives in North Carolina. In Pettigrew."

The two adults behind me descended on the old man like an ER team, doing everything but cover his mouth with their hands. Looking back on that day, I think if they hadn't been so obvious I wouldn't have gotten so suspicious. I would have marked it up to another Mimi incident. Maybe he had had more than one tryst. He was a handsome old guy with those eyes and that square jaw, and probably had played the field as a younger man.

"What's going on, Chloe?" asked Granddaddy. His body fell back onto his pillow and he gasped. "Good Lord, help us all."

Ulysses Hunt, the man I had grown to love and trust and learned to call Granddaddy Ulysses, died the next morning. Two days later, I hired a private investigator to help me find this Betty of Pettigrew.

chapter 1

"life's a wild ride and then you die," I muttered the words of a song to myself as I put my dinner together. Stone had set tonight as a date for our last meeting. He would have the address of my mother, a woman referred to as Beatrice Anne Douglas on the decree of adoption he found, and at least one picture of her. *A picture.* My heart raced at the thought. In exchange I was to have the balance of what I owed him. He was an inexpensive and slightly unorthodox private investigator but nonetheless thorough. I appreciated that. And I'm sure he would appreciate getting paid real soon. Trouble was, I had nothing left.

Tate walked into the kitchen and looked over my shoulder. I hadn't really been following his monologue but that didn't seem to matter to him.

"Isaac, you listening, man?"

I sighed and gave him a sidelong glance.

"I told you last week," he said. "We're going to a play tonight. My treat. Karen and JaLisa will be here any minute, man. Put that sandwich down." He curled his lips and pointed to the food in my hand. "What is that?"

I ignored the question and used my tongue to push the corn chips back in between the bread. The mayo wasn't quite keeping them in check. "You need to go shopping."

He stretched his brown face and turned his head to one side, looking too much like Mr. Happy, the wirehaired fox terrier I had in high school. *"Me?"*

Of all the people to set me up, I least expected Tate. But looking back I should have known something was building. Tate had become a good Christian boy behind my back. Although I had to put up with the occasional sermon, he'd agreed to let me stay until I finished my degree and started work. Barely paying me any attention for months, lately he'd been asking questions about my employment decisions. I expected him to eventually start asking me to pay rent or something but certainly not, "Let's double-date."

"Isaac Hunt, you know what you are?" Tate asked, rising from his chair and taking on his I'm-tired-of-your-foolishness stance.

I checked my watch. *Going on eight o'clock.* "No. Tell me, Tate Michaels." Stone should have called by now to tell me where and when to meet him.

"A spoiled rich kid."

I gave him a wry smile. Spoiled? Being an only child, maybe so. Rich? The two people that raised me were certainly made of valuable green paper. Looking back on the night I left, I should have listened to the voice in my head: *Take cash or at least its plastic equivalent.* Suddenly I missed Ulysses Hunt but for the wrong reason—his potential for providing money.

"Thanks for not adding *that* word," I said, temporarily shifting my money woes into neutral.

"What word?"

I chuckled and pressed past him into the living room. He knew what I meant. Only last week, in a similar rage, Tate had rudely offered his estimation of me. "Why do you act so white?" he had yelled.

I wanted to say that just because a man can pass for white doesn't make him white (unless that man chose to live a lie, I suppose). No more than his darling JaLisa could pass for a man just by wearing my favorite 42-long hounds-tooth jacket.

I considered myself a black man. Okay, maybe not as dark as Samuel L. Jackson or even Laurence Fishburne, but nonetheless a member of the race of people taken from the African continent and sold on Carolina auction blocks. My blue eyes, curly blond hair, fair skin, notwithstanding.

My mind went to the night I ran from the sprawling 1950 bungalow on Feldspar cursing, vowing never to return. The night I saw the true colors of the black man and woman who had raised me.

While Councilwoman Hunt trampled on the papers

from my partially paid private eye and screamed about me insulting her motherhood, Judge Hunt thumped the counter-top with his fist and launched these senseless words at me: "What's this adoption foolishness? You're our son. You do not have white parents. You're a black man just like me. You like all the things black men like: black women, sports, and the like. You're afraid of all the things black men are afraid of: flashing blue lights in the rearview mirror—and don't get me started on how we need to protect ourselves from some of the same stuff from back in the day on the issue of white women."

Tate brought me back to the present with a slap to the TV screen I was preparing to watch. "Look, Isaac, man. I'm going to finish getting dressed. JaLisa and *your* date will be here any minute."

"Hmm." I faked interest and adjusted myself on his beat-down plaid couch. Where was that remote?

"You've got to get out of the house more," Tate continued from his bedroom. "Get your face out there, man."

Was this a date with a girl or a modeling agency? Maybe there was a documentary on A&E. Anything to drown out my social advisor. I had no intention of going out. I wasn't quite sure about my next move after graduation tomorrow, but it did not involve a woman unless, of course, her name was Beatrice Douglas.

I had gone to N. C. State to get out of the house, and majored in computer engineering to satisfy my curiosity in the subject (and to annoy my parents). Albeit my brush with the Red Planet on the NASA project during my senior year was exciting. But thanks to Ulysses Hunt, I had something beyond the intrigue of the cosmos to fill my nightmares.

Tate appeared, a toothbrush dangling from his mouth. "I forgot to tell you that your mother called."

"Who?"

Toothpaste froth splattered. "Oh, please, Isaac man." He swallowed hard and wiped his mouth on the back of his hand. "You're graduating tomorrow. *Your* mother, Chloe Hunt, wants to come. Get off this adoption thing. Forgive and forget. Get on with your life. I'm tired of your whining, man. You don't do nothing around here . . ."

I stood and raised my mood and voice to match his. "Why don't you tell me what you really think? I suppose you want me to give NASA the nod. Or worse, move back in with those people that call themselves my parents and continue to live the lie. Is that it?"

"Man, you don't know how good you've got it. God has blessed you beyond belief." He jabbed a finger at the door. "Why don't you just get your lazy, ungrateful behind—"

A knock on the door cut Tate short. He dashed to the bathroom.

I brushed crumbs from my T-shirt and snatched the door open. "Hi, JaLisa." A solitary black female—a nut-brown vision in a pink dress and a shiny purse to match—smiled back from the other side of the threshold.

"Hey, Isaac. Karen's parking the— You're not wearing that, are you?" She pressed past me, slapping me with her braids. "Tater, honey, did you tell him about Karen?"

I peered nervously out of the apartment. A car passed and I ducked back in, pushing the door shut. I could say I didn't feel well. That wouldn't be a lie. That sandwich had smelled better than it tasted. The phone rang.

Tate gave me the eye as he wrapped himself around JaLisa. "He was just getting dressed."

I had to fix another sandwich, I decided suddenly. A glint on JaLisa's left hand caught my eye as I went for the phone. *An engagement ring?*

"Have you set a date?" I asked casually as I picked up the phone in the kitchen.

"What are you talking about, Isaac man?"

"Nice engagement ring."

Tate rolled his eyes toward JaLisa. "Baby, I thought we agreed you wouldn't wear it until after, you know . . ."

His future wife studied her new nail job.

A ring. That sinking feeling in my stomach now had a reason to grow. There was more to Tate's interest in my love life than friendly concern. But the sight of the ring had given me an idea, an answer to my money problem, at least temporarily.

I turned my attention to the phone. "Hello." Stone greeted me in his usual rushed way and told me to meet him at the corner in five. He had an address and a picture.

Five minutes. I had to find my class ring and get downstairs, hopefully without seeing anyone named Karen, in five minutes. I started rummaging through the junk drawer beside the fridge.

"Isaac, what are you looking for?" JaLisa quizzed.

"Cuff links for the tux I'm wearing tonight."

"Cute."

Someone knocked. "I'll get it," she volunteered.

A tall, very dark-skinned woman entered. The flowery

24

dress she wore was a bit tighter and quite a bit shorter than her girlfriend's. The short hairstyle and bright red lips made her head seem more prominent, like she was taller than me. And maybe she was. But I wasn't going to get close enough to find out. Because I wasn't going anywhere with her. I had a date with a guy from Jersey.

"It's nice to meet you," I started, tucking the class ring in my pocket and giving my best Denzel smirk. "But it's just not going to work out this time. I have another engagement. No pun intended, Tater honey. I'm sorry." I left without putting on my shoes.

Buddy Stone stepped from his black Jag with too much drama for a man with good sense. He smelled of fried chicken. What should I care; he was doing a good job. He reached inside his big black suit coat, tugging at the lapel like a detective lifting evidence, and produced a manila envelope. Eight rings flashed on his greasy brown fingers. What was the chance that he would need another?

I produced the ring. "Look, Stone, I know I owe you—"

"I can't take that." He took it and held it up in the streetlight. "A class ring's hard to hock."

I was ashamed to admit I honestly knew nothing about the hockability of anything. "How about my watch?"

"Hold ya horses." He studied the ring more. "Least it's not engraved. Real diamonds?"

I nodded. The class ring had not been my idea; it would be no loss to me, especially considering what I would gain.

"Hmm. Worth $650, at least, if they're real. More than what you owe me. Go on. Open the envelope."

I swallowed hard. "I'll wait." If the contents of the envelope were the type to make a grown man cry, I sure didn't want an audience.

chapter 2

"you disgust me!" Tate screamed through the closed bathroom door.

I had spent a sleepless night thinking of my mother. I had been a fool to think that finding out more about her would calm my fears. My fears had increased at least five-fold. And on top of that I had a growing uneasiness over the contents of the envelope from Stone.

What if he had the wrong Betty Douglas? What if he was just pulling my leg, making it all up? What if . . .

"Stop it, Isaac," I told myself. She *was* my mother. I had to believe that. Her picture in Stone's half-page report looked like me. It was a color printout from a class reunion Web site. *Class of '74—Tallahassee Central High,* the title read. I had been glued to the picture for what seemed like days. I had her eyes—albeit, a different color—and mouth.

In the wee hours, I had checked the school Web site for myself. There she was, somehow more animated, more real, more shocking on my flat screen monitor than on paper.

This honey-brown child-woman with large gray eyes, would she remember me? I hoped so, though it pained me that I didn't remember her. I longed to have her touch me like a mother would a son, nuzzle me with her nose and cheek. I'd seen a black-and-white of Jackie O with young John like that. Had anyone done that to me? Chloe Hunt never had. Would Betty?

Tate was now pounding on the door and shaking the knob. "Unlock this door!"

"Just a second," I said, trying to sound normal as I dried my eyes.

"Just a second, my foot."

The door burst open. Tate stood behind me, jabbing a key.

"You disgust me, Isaac. That stunt you pulled last night. It topped all the crazy, selfish, stupid things you've done since finding you were adopted. You showed no respect for me and JaLisa. No respect for Karen. JaLisa and I took her out to try and make it up to her."

I tried to look apologetic.

"Don't give me that look. You just walked out on us. Then you had the nerve to walk back in like we should just let you slide. What's happening to you, man? Say something."

I listened to him rant. What I had done was done. I had no regrets.

"I've got a lot on my mind right now," I mumbled, finally.

He sighed and threw up his hands. "I don't know you anymore." He turned to go, but spun around with his finger aimed at my chest. I resisted the urge to knock it away.

"Wow," I said. "You went on a date with JaLisa *and* Karen? That means you had a girl on each arm last night at the play. And you call yourself a Christian man." I feigned shock and pushed past him into the hallway.

"What?" He turned and stood with his mouth open, head shaking for a few moments before he sighed and threw up his hands. "Stupid. Flat-out stupid. Stupid. Stupid. Now I *know* I don't know who you are."

"Well, Tate, maybe you never did."

"I guess you're right. I always thought we were friends. Always had each other's back."

"Always tell each other the truth? Confide in each other? When were *you* gonna tell me about the future Mrs. Tate Michaels? After the honeymoon? Yeah, Tate, we're real tight. Brothers."

"I was holding up my end, man. But I had the wishes of JaLisa to consider. Something you don't seem to take into consideration anymore. It's all about you. Matter of fact it's always been about you. You first. You get the most, the best. I've just been so stupid and blind all these years. Stupid! Letting you have your way 'cause I thought we were friends. *Brothers.* But we ain't brothers and we never will be." He stared at me, his face twisted in pain and anger. "Or at least one of us won't ever be a brother."

I flinched at his words like I'd been slapped. He had jerked the Band-Aid off of a scab from an old wound and he knew it. *Just call me white boy.* I closed my eyes to hold back the angry tears and swallowed the lump in my throat.

"Tate—"

"You don't even know what it's like to be black, Isaac. black folk don't vacation in Europe." He had his hand in my face ticking off his points with his fingers. "Black folk don't eat pâté and caviar. Black folk talk black. Black folk know what it is to suffer, to work for what they have in life. It's not just given to them 'cause they have—"

"White skin," I whispered.

He turned away from me and let out a heavy sigh. "My father, mother, and oldest sister worked like dogs so I could go to the same private high school that Ricky and Chloe barely lifted a finger to send you to. N. C. State had been my only hope of getting a degree. That *public* university was one of your many options.

"You want to be real about this, man? You wanna know the truth. Can you handle it? The only *real* reason they let me in was because of my color. Not my stellar grades. And they're good, man. You know they are. You've seen my grades. The truth is, Isaac, they let me in 'cause I fit in the quota, man. They needed another black face. Do you hear me? I don't think you're hearing me."

"Tate—"

He held up two fingers like daggers in my face. "I held down two part-time jobs during our senior design project. *Two.* And still made grade. *I* deserve to be at NASA not UPS."

"Tate—"

He was on a roll, but running out of breath. "You're not passing as white, Isaac. You're passing as black. And I'm tired of it. I'm tired of your foolishness. I'm tired of your selfishness. I'm tired of . . ."

I bit my tongue and held up my hand for him to stop. "Tate. Good-bye."

"Yeah, who is it?"

The voice from the other side of the purple metal door sounded tired. "Eva, it's me."

"Me?"

"Isaac."

There was a pause, then the door opened a few inches. Eva looked twice as tired as she sounded. But I could still see a twinkle of her old pertness playing around the corner of her mouth and that cute little nose. I was happy to see she no longer had the dreds. Dreds never looked good on a white person.

"Hey," I said.

"Hay is for horses."

I chuckled. We could still play our old game even though it had been many months since we'd split. It had been an agreeable though bittersweet split.

She smiled and pulled her fluffy yellow robe closer around her body. "How've you been, Isaac?"

"Okay," I said through the four-inch opening in the door. "I guess." I looked past her. She still had that red leather couch we had picked out. The only thing I'd ever bought for her. She had questioned the practicality of it. I had stressed the need for something to sit on besides milk crates and cinder blocks. There was a mug on the coffee table. Steaming with coffee I hoped. "Can I come in?"

She bit her lip and looked away.

"I'd love a cup of coffee."

"Um . . . "

She was biting the nail of her index finger and shaking her head. Somewhere above us in the building I could hear loud music, then shouting. I leaned in closer.

"Listen, Eva, I'll be honest with you. I need a place to stay. For a little while. Please let me in. I'm not trying to . . . I don't want anything else from you. I know this is crazy. You're probably saying, why don't I just drive across town to—"

"I've talked with Ricky and Chloe."

My jaw dropped. We had agreed that she would never talk with them, never make contact. They would never approve of her, the daughter of a retired millworker from Mississippi who had threatened me at gunpoint.

"Take your white/black, whatever you are hands off my Eva," her father had said while pointing the most ancient double-barreled shotgun I'd ever seen at my head. Although we didn't doubt the gun's or her father's ability to deliver bodily harm, Eva and I continued to see each other.

She sighed and pushed her short brown hair behind her ears. "I went by their house a few weeks back. I couldn't remember any of the phone numbers. I wanted to go to your graduation. Chloe told me everything. I didn't know you didn't live there anymore. Isaac, I'm sorry . . ."

I grunted. "So am I."

"Isaac—"

"Just one night, Eva. I'll sleep on the couch. That's all," I stressed. We had met at Starbucks over a year ago and spent four months together enjoying the excitement of forbidden fruit. She was wild and edgy, and I liked it for a while.

She sighed. "Isaac, I . . . um . . ." She crossed her arms and glanced behind her.

"You changed your hair," I said, figuring a change in subject would help her relax.

"Yeah, it was time to grow up. You haven't changed. Still ole blue eyes."

I groaned inside. *Blue eyes and white skin. Black man.*

"Eva, let's go for a walk. I'll wait downstairs and—"

I was cut short by a baby's cry from inside the apartment. By her wild-eyed reaction I could tell that she was not just babysitting.

We stood staring at each other.

"A baby?"

Tears trembled at the corners of her eyes. Her bottom lip quivered. "Don't worry, it's not yours."

I was numb. "Girl or boy?"

"I said it ain't yours, Isaac." She bit back a sob. "Now, please go. You can't stay."

"Why not?"

"Because I'm married."

chapter 3

"life's a wild ride," the voice echoed from a back room. I stepped into the darkness and listened to the raspy female voice coming from the back of the house. It was coming from a radio. Ulysses's "fishing" radio I figured.

"A wild ride. A wild ride. A wild ride, and then you die." The song faded into the hushed voice of the announcer.

I closed the door behind me and slumped against its coarse wood surface. Grateful that my key still fit, I closed my eyes and listened to the announcer wrap up his top ten at ten show and prepare to sign off.

"Take care, my friends. Have a safe and responsible

evening. And for all you designated drivers out there, this last one's for you."

A drink would be nice right now.

I sighed and opened my eyes. As far as I could tell, much of the furniture was gone from the first floor, especially the bigger pieces. I didn't hear the low tock of the grandfather clock that usually sat at the back of the hall. It was obvious Ricky and Chloe had been so busy looting Ricky's parents' home they hadn't bothered to put it on the market. What loyal offspring they were.

By the moonlight coming from the dining room windows to my right, I could see a couple of rugs rolled under Margaret Hunt's baby grand, her prized possession. The piano lid was down and books of every shape and size were stacked on top of it. A few small boxes lay open on the floor in the center of the dining room and nearby, like a deserted island, stood a brass urn.

I dropped my keys and overnight bag at the foot of the stairs to my left and went into the dining room. My sneakers squeaked on the hardwoods. The last song faded away and static buzzed from the radio. Somewhere deep in the house old ducts rattled as the air conditioner pushed air through the house.

I looked down at the urn. "Whatcha doing here on the floor, old man," I said to it. In the moonlight the urn looked more like a dollar store treasure than the final resting place of Ulysses Hunt. I picked it up and put it on the piano beside the books.

I stood there and studied it. It was nothing more than a fancy metal pot that held ashes. *Ashes and death.*

I shook myself. I couldn't let myself slip just yet. All is not lost. I thought of my mother. Those sweet eyes meeting mine, smiling, loving. There was still hope.

"But what if . . ." I shook my head. "Stop it." I thought of Old Ulysses. He would know what to do. We would sit on the front porch and he would listen to me ramble on, then he'd tell me what he thought was best.

"But you're gone now," I said to the urn. "Gone." Before I could stop myself I was pounding the top of the piano. The urn bumped around a little. Several of the books slid off the piano and onto my feet. I cursed.

"What am I doing? I need a drink. Where'd you stash it all, Ulysses?"

I picked up books from the floor and restacked them next to the urn, then stopped short at the sight of my name on a slip of paper poking from one of the books. I turned the small dark leather book in my hand and read the cover.

The Holy Bible.

I looked closer at the slip of paper, a white scrap with "For Isaac" written in black ink. For what seemed like forever I stood there barely breathing, trying to convince myself that it was not Ulysses Hunt's handwriting on that paper.

I pulled it out. There was more of his handwriting near the bottom, Matthew something. A passage from the Bible, I guessed, followed by my mother's name.

I cursed again and closed my eyes against the tears.

Life's a wild ride . . .

I threw the book across the room and screamed. "How long did you know, old man? How long were you gonna let me suffer?"

I sank to the floor and let the tears roll. The air ducts rumbled. Clouds passed over the moon. A cat meowed under the window.

I thought of Ricky and Chloe. They knew about Betty Douglas, just as Ulysses did, and yet they were willing to let me live in ignorance. Live a lie. My ignorance had been bliss for them.

Maybe Betty doesn't want to see me. Maybe she forbade Ricky and Chloe to let me know about her. Then they were simply honoring her wishes. But why did Ulysses tell me? He *had* started to slip near the end. *But why . . .*

"I need a drink."

I slipped my sneakers off and went to the kitchen where I hoped to find something to make this night bearable. In years past I could always find some of Old Ulysses' sipping whiskey or some of Margaret's baking spirits, as she called them.

The kitchen was bare. Even the island with the thick butcher-block top was gone. I had helped Ulysses put it in for Margaret's sixtieth. Chloe had always been jealous of it.

On the screen porch just off the kitchen I saw a wood crate draped with a white towel. A used candle stood in the middle. A half-empty bottle of Jack Daniel's stood to one side of the candle. A well-used glass stood to the other. And on the floor next to the seat, a five-gallon bucket of paint, lay a box of Dutch Masters, cheap Ricky's brand of choice.

A thud on the back step made me jump. I thought of Margaret Hunt, how her foot would fall heavy on the top step leading to the screen porch before she would fling open the door. I flinched and almost tossed the towel over the whiskey bottle before I realized my foolishness. Old Margaret was long gone and the noise was only a cat on the prowl.

The fat tabby bounded to the ground and across the backyard where it scratched around the apple trees for a bit before it left.

But wait, Margaret was still there, perched on her stool at her butcher block, looking across to where I sat on the porch. She was wagging a finger like she liked to do, talking to me in that half-whisper. That voice she would use to tell me about Jesus when I was small and gullible.

"Jesus lives in heaven, Isaac." Her eyes would twinkle and she would add in a tone I'm sure she meant to suggest angels and halos, "Do you want to go there, son? There's peace and happiness there."

Funny thing is, I was never "at peace" around her. Maybe because I always thought she was up to something. With all her talk about Jesus bleeding on the cross for me so I wouldn't have to die, she made my stomach turn. I told her as much on my tenth birthday. Our relationship went downhill from then on but she still used that whisper-tone when she wanted to "impart something special" but at least the word Jesus was never used again. And now to know that Ulysses had "turned to Jesus" made me even more nauseous. When had he turned? Why?

I remembered that shirt he wore the last day I saw him alive. I remembered his last words: "Good Lord, help us all."

None of that mattered now anyhow. What mattered now was I knew who I really was. And I knew where to find my mother. Now all I had to do was screw my courage into place and go see her. Maybe I would go next week on my birthday.

What mother could forget the day she gave birth?

I pushed the hair out of my eyes and lifted the bottle of Jack Daniel's. Nothing floating inside.

"Here's to you, Ulysses. For showing me the way. And to you, Margaret. Peace and happiness."

The "peace" lasted me until noon of the next day—when I woke and remembered that J. D. and I never really got along very well.

⌇

Abraham Benson ran his fingers over the snapshots spread on the table beside his bed. They were all recent snapshots of Olivia, his wife and business partner for the last eighteen years. Funny thing, she didn't look any older in these pictures than in their wedding portrait hanging over the fireplace. He owed that to the blessing of her Cherokee grandfather's genes. Abraham's own skin and hair showed the price of forging an empire from the land and sun, but not his beautiful Olivia's. Her native blood had stayed the rake of time from her face. She would always be a slender shaft of light playing in his shadow. He longed for her youth now, nestled like a bright kernel in the hollow of his graying frame. Each day he had died a little more as he watched cancer take her away.

And the previous year, a grain elevator explosion had taken the lives of three of his men. Among them, his friend and mechanic Henry Wright. Where was God in this? Taking the good people from him and leaving the bad. God was a tormentor, that much was sure. Why would Abraham be asked to keep loving only to lose again? He didn't know and he was tired of trying to understand life and God. All his money could not stop time or life's end.

Why keep it? He had asked himself at Olivia's graveside. As he studied the coal-black clumps being pushed onto his wife's coffin, he vowed that he would give all his money away. What was it, anyway? So much worthless paper in the long run.

Everyone in Pettigrew was saying he was crazy, he knew it, but they hadn't lost as much as he had. He didn't care if he lost his mind. In fact, he wanted to, particularly if doing so meant losing the memories and the guilt that plagued him. Forgetting the secrets he was forced to carry. The townspeople that benefited from the Benson secrets, they were bitter, hateful people. They deserved to be erased from the earth. As did those few Bensons left, perpetuating the evil with their silence.

Thousands of acres of the most fertile black earth could never fill the hole inside him. A hole that had been made over years of doing only what his family wanted—living for the sake of farm and family.

He lay back across the bed and fingered the pink satin and white crepe gown spread across the other side of the bed. It was one of Olivia's favorite gowns. Some mornings, for no good reason, she would wear it as they ate on the balcony.

Breathing shallow, he hoped he could hold the smells of morning in his body forever—honeysuckle and young corn, smells of Olivia. As the May morning ripened, he thought about praying. Would there be corn and honeysuckle in heaven, he wondered with a weak chuckle. Would Olivia be there among the heady green stalks, singing and harvesting? Would she be arranging bunches of honeysuckle for the Lord's table?

Singing came to him from down the hall. The smell of freshly pressed cotton fabric followed. It was Catherine, Henry's only child—hired the week before to help with the housework.

Ironing and singing.

He closed his eyes against burning tears and imagined the sounds came from Olivia. Catherine—she was decent and honest and trusting. Now she was singing, and probably ironing his shirts and pants that had grown too big over the past several months of his wife's sickness. She couldn't know how these sounds and smells soothed him.

A young traveling minister had come out from the migrant camp today. To talk, he said. "You need to talk about your grief. To help sort out what's on your heart."

Henry's girl couldn't know all the pain he felt but she had lost her father only last year. Could she help him sort out his heart, he wondered. No, no, she was only a child herself, barely out of high school. But maybe one day he would tell Patrick, his seven-year-old son about the memories, the family secrets. But not now, that kind of talk was too painful.

"Olivia," he whispered. Abraham rolled onto the gown, his chin hairs scratching the fine fabric. His friend and confidante was gone forever. "How I loved you."

He heard the creak of his door being pushed open wider and the squeak of sneakers on the wood floor. "What is it, Catherine?" he mumbled through his satin mask.

She gave a nervous chuckle that reminded him of Henry.

"Finally finished all those clothes, Mr. Abraham. Just got your shirts here, sir."

In his mind, Abraham could see the thin girl, her dark brown face lowered at the sight of her new boss in his underwear. He'd seen her do that several times during the past week.

"I'll just hang 'em in your closet." From the depths of the walk-in, he heard her continue, "I've hung your robe on the inside of the door."

He didn't answer.

"Um, Grandma Lu wants to know if we can take Patrick off your hands for a few days."

He jerked his head around to look at her. She flashed her brown eyes at him, then studied her feet again. Did Miss Lucretia understand what she was getting into? Was her grip on reality beginning to slip too?

A black woman caring for a white child was fine in Pettigrew, or any southern farm town, but only if she was caring for him in his own home. To take in the child of a Benson was asking for more than the usual amount of scrutiny and trouble. But none of Abraham's own family had made such an offer after the funeral. In fact, they had distanced themselves, furious over Abraham's decision to scatter the family's assets.

Abraham rose from the bed, allowing the offer to hang in the air while he put on his robe. *Why not?* The boy needed to be around lively, happy people. Despite what his family believed, the color of those people didn't matter to him.

chapter 4

pettigrew. That was the last known address on the report Stone had given me. But a lot can happen in eighteen years. Was she still here? Had she tried to contact me in all these years? Or would she turn me away? Would she even remember today was my birthday?

Don't pay beach prices, the gaudy billboard before me urged. I had no intentions of beach hopping. Tomorrow or the next day, I would be back in Raleigh, job hunting. I returned the nozzle to the pump and pulled out my wallet. Stone had hocked my ring, taken his cut, and dropped the rest in my lap.

"My mama didn't raise no crook," he said and added a wide gold-studded grin. "I don't do this for all my clients, you know. You got an honest face. God bless you, Mr. Hunt. Keep in touch."

I rubbed a hand over my new haircut and studied what I could see of my birthplace—the last gas stop before the beach. How far to the beach, I couldn't tell, for all I'd seen along the way were rows of trees, ramshackle houses, and farm fields. Across the highway in the largest clearing I'd seen in miles stretched a strip mall of sorts. Complete with a junk shop, a mom-and-pop grocery, and a craft store where two women sat outside on a bench. Further down, just before the blacktop rippled in the heat, I could make out a tractor crossing from one field to another. I hoped that a good price on gas wasn't all I would get in this sleepy little town.

Maybe I could get a cup of hot caffeine in the shack of a store behind me. I yearned for Starbucks, but taste and ambience didn't matter at this point.

Every waking hour since I'd seen my mother's picture was filled with thoughts of her. How did she look now? How much did I look like her? All my hypothesizing had made for a rough week at Old Ulysses' and a rougher three-hour drive from Richmond.

How I hoped she would find a place for me in her life again. I pushed down the lump in my throat and thumbed through my wallet.

Why did life have to be so gut-wrenching? "Happy birthday, Isaac Hunt."

"Talking to yourself, young man?"

I turned around to see a greasy-haired white guy in overalls.

"What?" He had a gunnysack slung over his back that looked cleaner than him.

"Lost?"

"No, I'm not lost." I handed him my new checkcard. "You take Visa?"

"Who's Visa?"

"Don't you work here?"

The man studied my card then my face. It didn't look like he had any intention of answering my question or taking the card.

The door of the store opened behind us. A voice boomed. "Get outta here, Crazy Eddie. Stop bothering my customers. Go call your mama."

I turned to see a woman in baggy clothes, smoking a cigarette. "Come on in, sugar," she said to me. "Don't mind Crazy Eddie," she said as I stepped into the store. "He's not all there. If you know what I mean."

As the woman ran my card, I watched the so-called crazy man through the front window. He trotted across the gravel to a pay phone under the billboard. He talked excitely to someone, all the while pointing toward the store. I don't think he was telling someone that Casey (I read her name badge) here had exceptional coffee. There was none in sight.

"First time through, Mr. Hunt?" Casey asked, eyeing my card before she handed it back.

I decided to answer with a thin smile. She smiled back. How old was this woman, I wondered as I studied her crow's-feet, the pucker lines around her mouth. Would she know Betty Douglas? "How do I get to Water Street?"

She told me between puffs and then gave me some advice.

"Watch out for low spots 'longside the road. They don't call it Water Street for nothin'."

Crazy Eddie was just hanging up as I climbed in my car. He flipped his sack onto his back and set out. He pumped his arms and, with each step, seemed to be pulling his feet out of a puddle of glue. Even with his back to me, I could hear him yelling, opening his mouth wider than Guy Smiley. I pulled to the edge of the gravel lot and watched him until he looked like a deformed tree waving in a distant breeze. I was in no rush to go to Water Street. That was obvious. But also, something about Eddie bothered me. That bag. What would a crazy man need to carry around?

One turn off the highway and I was on Pettigrew's Main Street. The wooded corridor I had driven along the highway thinned and gave way to yards and houses, then there were sidewalks and a handful of ancient storefronts.

The business district. I chuckled. I eased my Saab past pickup trucks and late-model cars as close to the posted 20-mile per hour limit as I could bear.

A sign caught my eye in a window: Hot Coffee. I could stop long enough to get a cup. The eyes of several overall-clad men loitering around on the front stoop followed me in.

"Hey. Welcome to BJ's," called a bubbly blonde, in a cropped T-shirt, from behind the bar. Cowboy-hat earrings and a ponytail completed her cowgirl look.

"Hi. Coffee, please." I looked around hoping to see a we-accept-Visa sign somewhere. Nothing but a few round tables and a jukebox against the far wall. Beer ads and banjos hung behind the bar alongside glossies of celebrities in cowboy hats.

Over the door above the exit sign, hung a metal sign with an elaborate corn design. The words "faithful and pure" curved around it.

As I turned back around the blonde pushed a Styrofoam cup across the counter. She was staring at me, her fingers lingering on my cup, her eyes getting narrower by the second like she was trying to figure me out.

Is he white or black?

I smiled at her and reached for my cup. "How much?"

"My treat, sir. Betcha you're on a business trip. Going out to the Farm?"

Ignoring the question, I thanked her for her kindness. I was thankful that the cup had a lid. I'd hate to spill coffee on my "business" clothes.

Water Street ran east to west, the same as Main, but about half a mile to the south of the business district. It was a short street, solely residential, with shallow grass-lined ditches cutting a square around each property. One-story shotgun houses seemed to be the theme with the occasional two-story.

As I searched for house numbers, I thought of Casey's warning about low spots. I was challenged to find anything but lowness. Further south stretched a stand of evergreens, as far as I could tell. I couldn't see a swamp, but the smell of aged gym socks seeping through my car vents told me it was nearby.

Sixty-five Water Street was a two-story with a screened-in porch and peeling yellow paint. I edged my car onto the shoulder. A pink-clad form sprang from one of the porch chairs and darted into the house.

I collected my courage and stepped across the weedy front yard, making sure I used the path of crushed oyster shells. My knock was met with silence. "Hello," I yelled politely, then tried the screen door. It was locked. Beyond the screen I could see three rocking chairs and a white door. I yelled again, "Hello, my name is Isaac Hunt. Is there a Betty Douglas here?"

The sun had warmed my black shoes to a temperature suitable for baking cookies by the time the door opened. A girl in a pink nightgown stepped onto the porch. Red spots covered her light-brown cheeks and forehead.

"What you want?"

I smiled. "Is your mother home?"

"I'm not supposed to tell you."

"I'm Isaac Hunt and I'm looking for Betty Douglas."

"She ain't here either." Her eyes bugged and she clapped a hand over her mouth. Then she disappeared.

I returned to my car, resigned to waiting. It was about 11:30 a.m. Maybe Betty would come home for lunch. I turned on the radio. Country. Country. Country. I turned it off and leaned my seat back. I could wait in silence.

"Isaac," a woman's voice cut through the silence.

The scent of flowers. Thick like Easter lilies. "Isaac," came the voice again. From the flowers? Everywhere. Flowers filled the street, my car. Cool and waxy on my face. Their green arms around me. Such a soothing voice, they had. "Isaac."

There was crying. Beyond the flowers, there was a woman, crumpled under the flowers. Muddy water poured from the face that she covered with brown hands. I reached for her. *Stop crying.*

But then there were kisses. The flowers were kissing me. My forehead. My cheeks. "Isaac."

"Wanna know what's in my bag?"

I jumped, fully awake now, and looked into Crazy Eddie's watery eyes. Next to my door, he was crouched over his sack, struggling with the cord at the top. The bag? There was something about that bag that was bothering me. But then again maybe it wasn't his bag. Whose bag? My bag? Was there something I forgot to pack?

I shook my head, hoping my silly preoccupation would go away. I pointed to his bag. "What's in there?"

He pulled out a toothpaste box, empty by the way he moved it. "Cell phones," he announced like a true salesman. "My bag's full of 'em."

I looked down into a bagful of used boxes.

"Want one? Half-price today. They work real good. Here let me call my Mama and show you." He stood and punched the letters on the box with his finger.

I tried not to smile. I was certainly not about to give him money for a phone, half-price or not, but if he kept up this act I might be forced to pay him for the entertainment. "No, thanks." Then a wild thought hit me. "Do you know where I can find Beatrice Anne Douglas? Folks would call her Betty, I guess."

"Burned," Eddie replied and went back to talking to his mother on the toothpaste-box phone, waving and gesturing with his arms and body as he spoke.

Burned? That didn't make sense. Did he mean she'd been in a fire?

I glanced at the house again and then at the paper in my

hand: 65 Water Street. Surely there wasn't another such street in this one-pump town. There didn't seem to be any signs of fire damage to the house. *What? So they rebuilt the house? Did she move away then?*

I grabbed Eddie's wrist to steady him. "Mr. Eddie."

He turned to me sharply, his eyes narrowed. For the first time he looked like a man only pretending to be mentally unstable. He leaned in, two inches from my face, and looked at me from eye to eye, then at my hair. Could he tell my thoughts? He had guessed my curiosity about his bag. Did he also know I thought he was a con? That his act was contrived? I was starting to feel like his biology project.

I looked away and saw a woman standing in the shadow of a cedar across the street. She stepped forward, the sunlight dusting her black face as she waved me over. She wore a simple white blouse and black skirt, pantyhose circling her thick ankles, surely not the outfit of a temptress. She cupped her hand again and fanned it inward with short jerks like she was just calling me over to share a cute joke, the kind you told your grandson.

I let Eddie go and got out of my car. He donned his insanity again and scampered down the street. I'd talk with him later about this burned house. Right now I had a little old lady to grill.

chapter 5

i'll be honest. I can't say I've had a best friend, the kind of person who knows you inside and out and will still move the world for you. My friendship with Tate is the closest I've come to that sort of relationship. We have a strange love-hate relationship that's been mostly hate of late, thanks to JaLisa dear (or thanks to God). But if I had a best friend I would want him or her to fawn over me and cook like this little old lady who sat across from me.

Lucretia Jane Price. A sweet name for a sweet lady that smelled of roses, spoke with a sweet drawl, and was surely made of all the sweet country things a man who hadn't eaten a good meal in a long time could imagine—molasses, sweet peas, sweet corn, freshly churned sweet butter. I was sure there wasn't this kind of sweetness in all of Raleigh, at least not in the white-linen set I knew too well.

Miss Lucretia, as she wanted me to call her, wrapped her gnarly brown knuckles around a fork and pushed it into a thick slice of country ham. I nodded to her for some more and she let the meat fall beside the half-finished slice already on my plate.

"So, you're thinking about moving to the area. A lot of people are doing that. Mostly to Manteo, though."

I nodded, nibbling at the edges of my biscuit and staring at her stark white shirt, buttoned high and tight around the dark folds of her neck. I had lied to her, and I didn't feel the slightest bit guilty. Some of it was true anyway. I had yet to approach the subject of her neighbor Betty Douglas. Didn't know if I would. Why did she have to know about me and my business in Pettigrew?

"I'll get you some fig jam for those biscuits." She shuffled to her feet and made for a curtained-off doorway in the corner behind me. "I'm sure I have one left. Gladys makes it special for me."

With the slightest shift to my left I could look through the house to the front screen door. Through it, I had an unhindered view of 65 Water Street. I had found a pleasant, albeit small, spot to wait. Every window I could see was open with thin curtains sighing in the breeze. On the kitchen counter to my right fluttered slender yellow and white flowers in a large mason jar.

I could not ignore the scent they produced even over the

wonderful smells of the hefty brunch on the table before me. It was lighter than the smell of lilies that had filled my dream, but in its own way strong and insistent, piercing. I closed my eyes and inhaled, pulling from my memory the picture of my mother in cap and gown. How would she have aged? And those eyes, those sweet, insistent gray eyes, how would they see me now?

I opened my eyes and caught movement to my left. A door that had been closed when I arrived was now cracked. Had it just been the wind? The old woman continued to rummage in her pantry. I could hear her talking to herself over the clinking of glass. In my mind's eye I saw rows and rows of glass jars full of muted red, green, and brown blobs. Glass jars with dusty metal lids. Rusty metal lids. Bulging rusty metal lids.

The door moved again, a little wider. Suddenly I was more curious about what was behind door Number 1 than what was under the lids of Miss Gladys's ptomaine preserves. I stepped across the braided rug, careful to avoid the curling edge, and pushed the knob.

At first all I saw were paintings and drawings of every variety on the floor, then I saw the boy. He was sitting on the edge of the bed just to the left of the door. His bony white knees, just inches from my legs, were as pale as his arms. In fact, he was pale all over like a lab rat. When he looked up into my eyes I expected to see shiny pink dots. But his eyes were dark brown like what was left of his hair, which by the looks of it had been cut with a steak knife.

"Hi," I whispered.

He stared at my mouth. Could he talk? He had been

watching Miss Lucretia and me from his perch on the edge of the bed. Why? And what, I wondered, was a little white boy doing in this house? *None of your business, Isaac Hunt.*

He looked me up and down—the movement of his head and eyes seemed to pain him—then he looked to the pictures on the floor. I followed his gaze.

"Did you do these?" I stepped closer to the makeshift gallery, not really expecting an answer from the mouse boy. If he was the artist, he was a very talented mouse boy. What I saw startled me.

I knelt to touch the one closest to my feet—a close-up still life of peas spilling from a pod onto a wooden surface. Oils, I guessed by the sheen, had been used on the two-foot square canvas in a way that made me want to like peas. There was a realness about it, not Norman Rockwell real, but a something about it that made me think that if I stroked the surface I could feel the peas' satin skin and the rough grain of the wood.

There were other fruit and vegetable works done up in the same treatment. Who would paint peas and corn? C. Wright or CW was scrawled in the corner of each piece. There was at least one judge's wife in Raleigh who would be slobbering all over this investment opportunity. What would she offer this CW to own the collection, to be the one to have discovered such an artist?

I turned to the boy and started to ask, "Who—?"

"Patrick," came Miss Lucretia's call, stronger and harsher than she had talked to me. I turned to see her frowning. "What have you been doing in here? Put Catty's paintings back in her case and put the case back under her bed." She pointed to the front of the house.

The boy slid from the bed and started shuffling the paintings into a stack. Miss Lucretia moved in closer to supervise the work.

Catty? I watched with disappointment as the stack was placed in a black portfolio. This discovery had been a rare find, a refreshing diversion from my dusty path. And now the art was gone as quickly as it had materialized. It was unsettling.

"Who is Catty?"

The old woman eyed me with pursed lips. "My granddaughter."

What was I doing? Chloe Hunt had trained me well. Now her influence was pulling me away from the real reason I was here. *Focus.*

"That girl is always painting," Miss Lucretia said. "Wasting her time with those smelly paints. She's a better cook. Cooked all the food you ate. Did a fine job, wouldn't you say?"

I nodded and stepped back into the kitchen, giving the street what I thought was a casual glance. No car at house number 65.

"Looking for something?"

"No, uh . . . I'd better get going, Miss Lucretia. Thanks for opening up your home to me."

"Well, you looked lost and hungry, sleeping on the side of the road like you were."

"I think I'm on the right track now thanks to your kindness."

There's something about simplicity, I concluded, standing at the car. It makes its bed with kindness and generosity.

This little town, these people, even clueless Crazy Eddie, were all bedfellows. Would Betty Douglas be as naïve? I had no way of knowing, but I hoped she would. It was cute and endearing. It would take me for who I professed myself to be.

My dashboard clock read 12:45. It was doubtful that my Betty would show up for lunch, but certainly after 5:00. What to do between now and then? Maybe visit this Farm I'd heard about. Maybe head to the beach for a few hours.

I looked to Miss Lucretia's sweet stooped form, pink rosebud lips pursed in the nicest smile, waving to me from the front step of her house, probably the same house she was born in, the same house where she cried out in pain as her own children entered the world. Had she known anything beside her simple house with its vine-covered porch and tin roof? I doubted it. With one foot in my car, I smiled and wiggled my fingertips at her.

The tortured yelp of a dog came from a white pickup parked in the middle of the road a few houses down. Headlights on, diesel engine rumbling, but no driver and no dog. Another yelp and, from behind the truck, the flash of a bottle in a man's hand. I stepped out of my car and walked toward what was shaping up to be anything but a scene of kindness and generosity.

"Hey," I called.

Nothing but the sound of a whimpering dog. I walked faster.

"Hey, you. Stop!"

Nothing, not even a sound from the unseen dog. The unseen assailant had stopped beating the dog. I stopped short of the nose of the truck and looked behind me. Miss Lucretia stood wringing her hands in her driveway. My car door hung open into the street across from her. The little nightgowned girl peeped out from the safety of her porch. I could turn and . . .

"Hey, mutt-lover," a man said. The dog yelped again. I turned to see a shaggy brown animal. Its eyes reminded me of Ulysses Hunt's the day before he died. "You want him? He's yours." Another yelp as the toe of a work boot sank into the animal's side.

With the dog writhing at our feet, the man pounded an empty glass soda bottle in his palm. Tall and dirty, about my age, I guessed, though it was hard to tell with his face shadowed under the curled bill of a baseball cap. The logo on his greasy T-shirt matched the one on his hat, the letters BRF with partially shucked ears of corn on either side. He waved the soda bottle in his right hand, and shared words about my mother that I didn't appreciate.

It dawned on me a few seconds later that this dirty man with the dirty mouth had no way of knowing about my Betty, but it was too late, I was already two inches from his face telling him about his father.

Later, much later, from a soft pillow in a darkened room, I remembered that it is often the unexpected things that cause the most damage. During my discussion with the abusive stranger, I had kept my eye on his bottle. I was not about to go the way of the mutt. I had no way of knowing that the bully was ambidextrous or that I would go down so easily.

chapter 6

having to see Patrick occasionally was
one thing, Catty realized, but having to see his pitiful
scrawny body every evening was beginning to be more than
she could bear. And now her grandmother had taken in another stray. A strange man with a fancy car. Sleeping in her
bed, the nice bed her father had given her. How far would
she let her grandmother go with this meddling before she
objected?

She had given notice to Pettigrew High. Only two more
half days there and she would be rid of serving up mystery
meat and putting up with perverts with peach fuzz. No reason

to split her days between two jobs to come all the way into town. Working for Mr. Abraham had been paying well. He was a good man, sad of late, but decent. He had offered to let her stay in the old Ross house that had belonged to his wife's family. Her oil painting would not be a problem there.

Her old classmate Cynthia had approached her about splitting rent at a mobile home park outside Finleigh, the county seat thirty miles to the east. Catty had almost accepted on the spot. The thought of getting out from under Grandma Lu and to a town with a movie theater and a library was appealing. But then she'd have to give up work at the Farm. Maybe when Mr. Abraham was on his feet again, she'd move.

"Either way, no more painting in the smokehouse," she whispered to herself as she loosed her thick braids. Patrick stirred on the bed behind her. His arms and legs spread to the four corners. "No way am I sleeping in the same bed with you, my little octopus friend."

Catty switched her desk lamp off and slid to the floor under the window. She had folded two quilts and placed them there earlier, before the last of the light had slipped over the trees behind the smokehouse. A stack of pillows and dinner, a bowl of sliced apple and cheese, waited for her there. With a third quilt and two chairs from the kitchen, a tent was added to her oasis. Inside, she could barely see the slab of light from the crack under the door. She fished out a flashlight from under the pillows and clicked it on.

A well of coolness collected quickly inside her quilted cave. She stretched out, careful to thread her legs under the chair footrail. The books near her left elbow, *Wuthering*

Heights and an ancient collection of love poems, distracted her with their musty breath.

They had been a gift from Mr. Abraham, part of his wife's collection. Miss Olivia had had so many nice books. Catty had spent the past two afternoons at the Ross house boxing them up—caressing each leather spine and gilded edge, attempting to push her envy down as she taped each box. Mr. Abraham's gift had made her cry.

The books would have to come later. First things first, she thought as she pulled her Bible from beneath the pillows and rested her chin on folded hands.

"Dear Lord, for this spiritual food—"

A knock at the door broke her prayer.

She winced and glanced toward Patrick. He was still asleep.

"Catty, mind if I eat the last of this fried chicken?"

This was the last person she wanted or expected to see on a Wednesday night, Trip Robertson, Miss Lucretia's occasional boarder and a young traveling preacher. Most nights since the beginning of the growing season, especially Wednesdays and Sundays, he spent time with the migrant workers west of the Farm.

Catty gritted her teeth and squeezed out of her tent.

"Catty," Trip called again, trying the knob. "If the answer is yes, snore two times."

She unlocked the door and opened it enough to see Trip's right eye and half of a grin. His brown curls had been shaved, she noticed, probably because of the lice in the camp. "How'd you know I wasn't in my room?"

"Good evenin', Catty. How was your day? The weather

sho' is warmin' up. Kinda warm for this time of year, though, don't you think? Oh, yeah, there's a man in your bed." He let his head fall back and he laughed. "A man," he added, drawing the word "man" into two syllables.

"Shh." Catty scolded him and slipped into the kitchen, closing the door behind her.

"My, my, my. A man in your bed, Catherine Wright, what would your grandmother say? Oh, yeah, I forgot. I helped her put him there." He pointed to the foil-wrapped chicken in his hand and asked, "Now, about this here dead bird. Mind if I put it in my stomach?"

Relieved that the preacher wasn't asking her to explain her absence at his church, Catty relaxed. "No, I don't mind. Now, I've got a couple of questions for you. Who is he? When is he gonna be gone? And where is my grandmother?"

"That's three questions," he mumbled through the chicken he held between his teeth. "Granny is across the street gossiping with Gladys. That man in your bed is named Isaac Hunt. From Raleigh, here visiting family. That's what he told Miss Luc. No wallet on him." Trip swallowed and got comfortable at the kitchen table. "Sit down."

Catty chose to stand behind the chair opposite him.

"I'm not gonna bite you, Catty, just this good chicken. And I'm not gonna pressure you to come to my church. Leastways, not this week. I want to talk to you about your grandmother and this tendency she has for taking in every Tom, Dick, and Isaac."

"Mmm. Strays."

"First it was Patrick, now this Isaac fella."

"No, first it was you."

"Did you mean to brush out your hair a bit?"

Catty tossed her thick wavy hair. "Never mind my hair. Tell me how I come to have a man in my bed."

"No, wait. 'Bout your grandmother, and to some degree, I see you doing the same thing, young lady."

Catty pulled at her hair and studied a frayed edge of the braided rug. She would need to mend that again soon.

"What is that, you ask? You and your grandmother are locked in cycles of guilt over your father's death. We need to talk that out. It's not healthy, young lady. Last time we talked you told me about the unforgiveness God freed you from. Well, guilt is just as deadly."

Catty studied the heavily tanned white man across from her and smiled, wanting to say *You're sounding like a preacher for sure right now.* The way he switched from teasing her to preaching was amusing at times. His face, his body, even his voice changed. It occurred to her that it was like he had two personalities. One was a hick with a drawl and a toothpick dangling at the corner of his mouth, the other was Charlie Gibson with a mike and a concordance dangling from his wrist.

"Miss Luc is surrounding herself with males, trying to offer them what she didn't give her son-in-law, your father. You, look at you. You've lost all this weight. How long has this chicken been in the fridge? Two, three days? Why didn't you eat it tonight? Working yourself like a maniac on so very little food. You're killing yourself slowly. Catty, look at me. This thing with Henry Wright's favorite spoon and his clothes . . ." Trip paused and wiped his mouth. Catty glared at him. "Okay, okay, I'll leave that alone for now. I'm just saying you and your grandmother can help each other, but you need to talk."

Catty brushed her fingers through her hair and studied the rug some more, praying that this pause meant the sermon was over. She wanted to grill him about a certain rumor she'd heard, but she knew she'd be speaking out of turn. He was, after all, a preacher. Small-town people say rude things about outsiders, most of which is as false as a hair weave.

He sighed and slapped the table. "Okay, 'nough said for now. Could you pour me a touch of milk, Catty girl? Thanks. About our mystery man in your room. I was pulling onto Water Street, coming by here for a late lunch, when I saw Jack Kepler's truck in the middle of the street. I didn't know it was his at first, but I could see that it was a Benson Ridge Farm truck. Then I saw him kicking Mr. Bill."

Catty drew a breath and turned so quickly to face Trip she spilled the milk. Mr. Bill was the stray dog that she had been trying to win favor with.

"I think your dog is okay," Trip assured her. "Then I saw that Jack was talking to somebody—our Mr. Hunt. But he wasn't just talking to him. He was giving him the business, you know. This led to that and before I could get to them, Mr. Hunt was out cold in the street. Meanwhile, Jack the Menace ambles off like he's done society a favor.

"Your grandmother saw it all and says Jack was viciously beating Mr. Bill. Our Mr. Hunt was trying to save the mutt from an untimely death."

"Why?"

"Don't know," Trip spoke through chicken. "Maybe he's

a mutt lover like you. Got any tater salad, macaroni and cheese . . . ?"

Catty let Trip's words flow past her as she wiped up the spilled milk. Her mind went to the long pale form she'd seen earlier in her bed. The muscular arms lifted above his head like a child at rest, the beautiful head with its full lips brushing her pillow. What kind of heart did this mystery man have that he would risk so much for a dog? She pulled her lips between her teeth and prayed that Isaac Hunt would soon be gone.

I woke to the smell of aftershave at the edges of my consciousness. The scent would have been appealing had it not been for my throbbing and lurching insides. My head pounded as did my jaw, particularly the right side. The general thud in my lower body was concentrated in my abdomen.

What time is it? My watch was gone, as were my shoes and keys. I hoped my car was fine, and I hoped it wasn't too late. In the ebbing light I could make out floral drapes puffing in the cool breeze over blinds, and felt the scratch of lace against my cheek. Had I been moved to someone else's house? I didn't like the way this was shaping up. I needed to get back on track. I rolled to my side and regretted it. When the room stopped turning, I tried calling out. My voice was fine but my mouth wouldn't open wide enough.

My fuzzy brain remembered a man, much shorter and thicker than my assailant. "Take it easy, big fella," he had said, his lips close to my ear as I puked on the front steps.

Whose steps? Then there were thick rough hands on one elbow and soft knobby fingers on the other—leading me, lifting me. *Miss Lucretia and who else?*

But thinking was hard work, so I stopped and closed my eyes, listening to the sounds around me. The crickets, the rattle of Venetian blinds in the breeze, the voice of the man with the rough hands. He was asking someone about fried chicken. Another voice. A woman, though not Miss Lucretia. The words were muffled. *Catty? That's a strange name.*

There was a knock on the door, and she came in with the moonlight on her dark hair. She carried a tray. She moved closer and smiled at me with affection in her large amber eyes, stroked my head with long cool fingers the color of ginger.

And on the tray there was a plate of fried chicken and peas—large, sweet green pearls. She fed them to me as she hummed, then kissed my closed eyelids and left.

I opened my eyes to a very dark, very quiet room and panicked. *This isn't my bedroom.* Then the scent, the smell of a man who liked lace, brought me back to my senses. *Had it all been a dream?* Parts of me were still pounding but not so loudly, but my bladder needed emptying badly so I tried rolling again. When I moved, the rest of the room did not. So I felt my way across a shaggy rug to the door.

I was comforted by the streetlight that flooded the room I stepped into—a riot of furniture wrapped in clear plastic. The sight had been my first impression of the world the sweet old woman had proudly introduced me to. I was still at Miss Lucretia's and I breathed a little easier. A man lay snoring on one of the sofas. Through the door to my right, I could hear someone else snoring.

Feeling a little like a polite prowler, I padded through the next room, a smaller sitting room with a TV and a window AC unit, and then into the kitchen where a Donald Duck nightlight burned in the socket next to the sink. A half dozen eggs and a stick of butter sat sweating on the counter next to a black skillet. The chair where I had sat so many hours earlier was draped in a large purple towel. Five cuckoos came from somewhere behind me. *Five o'clock.*

The door of the bedroom where I had met Patrick stood ajar. Did I hear voices coming from the room? No, it was a radio and it was coming from behind the door next to the boy's room.

The muffled voice of an announcer seeped through the door. Then there was music. Classical. It was joined by the sound of a shower, which only helped magnify the scream from my bladder, and there was humming. A woman's hum. *Catty?* I crossed my ankles and leaned against the wall, enjoying the hum.

The door opened. I stood at attention but it was too late—the door had hit my right big toe. I heard a muffled scream and the scrape of a chair from the other side of the door.

"It's okay," I said, trying to sound harmless and unhurt. "My name is Isaac Hunt. I was beaten up in the street today and your grandmother took me in."

"I know."

It was awkward talking through the door. I didn't look my best but I hoped she would understand.

She drew a breath and almost shouted for me to stop in a drawl thicker than any I'd heard since arriving in Pettigrew.

Four slender fingers were wrapped around the edge of the door. The door was pressed closer to me. I could hear quick breaths and the scent of herbs. "I'm going to pull this door closed. Don't move. Do not move. When you hear the lock turn, I want you to leave. Do you understand?"

Her words made sense. I wasn't offended in the least. I would wait for the click of the lock and leave. In her shoes or, as it were, wet towel, I probably would have reacted the same way to a strange man, my only weapon being a flimsy wood door. I wasn't bothered by her tone at all. I was bothered because, at the sight of her fingers, I realized my experience earlier with the woman with the tray had only been a dream. The proof being in the color of those four damp fingers pressing the door against my throbbing toe. They were not the color of ginger, but more the color of coffee grounds—maybe darker.

chapter 7

it's funny how pain colors a person's interpretation of reality. Like the absence of light in a painting, everything comes across flat and featureless, matter-of-fact. Pain, immediate and past, I reasoned as I stared into my coffee cup, had played a factor as well in my misperceptions of the previous day and night.

This little town was not a wonderland where sweet cherubs sprinkled elfin magic on all wayward travelers. There was evil here too. Pettigrew was no different from Raleigh or Richmond or anywhere else in the world. I would not settle here, a notion I had been allowing to simmer on the back burner of my options. When my toast was ready, I would take my leave, try one last time to make contact with the elusive Betty Douglas—her car stood in the driveway across the street—and make my way back to Tate's. Hopefully patching things up with him would not be too difficult.

No one here, except for maybe Miss Lucretia Price, wanted me here anyway. Certainly not the dark-skinned princess of silence who had poured my coffee. Pale Patrick was sitting on my left, imprisoned by some deep sadness, oblivious to the world around him. Miss Lucretia's boarder Reverend Trip Robertson had two things on his mind—food, and migrant workers. This was not my place. Too many angry, hurt people. I already had one too many of those.

"Isaac." The shabby minister across from me spoke through his half-chewed breakfast. He had a disgusting habit of doing that. "Sure you don't want some eggs? Catty's eggs are great." I studied the man, thinking of what minister wanted to be called by such a name. A minister with an under bite like that.

I smiled and shook my head. The smells were great but my stomach was still a little unsure of itself. "Just toast." A plate was placed in front of me with such force that the toast bounced. "Thank you." I bit back the other words I wanted to say. *Just a few more minutes and I'll leave and lock the door on this chapter. And throw away the key.*

Milky morning light filtered in through the kitchen window. A cloudy day. *So much for going to the beach.* I watched the yellow and white flowers tremble in the breeze as I ate, allowing the people around me to do what they wished. *A few more minutes.* The little yellow and white fingers ticked off the seconds for me.

Patrick rose, uneaten eggs and bacon still on his plate, and went to his room. Miss Lucretia entered from outside, stuffing a couple of large cabbage heads in a plastic bag and talking about someone named Gladys. The minister rambled on, to me I suppose, about a migrant worker named Miguel. A *few more seconds.*

I brushed the crumbs from my white oxford shirt and gray slacks, then stood. *How much should I pay Miss Lucretia for the room?* I thumbed the wad of bills in my pocket.

"Miss Lucretia." I spoke to the form bent over with her hands riffling through the bottom drawer of the fridge.

She turned, looked at my hands, and came over to me to slap them like a grandmother would. "Put your money back, child."

"But . . ."

"Keep your money. Was my pleasure to help you out."

"Thank you. And thank you," I said, turning to Trip, "for letting me use your room."

He jerked his head toward me, a corner of toast clenched between his teeth. He chewed and swallowed quickly. "Huh?" His face widened into a grin, and then he did what I guessed, by the crinkles on his long deeply tanned face, he did often. He laid his head back and laughed, slapping his knee, like I had told my best joke. "That lacy, flowery room, young man, does not belong to me." He sprang at me and turned me to the woman at the sink, the woman glaring at me with enough eye power to toast bread.

I stammered. She rolled her eyes and went back to washing

dishes. Miss Lucretia snickered. Trip continued to laugh while I stammered apologetically until someone tapped my elbow. I turned to see Patrick there with a slip of paper in his hand.

"Mr. Isaac."

His lips had moved, and he had spoken to me, with a light drawl, in a proper sounding way as if he were my manservant.

"My sweet Jesus," Miss Lucretia exclaimed.

I stared at the boy, as did the others around us, judging by the silence.

"Yes, Patrick," I managed to say.

"This is for you. I made it."

I cupped my hands and accepted the gift, a card with a rainbow on the outside and the words "Get well soon" written inside.

"When Jack hit you and you fell out, I got scared. So I prayed and God told me to fix you a card."

How do you tell a kid you don't believe in God any more than you do Santa or the tooth fairy? Smiling again, I stooped and looked him in the eye. Although I didn't agree with his theology, I did appreciate his concern for my well-being so I said, "Thank you, Patrick."

He smiled with eyes the size of lightbulbs and then wrapped his thin pasty arms around my neck and kissed my bruised jaw.

There was a collective "Aw" around us, then Miss Lucretia exhaling, saying "Sweet Jesus" as she dialed on the phone that hung next to the fridge. With the phone to her ear, she pulled the boy into a hug like she'd just seen him raised from the dead.

When I stood again, the preacher gave me a slap between my shoulder blades. "You know, Isaac, your run-in with the infamous Jack was a blessing in disguise."

Neither my brain nor my body agreed with that assessment, but I smiled nonetheless.

I glanced at my watch. Was seven thirty too early for a man to call on the mother he hadn't seen in eighteen years?

"Isaac, I've got a great idea," Trip said. "I want to get a picture of you and Patrick. My camera's in the truck. Wait here."

The man left before I could protest. I hoped he didn't see my look of dread. Miss Lucretia and Patrick hadn't; they were chatting it up with someone she called Mr. Abraham, Patrick saying far fewer words than she was. I glanced at Catty by the sink. She had seen my expression, I was sure of it. But Catty's was not one of distaste or disapproval. In her dark brown eyes I saw a question, or was it fear. She turned around and gripped the edge of the sink, then turned to face me again.

"You probably think we're all crazy." She paused and dabbed at her eyes with her pinkies. Her words were slow, shaky—the drawl heavy but no less sweet. I looked at her full in the face for the first time. Even with her forehead knotted and her eyes tearing up, she was very pretty. A heart-shaped face, drawn to a soft point at the chin where her full mouth, wrinkled and shiny like a date, trembled, drawing down her small flat nose even more. Her hair was pulled up with a thick rubber band into a large broad afro puff at the top of her head.

Crazy? I was the crazy one, for all I could think of in her moment of sadness was taking her in my arms and caressing that beautiful wild mane with my cheek, smoothing my palm over the freshness of her white cotton blouse.

She found her voice. "Patrick hasn't talked since . . . well, in months. Not since his mom . . . got real sick."

Trip returned with his camera. "Now, I want y'all to come outside. Miss Luc, get off the phone. We got a little window of sunshine. Won't last long."

We gathered in front of Miss Lucretia's sweet little house, and I smiled as genuinely into the Polaroid as a man who wanted to be somewhere else could. I eyed the car across the street, a Seville I could finally discern. Trip snapped a few different angles, then took my address.

"To send you copies," he said.

I gave him Tate's address. He urged me to file a complaint against Jack Kepler but I refused, wanting to make a clean break of this town. My solution in this situation was what the butcher and the baker must have said to the candlestick maker, "Don't make waves."

We all hugged. Or I guess I should say, I was hugged by everyone, even Catty. Though her hug was more like a two-handed pat the school bully would get from the principal. It was better that way, I figured. I didn't want to be tangled up with a relationship and everything that meant. She was just another pretty black face that would spurn me anyway. Disgusted by my "whiteness."

Her words from the wee morning hours came back to me, "I want you to leave. Do you understand?" It became evident that she was not merely wishing me away so she could shower in peace; she was willing me to leave her life, her lacy, flowery aftershave-scented world forever. Had she had a man

76

there and didn't want her grandmother to know? That was none of my business. Her choices were her choices. If anybody understood the desire to be able to choose freely how one's life played out, I did. But what I did not understand was why she hated me so. It bothered me. And at that moment, perched on a meeting that would change my life forever, I didn't want to be bothered.

"Good-bye and thank you," I said as I swung my body into my Saab. Like a man with places to go and people to see, I went through the motions of driving away, through downtown, and then back to Water Street. To my relief my hosts were back in their house and there was still a Seville at house 65.

I parked behind the car and wiped my sweaty palms on my pants. I suddenly felt like I was made of sweat. Sweat and butterflies. Now was not the time to throw up. *Breathe. Breathe. Breathe.*

My knock at the screen porch was not answered right away. Waiting on the doorstep, bees tracing around my head, it occurred to me that I didn't quite know what to do if she was happy to see me, took me into her world. I was prepared for rejection; the past several months had taught me how to deal with that kind of disappointment. But what was I to do if she accepted me? She didn't know me; I was not the little boy she gave away. I had been a teenage boy and done all the mean-spirited, thoughtless things a teenage boy could do. Now I was a man and had done my share of man things, which had not exactly improved too much on my teenage years.

I turned and looked at the sweet little house across the

street. Under that small tin roof there were people who had accepted me, comforted me. Why had they done that? Why did it upset me so?

Behind me the door opened. I turned to face the wrinkles and gray hair of a woman who, I hoped, was not my mother.

"Yes?" she croaked.

"Hello, my name is Isaac Hunt."

She slammed the door and stepped back. "No," she shouted. "No, you're not. You can't be."

This was not the reception I expected. "I am. I'm looking for Betty Douglas."

"No. Good Lord, no." She continued to back up. Behind her through the door, I saw the wide eyes of the same little girl I'd seen the day before.

"Can I speak with Ms. Douglas?"

"Go away or I'm gonna call the police. You come here again, I'm calling the police. You hear me?" She retreated quickly behind the white door and made a big show of locking it.

"Why?" I shouted and backed up, bumping into the side of the Seville. I thumped the car's broad tire with my heel. "Please, talk to me. I don't mean you any harm."

The crunch of gravel made me turn around. It was Patrick. Alone, except for a dog that danced behind him, the same shaggy mutt that had caused my beating.

"Patrick? What is it?"

"I know where she is."

A black man will do unbelievable things in times of indecision and desperation, even follow strange white children to find his mother. These were desperate times. With a minimum of words, Patrick directed me through town and across the highway down a straight road, its husky surface crisscrossed with black welts that made for a bumpy ride. Corn plants resembling dense loaves of green with a crust of brown abounded on each side of the highway. The fields stretched for miles it seemed in all directions, stopped in some places by a ragged gray-green line of trees in the distance. Stormy skies rumbled overhead.

A light rain had started when Patrick instructed me to turn onto a dirt road. A gate stood before us with a sign: "Property of Benson Ridge Farms" above in big black letters, with a warning for trespassers below.

With a flippancy that reminded me of myself at times, Patrick assured me that we would not get in trouble, then jumped out and pushed open the wide gate. He directed me a half mile along the road, shadowed deeply in places by low-hanging boughs tangled with flowery vines. Even in the rain, the sweetness from their blossoms infected my mood. I felt hope for the first time in months. I hummed and rolled down my window, sucking in the moist fragrant air.

My left side was fairly damp by the time we arrived at another lane. Patrick told me to stop and he jumped out. Through a neatly trimmed hedge I could see a white-trimmed house of blue clapboard. I got out and stood by my door. *Breathe. Breathe. Breathe.*

"Come on," Patrick urged. He took off at a trot. I followed a little more slowly. I watched him run across a freshly mown lawn, scamper across a low front wraparound porch, and disappear around the back of the house.

Should I knock or follow the boy, I wondered as I stood with one foot on the front step. I had taken him without letting anyone else know. He was under my charge out here in the sticks. If he got hurt, I would be responsible.

I followed and found him kneeling at a tombstone, his hands folded, his lips moving. *What was the sense in praying at a grave?* I waited until he was finished, then approached him.

"Patrick?"

With tears trembling in the corners of his eyes, he pointed at the marker engraved "Olivia Ross Benson, beloved mother, wife, and friend."

"My mama."

It was his mother's *death*, not merely her sickness that had robbed him of any will to speak. I felt like a heartless idiot. But those feelings turned quickly back to indecision and desperation. It was clear now that Patrick had led me here to see *his* mother, not my own. Olivia Ross Benson, *she* was here in his young mind. Not Betty Douglas. *Where to now?*

Patrick stood and began walking around what I saw to be other grave markers, low to the ground and moss covered. As far as I could tell, they were all Rosses except for a small one labeled Patricia O. Benson, with a small stone angel perched on top.

Patrick pointed and whispered as he walked through the graveyard, "My grandfather. My grandmother. My Uncle Bobby. My baby sister who I never saw."

The rain fell heavier. Thunder shook the skies. I wanted

to leave but Patrick walked on, his light blue polo plastered to his back.

"Patrick."

"Come. Here," he shouted back over his shoulder and pointed to the ground.

By the time I caught up with the boy, he had knelt again. After a short prayer, he started pulling at some vines. I saw the top of a marker through the mound of brambles. *Another grave.* He seemed infatuated with death.

"Patrick, stop."

He continued to pull.

"Please stop. You might get poison ivy or something. There could be snakes in here. We need to go." I placed my hands on his, then caught my breath at the letters I saw beneath our hands. B-E-A. I pushed back the vines a little more. T-R-I-C-E.

I didn't need to see any more.

chapter 8

bare-chested, Jack stepped out onto the porch and stretched in the cool morning air. He stood in the shadows, sipping his coffee and warming his toes in the sun that sliced through the clouds overhead. His time on Water Street had not disappointed him. A soft bed with a soft body beside him, food, good drink. A measure of peace and quiet, with the exception of the mutt that refused to move out of the center of the road and the rude stranger that wanted to play savior.

He had planned to spend only the afternoon on Water Street but the possibility of the law trying to find him had extended his stay. Jack leaned against the porch rail and worked a toothpick between his back teeth. Trina wasn't a good cook but that's not what he had paid her for anyhow.

The bark of a dog brought back thoughts of the pale stranger. What had been so important about that old raggedy dog? The fool would probably think twice, Jack reasoned, before he did that kind of thing again. Who was he? Why was he on Water Street? Obviously new in town. Lost maybe. Not visiting family. That high yella fella, he'd be looking for family on Freeman Street, maybe even the Projects, but not among the folks on Water.

Jack pushed his ball cap back and scanned the long wide street for the stranger's Saab. A handful of black men were milling around a light post three houses up. Smoke curled around their heads in the heavy air. A little further down he saw two stooped forms chatting in front of Miss Lucretia's. No sign of the stranger's fancy car, but there was a blue pickup making its way toward Trina's. He left his coffee cup on the porch rail and stepped back into the shadows and tucked his chin against his chest, wishing the company truck was anything but white and wishing he had parked it deeper in the kudzu behind Trina's. The screen door behind him banged. Jack jumped.

"Look like to me," Trina said, setting a pair of men's boots on the porch and slipping her brown hands in the pockets of her robe, "that you as jumpy as a wanted man." She held out a T-shirt to him. "Here's your shirt. I washed it last night."

Jack grunted and ignored the shirt, giving the truck a sidelong glance. Jack was relieved to see that the driver's face was black.

"You scared of an old man selling fish?" Trina chuckled and waved at the driver of the blue pickup. "Or *my* old man?"

"I ain't scared of no-count jail bait that don't know how to keep a woman."

"Like you do yourself."

"Your so-called husband don't spend no time 'round here, that's for sure."

"That ain't the point, Mr. Big Shot. I know what you done yesterday. My girlfriend called and told me 'bout it while you was in the shower. You running scared."

"I didn't do nothing wrong. Defended myself. Ain't scared of the law no way."

"I ain't talking 'bout the man, Jack. I'm talking 'bout another man who drives a blue pickup. A *white* man driving a *blue* truck."

She talked too much, Jack thought. Who did she think she was, suggesting Jack was afraid of his own father?

"Shut up." Jack lunged at the thin woman.

She didn't flinch. "I don't want my house shot up again, Jack. Take your mess." She threw the shirt at him and kicked his boots into the yard.

"Woman!" Jack stumbled into the yard after his boots. Rain had started. She was not going to be the reason for his boots getting moldy. He shoved his feet in them and headed for his truck.

"Leave. Don't come 'round here no more. I don't care how much money you got."

Jack left Trina cursing him on the front porch and backed his truck out of the bushes. She would change her mind when she needed money for her kids, he knew that. No reason to pick a fight now.

He was better than these people, he told himself constantly. He would never let himself be taken advantage of so easily, relegated to land unsuitable for animals, blacker than the swamp waters that flooded their homes during hurricane season.

He adjusted his hat and waved to the black woman fuming in the rain. Work was waiting for him on the Farm. He laid on his horn as he passed the men, now seeking shelter under a nearby tree. *At least I have a job.*

Somewhere along my college experience I read that the average person tells one lie for every seven truths. One thing occurred to me as I knelt by my mother's grave, rain soaked and cold: I lie at least twice as much as the average person, and lately I've told the bulk of those lies to myself.

Life's a wild ride and then you die.

As sure as a person has a birthday, there is a day of death, a sure end. I rose and decided that this would be the end of sorts for me. My search was over, as was my delusion. Tate had been right all along. That would be the first thing I would tell him. He would like that—me saying to his face that I'd been wrong.

I wiped my face, tasting the salt of regret and shame that poured from my eyes, then turned expecting to see a thin child behind me. Patrick was gone. I called for him as I retraced my steps through the Ross family cemetery and back to the house. No answer. Thinking he had sought shelter in the house, I tried the doors and peeped through the windows. Nothing but boxes and bare floors inside.

I drove to the main road hoping to see him wandering back toward town. How was I going to explain losing the boy? Through the deluge, I could see a speck of a white house farther up the road. A couple of miles, I guessed. Could he have walked there? How long had I been at the grave crying? I pointed my car in the direction of the house. If he was there, fine. If he wasn't then maybe they would let me use their phone—my cell was dead.

With dread like I'd only felt scuba diving, I rolled my window down and scanned the ditches as I drove. What color was his shirt? Blue? What about his pants? His shoes?

"Patrick," I yelled, crying for a new reason.

Up ahead a truck, white with an all-too-familiar insignia on the side, pulled onto the main road from a dirt side road and came to a stop in the center of the road. The truck's headlights flashed on and then off. I stopped short. Through the curtain of rain that stood between me and the driver I could make out the outline of rounded shoulders and a ball cap.

Another headlight flash and the truck came closer. Slow at first, then faster. I was not about to play this game. I didn't have it in me. Jack, if this was the same character, had bad timing and a bad sense of humor.

Uncle, call me a chicken. I jammed the car in reverse, hoping to make it back to the last turnoff, but the truck clipped me on the front bumper, passenger side, and sent me spinning. When the greenery jerked to a standstill, I was in the middle of the road, facing town. I placed my foot on the gas, ready to run.

Like the bite of battery acid on my tongue, something hit me. Maybe it was the taste of a death before it settles over a man. Or maybe just the sheer stupidity of a man not wanting to be struck down twice in one day. I don't know. What I did know just for that split second was that I could not run. What did I have to lose anyway?

I turned the car around, the scrape of the bumper on the road reverberating through the car, and faced my aggressor less than two car lengths away. He smiled at me—the same grin I saw before kissing gravel on Water Street.

I put the car in park and stepped out into the rain. I watched the truck creep toward me. Jack was smiling even broader as he pulled up beside me, the stock of a rifle peeping over the edge of the window. *I need a weapon?* My mind raced.

"You hit my car. On purpose."

He rolled his window down. "You were in the middle of the road."

I knew this little game. No witnesses. My word against his. I'd played the game before and wasn't in the mood to play it today. But I couldn't alienate this clown.

Unarmed, I put on my best Ricky Hunt. "I'm having a little car trouble."

"How's your head? Nasty bruise there on your jaw."

I continued, "My front bumper got . . . loose on the passenger side, and I was wondering if you can help me fix it."

He threw his head back and laughed. "You think I'm a fool, don't you?"

He asked for it. "A man I knew named Ulysses Hunt once told me that if a man acts like a fool then he is a fool."

His smile melted into a crooked-toothed grate. "Well, sounds to me like Ulysses Hunt was a fool."

I lunged for him, wrapping my hands around his neck. He cursed and clawed at my fingers, then nicked my brow with his left elbow before gunning the engine. As he pulled away my body went with him for what seemed like a few hundred bone-scraping yards. Then I felt a blow to my temple from the side of the truck, followed by a couple of good bangs to the jaw as I rolled on asphalt.

Through the stars that danced across my vision, I saw him turn the truck around and ram my car. One hit, two hits . . .

"Stop!" I screamed, as if a simple word could control the descent of my car into the drainage ditch. He did not direct his two-and-a-half-ton weapon at me next as I dreaded. Instead he turned back around and drove a leisurely pace back the way he'd come.

Then there was silence and cold, cold water mingling with the warmth of my own blood down my face. Then, darkness.

Images came to me in the darkness. Pictures of the one man who had treated me like he was glad I was alive—Ulysses Hunt. Was my life flashing before my eyes? I didn't know, but at least they were pleasant flashes.

We were sitting in a porch swing at his house in Richmond. That was back after Grandma Margaret died when I lived with Chloe and Ricky near Old Ulysses' quaint Victorian in the Fan. Ulysses and I were eating chocolate kisses and talking about the statues on Monument Avenue; we could see Jeff Davis from the swing. Many times we would sit on the steps behind the statue and watch traffic circling.

Then, for no good reason, he changed the subject, grew more giddy and friendly. Started pushing the swing faster. Maybe it was the chocolate. How old had I been then? Five? Going on six? Thin and quiet. So thin that he could pull me up in his lap with one hairy arm.

"What do you want to be when you grow up, Isaac?"

I remember saying lawyer because I thought that that was the right answer. He had been a lawyer and his only son, Ricky, was a lawyer.

Old Ulysses chuckled and pressed his lips to my ear, his coarse mustache scratching me. "What do you really want to be, little bug?"

I lowered my head and whispered, "Your son."

He hugged me and kissed the back of my neck.

I thought of our "fishing" trips on the James. He called them fishing trips, and sometimes we really did do a little fishing, but mostly we goofed off, ate junk food in defiance of his high blood pressure, and talked. I remembered the time I fell in. He let me strip and wear his shirt while my clothes dried on a bush. It was during that trip that he told me about sex. I was ten and I didn't believe him. Surely girls weren't that different. It may have been shortly after that that I tried my first kiss.

He taught me that you make your own destiny, your own future. No person has that kind of power over another's life. And certainly not God. Something that didn't exist could not control you. A real man made his own life, one day at a time.

He taught me how to "shoot the bones" and dance like

Fred Astaire. He taught me how to fix a lawn mower and clean up so his daughter-in-law never had a clue I'd done something beneath my station in life. He taught me love. Now he was gone.

My images of him melted into the sounds of footsteps and talking.

"Mr. Isaac."

Patrick. There he was, smiling at me through tears. He was wet and dirty, hair sticking up even more. I wanted to kiss him. Two sets of muddy boots stood behind him. The blackness came again. Shaking, rocking, lurching. Lifting, wiping, splashing.

Patrick's face came to me again, then Trip's inches away from the boy's, with a heavy hand on my chest. Asphalt grated into my wet back and buttocks. My feet were propped up on something soft.

"Easy, big fella."

I tasted bile. Had I thrown up? My face hurt. My head hurt. My brain hurt.

The other person knelt behind him. A man? I studied his NASCAR belt buckle in a daze. He was a very large man with abnormally thin white fingers wrapped around a thermos that he handed to Trip who pulled my head toward the plastic lip. Then the large man stood and walked away, so that all I could see of him was the back of his Levis and rain parka.

A familiar voice, edgy and high, came from the other side. "He ain't dead, is he?" Crazy Eddie sounded like he'd be disappointed if I survived this brush with death. "'Cause if he ain't then I need to call my mama to let her know that he ain't coming."

chapter 9

he unhitched the mangled bumper of Isaac's car from the old Farm-All and pulled the ancient tractor onto the concrete pad in front of the garage. He would have one of the men park it under the back shed with the other older tractors before dark. Of course Patrick would be happy to do that when he woke up from his nap, Abraham thought, smiling at the thought of his son's energetic return and his nonstop chatter about Betty's son. He hadn't said more than two words since January and now he was making up for it in two days' time. Not a sentence that didn't have Isaac in it.

They had not yet talked about the grief they shared and

that was a good thing as far as Abraham was concerned. Why talk about something that was beyond man's control. It would work itself out in time.

The cell phone in his shirt pocket buzzed.

"Hello."

"Hello, Abraham," came a familiar voice.

Abraham paused, the hair on the back of his neck crawling. "Hello, Mr. Highsmith."

"Call me Mitchell, Abraham. Long time, no see."

"Yes indeed." In Abraham's mind he saw the man. A thin man with watery blue eyes and shiny black boots. Of course, it had been more than ten years since he'd seen him last, but he doubted much had changed in the way he related to people. "How have you been?"

"Fair. Listen, I've just heard about your wife. You have my condolences."

Abraham drew a breath. "Thank you. I'm not interested in selling Benson Ridge."

"Well, Abe, I see you haven't changed. Right for the heart of the matter. That's not why I'm calling, though." He lightly chuckled.

"Then why are you calling?"

"I'm interested in how we might enter into a partnership similar to the one I had with your father. Mutual benefit."

"Benefit for the United Front, you mean?"

"Well, yes, this arrangement would benefit the Front but it would mostly benefit Benson Ridge, your entity being more public, if you know what I mean."

"I'm not interested in getting involved in a hate group."

The man chuckled. "Now, Abe. Hate group—"

"I've got enough shame in my past. Good-bye, Mr. Highsmith."

Abraham shoved the phone in his pocket.

How'd he get my number?

Three refrigerated semis rumbled by on the main road, ruffling the Leyland cypress screen that fronted the main farm complex. Abraham took off his hat and waved it to the drivers, men from Dakins Packing, one of two produce packers Abraham used, on their way to the grader.

There was a peace in just knowing people for the sake of knowing people, Abraham reasoned as he watched the trucks disappear down the road. A peace in being kind and decent to folks. Peace was something he was just starting to feel again. A thing he was sure men like his father and Highsmith didn't know a thing about.

The Farm, originally a forty-acre plat sliced out of some of the most fertile land in the Great Dismal Swamp chock full of age-old peat deposits, had been a source of peace as well. It had been built into a 35,000 acre mega corn farm under the combined genius of Abraham and the two owners before him, his father and grandfather. Countless people had benefited over the generations—migrant workers from Florida and Delaware, as well as Haiti and Puerto Rico; the local folk working the fields and the grader; the smaller farmers who rented Benson land for hog and chicken farms; university researchers; and the Bensons themselves.

Abraham thrived on the idea of providing for others. He was glad his younger siblings, three sisters, were well-off because of Benson Ridge. But it was more rewarding to see those who had known nothing but lack all their lives gain the ability to provide for their families and see hope that their offspring would never beg again. That was his pride and his weakness.

Abraham Benson was a born farmer; he lived by his senses, his wits. He took pride in being able to squeeze life for so many out of the black dirt that lay beneath his feet—to turn the inanimate, the seemingly dead, into a thriving creature.

He paused, surveying, the garage fifty or so yards behind him, his house another fifty before him, and listened. To the diesels in the distance slow at the Y and veer left, to the puff and sigh of pecan trees beyond the house—a living thing, if a house can be said to grow and breathe, from generation to generation. His legacy—the land, this house, the Farm— Benson Ridge. Dare he leave it behind? Surely, he reasoned, he could find another plat of land that he could make thrive. A plat that held promise but not so many memories and so much pain. The pain, he realized, of losing his wife was ebbing, but not the pain of a lifetime of bad choices. That pain would never leave him, he figured.

In the few hours he had by himself, Abraham had decided to make a few phone calls, then he would go through some of Olivia's boxes in the library before he decided what to put in storage or on the empty walnut shelves that lined the walls. It would be better that way. Catherine had offered to help but he had sent her away to sort the things in the attic at the old Ross house.

Abraham slipped his boots off in the kitchen where he grabbed two apples and padded across the flagstone court-yard to the library. The last of the afternoon sun was slipping behind the trees that flanked the house to the south, leaving cool motionless air that reminded Abraham of his parents' crypt.

Through the half dozen towers of half-unpacked boxes stacked around the room, he saw a single sheet of paper on his desk. It was a note from Catherine. She had decided to drive over to Finley when she finished at the Ross house. He wondered what that was about. She hadn't mentioned it before. She was a mysterious girl, just like her father. On the other side of the sheet were instructions for cooking the roast he'd seen defrosting in the fridge. She treated him like a teenage son, or clueless husband, not like a CEO to a multi-million-dollar business. Had Olivia treated him like that? Probably. He didn't mind, though.

Women.

He moved behind his desk, unlocked a side drawer, and pulled out a briefcase. He ran his thumb over the scratched nameplate. *Karl Benson*, it read. The case had been his father's, but it could have easily been his. But they had shared first and last names only. The senior Karl had given his first and only son the middle name of Abraham, his way of hoping for many grandsons.

More Benson men to indoctrinate, Abraham thought.

He settled into the dark brown leather wingback and opened the case. The ancient lid eased open like it was stretching from a long, deep sleep.

How many times had he looked into the contents of that briefcase and how many times had he closed it without following through on his plan. Today he would do it, particularly with Highsmith's talk of reviving the Front fresh in his mind.

Abraham pushed the handful of audiocassettes aside and pulled out the letters. He took them to the photocopier and started copying. Three copies of each one.

He pulled his cell phone from his shirt pocket and dialed a number from memory.

"I'm sorry," the recording said, "you've reached a number that is no longer in service."

He frowned and hung up. He dialed information.

"City please."

"Charlotte."

"Listing?"

"FBI."

Within seconds he was talking with an actual person. He was relieved it wasn't the automated system that sent him to voice mail. What he had to say couldn't be left on a recording.

"Yes, I'd like to speak with Agent Charise Blue."

"I'm sorry, sir, she's out of the office indefinitely. May I direct your call elsewhere?"

"How about Agent Ulysses Hunt?"

"Sir, may I have your name and the nature of your call today?"

"My name is Abraham Benson. Full name: Karl Abraham Benson. I am calling to relay sensitive information to Agents Blue or Hunt."

"Mr. Benson, can you be more specific?"

"No, not over the phone. Might I speak with Agent Hunt?"

"Sir, Ulysses Hunt is no longer with the Bureau."

Abraham paused. There was something in the voice on

the other end so he pressed further. "But you know who he is, don't you."

"Sir, I'm sorry to have to tell you this but Mr. Hunt died last October."

"He's dead?"

"Yes, sir. I'm sorry. Would you like to arrange a meeting with another agent?"

"No. Thank you for your time."

He hung up the phone and leaned back. Ulysses was dead. *Killed?* It felt like something the Front would do. Was it because of the risk of reopening the murder case against them?

And Charise was gone. Had she been fired for what he had asked her to do? What next? Should he travel to Charlotte in person? Or D.C.? So many things to consider. One thing was for certain, Patrick would need to go away.

—

With his photocopying done Abraham decided to turn his attention to unpacking some of his wife's books. She had always wanted them in his library. He lifted a book from the nearest open box. It was an album, denim covered and bound with a leather cord. The handwritten cover took his breath; he laid it down and stepped back. What had possessed him to think he could do this? It was too soon. Catherine could do the unpacking . . .

His eyes stung as he reached out and fingered the cord that Olivia had tied, the letters M-E-M-O-R-I-E-S, that she had drawn in red. On a flap, turned down so he didn't see it at first, Catherine had written "Miss Olivia's albums." He would unpack this one box, Abraham decided, and leave the rest to Catherine.

With one of the apples between his teeth and the other under his arm, Abraham carried the box to the courtyard, stripped off his shirt, and sat on a chair in the last patch of sun. A light breeze rustled the crape myrtles along the dirt lane running from the house to the greenhouses. The lane ran red with the wine of two dozen trees, a soft playful elixir that stirred with the slightest breeze. It reminded Abraham of the moonlit night he first saw the woman he would love forever, running beneath the canopy of those trees shoeless. He had pursued her across the ultrasoft blanket of petals like silk between his toes, dampening each footfall. The only thing softer had been her lips.

He didn't check the tears this time. He let them slip down as he leafed through the book. There were so many pictures of Olivia and him together—the engaged couple with eyes only for each other seemingly, the blushing bride stuffing cake into his mouth. And there were pictures of Patrick. He looked so much like those Indian babies Abraham had seen during his one visit to the Cherokee reservation west of Murphy. Not in his coloring but in his wide, bold features Abraham saw a hint of the baby's great-grandfather. Had any of the other Bensons noticed, Abraham wondered? Of course, maybe he was just being overly sensitive. What did it matter now?

"He is *my* son," Abraham told himself and tossed the first apple core aside. He shifted his weight to grab the other apple perched on the top of the next album, making a picture fall from the back of the album in his lap.

Betty's face smiled up at him, wholesome and hopeful, happy with her son on her lap. How old was he then? Three or four. So smart and cute. Betty was so proud of him, you could see it in her eyes. If only he could have saved them both from the fire. If only he had not let his cousins talk him into drinking. If only . . . so many mistakes . . . so many regrets.

The kitchen door opened and Abraham's cousin, Ben Jacob, walked across the courtyard. He reminded Abraham of how his father, Karl Benson, carried himself in the days before diabetes took his legs—pushing his long legs and arms around with contrived bravado. Power, or the abuse of it, Abraham judged, had gone to Ben Jacob's head.

"What are you doing out here?" Ben Jacob asked. "Half-naked. Crying?"

Abraham turned his back and slipped the photo of Betty and Isaac back into the album, then wiped his face. "Did you find Jack?"

Ben Jacob shook his head and slumped on the two-foot wall encircling the courtyard.

Abraham eyed him as he ate his second apple. Making Ben Jacob manager had been a bad idea. But it had been one of his father's last wishes. "I don't know why I should trust you, BJ. You've taught Jack everything he knows. Why should you turn him over to me?"

Ben Jacob laughed and propped his feet on the low wrought-iron table between them. "What's that supposed to mean?"

"Tell me you're not protecting him, hiding him."

"I cain't believe you're talking to me this way. But maybe I shouldn't be, considering how you been acting. Like you're about to sell the Farm or something."

Abraham studied the trees along the dirt path; the sigh of the wind among the leaves was almost too much to bear. How long could he stay here, listening to that sound, all the sounds of the Farm that reminded him of a life of bad choices?

"You need help, Abe. Counseling. It'll help you get your head back on straight. As Farm manager, I'm telling you, you don't need to sell. Who'd buy anyway? The Italians? Like South River Farms did last year. The Bensons will not be doing that. Do you understand me? We're not selling. The Board would never go for it."

Ben Jacob fished out a cigarette from the crumpled pack in his shirt pocket and perched it on his bottom lip. It hung like a fragment of metal to a magnet while he continued his speech. "You don't need to be bringin' nobody else into the family business ventures. You understand me?"

He lit the cigarette and took a long drag. Abraham was weary of his cousin's babble and smoke. He stood and stretched. BJ's monologues could go on and on. They were as inspiring as some of his plans for grandeur and world domination. He'd tire, Abraham figured. And just like all of his other schemes, this one would run down like a disk harrow in clay.

Abraham glanced at his watch. He'd need to put that roast in soon and then walk over to the Ross house to see how far Catherine had gotten. Would she consider living in the old house, he wondered. *It needs a woman.*

"Abe, have you been listening at all? Good night, man!

You look like your mama did before they took her away." He threw down his cigarette and crushed it under the heel of a silver-toed boot. Abraham couldn't help thinking that his cousin didn't look well either. Hungover, most likely, looking even more pathetic in his attempt at sympathy. His wife, Selma, had probably put him up to it.

"You need to see somebody, Abe. A counselor, a preacher. Somebody to bring you back to reality. You've got a business to head up . . ."

"I know, BJ. Tell Selma I said hello. Thank her for the flowers."

"Say, where's that black girl that I saw last time mopping the kitchen? I just realized who she is. Henry's girl, right? They call her Cathy or something like that. Good night! She scared me. I come around the corner and there she was. blacker than your mama's skillet." Ben Jacob let out a bark of a laugh.

"Get out, BJ."

"What? You ain't sweet on her, are you? You are. Benson men always did like a little color in their bedrooms. Nothing wrong with that. Just gotta know how to handle 'em."

"Shut up!"

"No, you're the one who needs to shut up. Shut up and listen, big man. You and Olivia were as blind as they come. All them blacks y'all had working here at Benson Ridge back then. Started with Betty, then there was Henry, now his daughter. Some of that was Uncle Karl's doing too, I imagine, in the early days. Robbing the Bensons blind, they are."

Abraham stormed toward his cousin. He could hear the white supremacy speech coming. "Shut up and get out."

"But did *you* see it? Naw. 'We gotta help the little man.' I had enough of it. 'Specially the way you keep throwing your money at 'em now. Times have changed, Abe. Tolerance is out. Power is in. Our power. It's time, Abe. I'm not gonna stand for much more of your mess. You hear me. Get with the program or I'm gonna bring you down if it's the last thing I do. Like a big ole buck, Abe, you're in my sights."

Abraham doubted BJ had the power to come against him. No one else on the Board had voiced a concern. Besides, BJ wasn't even an officer. He was just his bigmouthed cousin.

"And this thing with Betty's boy," BJ continued. "It's not about him maybe suing us 'cause Jack, a Benson Ridge Farm employee, attacked him on company time and company property. No, that's not it. It's you and your guilt. You think you owe him something 'cause you didn't pull his mama from that burning house. Well, I hate to break this to you, big Abe, but you're not God. You cain't rescue ever'body. She was gonna die anyway."

Abraham stopped short of pulling himself from the chair. "What do you mean by that?"

Ben Jacob shrugged and pulled his cowhide vest around his thin body, tossed his ponytail. "I better get back to town."

Abraham stood and blocked his exit. Were his suspicions right about his cousin's involvement in the house fire? "What do you mean? What did you do that night?"

"Excuse me, Abe. Step aside."

"Did you start that fire?"

Ben Jacob's gray eyes smoked like hot oil as he looked into Abraham's face. "Don't be a fool."

chapter 10

in the darkness I heard voices, a small crowd carrying on what seemed like five hundred different conversations. It wasn't the darkness that I'd slipped into so many times since hitting the wet pavement. This was the darkness of night. A thick crust of quilts lay on me. Curtains, glowing like amiable ghosts in the moonlight, hung silent over two windows.

I couldn't tell if the sweat that washed me was from fever or heat wave. I pushed the quilts aside and sat up unable to push aside the questions, the images of a mother I would never meet. The eyes that would never look into mine and explain why she gave me away. The mouth that would never tell me she loved me.

My ears were ringing. Or was that the phone? I ran my hand over the unfamiliar flannel pajama bottoms I wore and groped for the door, toward the voices. I listened, barely breathing, scarcely thinking.

Mingled with the scrape and rattle of silverware on plates were scraps of conversations. Soft words like the mixing of overripe bananas. Hard words like rat scratches in the night. *Betty was a good woman . . . a sweet child . . . was them Bensons that drove her to do what she done . . . I don't care what the man told us, she was murdered, burnt alive.*

With no thoughts of shame, I pushed the door open.

The voices stopped. Their owners—ten or fifteen dark strangers—all turned toward me, half-words hanging from their thick lips. I batted at a moth, intent on beating its brains out against the frosted glass globe above my head and cast a questioning look at the only familiar face in the room.

But before I spoke, she started moving toward me with a dish towel, intent on covering my half-naked body with it, I suppose. She tapped the cotton against my chest until I backed into the shadows of the bedroom, the one Patrick had slept in the night before, talking to me like a child who had lost a puppy.

"It'll be all right, baby," she cooed.

I pressed back, despite the pain it caused to push against her gentle touch, to even move my jaw to talk. "No, it won't be, Miss Lucretia."

"Isaac—"

"Tell me why . . . someone said my mother was killed. Burned on purpose—"

"Now ain't the time, child. Later. You've had a long hard day."

"How is knowing later going to help . . . ?"

Trip's white face appeared out of the black masses like the chameleon I had figured him to be. He slipped his long face between Miss Lucretia's and mine and spoke quickly, sharply. "Back up. Take it easy. Just get back in the room. We'll talk."

He turned and whispered something to Miss Lucretia. She nodded and retreated.

"Have a seat," Trip ordered as he closed the door and switched on a lamp. I stood. He settled on the edge of the bed and studied the curtains. "Your car was totaled. We managed to pull it out of the canal with Abraham Benson's help. Got your stuff out and left the wreck there at Benson Ridge. Abe said you can claim it or leave it. It's up to you."

"Tell me what you know about my mother."

"You're wearing my pj bottoms. Catty's washing your clothes. I think she should be able to salvage most of what was in your bags. No hope for your cell phone and that digital calendar thing."

I stared at the door and fingered my bandaged face, trying to recollect the memories of being moved and cleaned up.

"The bus no longer comes through Pettigrew. You can catch one in Finleigh. You'll have to drive an hour north to Elizabeth City to rent a car. If you use the magic words you might be able to get one of us country bumpkins to take you. No charge. You know the magic words, don't you?"

He stood with a jolt and walked slowly toward me. "Look, Isaac Hunt, or whatever your name is. I don't know what kind of people you're used to, but 'round here when somebody scrapes your butt off the pavement twice in one day and lends you a pair of drawers, you say 'thanks'.

"And another thing," he continued, pointing a finger up at my battered face. "If you so much as hurt that sweet little old lady's feelings, you're in trouble with me. If you lay a finger on Catty you're in trouble with me. You understand?"

He sighed and scratched his stubbled chin, listening maybe to the sounds outside the room. People saying good-bye, dishes clinking in the sink.

"In the morning Miss Lucretia's probably gonna come in here and tell you that you can stay as long as it takes for you to heal. But . . ."

I don't know what it was, but I was getting the funny feeling he didn't want me around. "Don't worry, Trip Robertson, or whatever your name is. I heal real fast."

He huffed in my direction and left.

I eased my throbbing body onto the bed, skipping the quilts, and closed my eyes. A breeze, I remember thinking as I drifted off, would be nice.

I woke to darkness again, cool air caressing my chest and arms. The thin curtains, fluttering and flapping like tethered birds, still glowed in the darkness. I could hear the bark of a dog, a cricket chirping, and someone else breathing. That someone was awake, I guessed by the steady light intake and exhale, and it scared me. My mind raced as I sat up.

A weapon!

I jumped at the words, "Oh . . . you're awake."

They were Catty's words but they were quieter, sweeter than any words I had heard since returning to Miss Lucretia's and nicer than any words I'd heard from her. And it wasn't just because she was whispering.

She rose from the floor, apparently from a spot under the far window, and lifted something with both hands from a spot near her.

"I've got some food here on a tray. Something light. Are you hungry?"

She set the tray on the nightstand and pulled a chair over. Perched on the end of the chair, she tapped her fingertips together and watched the curtains as I ate. She was avoiding looking at me, like it was painful to do so. Did I look that bad?

"Thank you," I whispered between bites of what tasted like chicken salad with a crisp cool sweetness mingled into it.

"I could turn the light on if you like. I'm probably the only one who likes to eat in the dark." She went to the window closest to the bed and pushed the curtains wide. Moonlight cut a line around her narrow body, a dark robe pulled tight around her waist, thick ringlets radiating from her head like the points of a black sun.

"No, it's okay. So is the sandwich. Apples?"

"Yes. My daddy liked it with . . . there's a cup of water on the tray but if you'd like tea, I could get . . ." She sat abruptly and pulled at her hair.

"No, water's fine. Thanks."

"You're welcome."

I finished the water and wiped my mouth on the paper napkin.

"I'd better go," she said, taking the tray.

"What do you know about Betty Douglas?"

"Nothing . . . honest. Please don't— "

The tray trembled as she stood and stepped closer to the bed, into a slice of moonlight that cut the room in two. I could see fear glistening in her dark eyes, or was it a questioning look like the one she showed me moments after Patrick spoke. How could she not expect me to ask her what she knew? Catty had heard the conversations, every word, while I lay on this bed unconscious to the discussions concerning my life. How could she show pity for my stomach and not for my state of mind?

Her lips trembled.

What is it? I stood.

She stepped back. "No, I can't."

For several seconds, she studied the floor, the tray, the windows, anything but me. "I'm sorry," she muttered, "I can't—"

I wouldn't push, I told myself. When she wanted to talk, she would, I said. But still . . .

"Do you need aspirin? For your pain?"

I nodded.

She left and returned with a bottle and another cup of water, which she placed on the nightstand, then stood back like she was tending a wounded wild animal, daring not to come too close.

I shook out four pills and washed them down, all at one time.

"I want to thank you for helping Mr. Bill," she whispered, pushing the door closed behind her.

"Who?" I asked, forgetting to keep my voice low.

"Shhh. The dog that Jack Kepler was beating. I call him Mr. Bill. He's a stray that I feed sometimes."

"Why do you call him—"

"Mr. Bill? Sometimes when he's happy I can get him to talk. He says, 'Oh no' like Mr. Bill on *Saturday Night Live* used to." She made a sound, a sort of grunt, that I guessed to be her version of a giggle.

I smiled, remembering my own dog. Suddenly, I wanted to tell her about Mr. Happy. To talk about anything or anybody but the dead woman who dominated my thoughts, the pain that clung to me like a cold sweat.

"Thanks for helping Patrick too."

Patrick. I smiled, remembering the wet spiky hair, the tears, his crooked smile hovering over me as I lay on the pavement. "Where is he?"

"Back with his father. He wanted to see you before he left this morning, but Grandma Lu wasn't having it. Patrick's in love with you. He's not gonna let one little old black woman stand in his way." She grunted again.

The thought of a boy I just met loving me was a little strange but not as disturbing as the hate of the man I'd never met. A hate so strong that he did not think twice about harming me bodily or destroying my car. It was a painful thing to consider. Who was Jack Kepler and why did he feel I owed him my life? I considered myself a decent man. If I had wronged him unaware, I wanted to find out the whats and wherefores so I could set things right. If I had not, I wanted to set him right. Justice would be served.

My father was a lawyer after all—I caught myself mid-thought and shook my head. Ricky Hunt was not my father. I would find a way to pay him for his faithful "service" as well.

"I . . ." She started, then cleared her throat. I thought I could hear tears in her voice. "I didn't know your mother. She was . . . gone before me and Daddy came to live in Pettigrew. Miss Gladys and Grandma Lu knew her. Miss Gladys talked about her tonight. A lot of the older Water Street people did. It's like what happened to you today pricked something and all the pent-up air just came flowing out. Funny how curious they were about you. They all wanted to see you, but Grandma Lu held them back." She sighed.

"What did they say about her?"

Catty sighed again, not like she was sorry to have me in the same house with her but like she was sorry for my pain.

"Your mother came from Florida with her father. They were migrant workers. When he died she started work at the cucumber grading plant near the migrant worker camp. She was very likeable, pretty. Miss Gladys had her picture. Very pretty eyes. She stayed with friends at the migrant camp for a while after you were born and then with her friend Olivia Ross until Miss Olivia got engaged to Mr. Abraham. Then she moved in with Miss Gladys. Then . . . there was the fire. There was a lot of talk about that tonight too.

"They say that it wasn't an accident." Catty covered her lips like she was holding back vomit, then drifted off, looking to the billowing curtains.

"Go on."

"No. I won't talk about what I don't know."

"Why not?"

"Sometimes people tell lies or talk about something they

don't personally know about. Have no proof for. They repeat it so much that it starts to sound like the truth. I don't want to be a part of that."

"But what if it is the truth to begin with and not a lie at all. The truth is not always a pleasant thing," I said, thinking of the pretty lies I'd been told all my life. Lies that I was the son of a prominent judge and his loyal wife when I was really the illegitimate son of a field-worker. What about Betty Douglas? What lies had she endured from the white man who had made her pregnant?

Catty continued. "The people in this dot of a hick town, they're no different than the people of any other town. There's bad and there's good. And there are some who ride the fence depending on who's looking. Then there are some who have done bad in the past. white people, I mean, who have done a lot of bad to a lot of our people."

I was encouraged by that. Unlike Tate, she at least considered me to be black.

She cleared her throat and continued. "But those white people today bend over backward to right the wrongs of their pasts."

We sat quietly for a few seconds, then I surprised myself by speaking the words on my mind.

"But shouldn't they *pay* for . . ."

"No!"

She surprised me by standing and throwing a "no" at me. I don't know if I was more surprised that she spoke so sharply or that I was having this conversation at all with a woman I barely knew, a woman who had earlier treated me like an enemy, a threat.

The night before I had slept in her bed, smelled and felt what she had every other night before. I had deprived her of her privacy, something dear to her, and she had reacted the following morning by punishing me. Now she was rewarding me with her company and information I needed, and some I didn't. But the whole thing intrigued me. *She* intrigued and troubled me.

I challenged her simplistic argument. "Why not?"

Her shoulders sagged a bit. She turned to study the window again, breathing hard. "If a person's been forgiven, they don't owe anything to anybody."

Maybe she saw my frown in the semidarkness because she continued.

"If God's let them off the hook, then who am I—another human with no more power over my anger than the next person, liable to sin or fail—to demand anything of them? It shouldn't matter anymore after they've been forgiven."

That made no sense to me, and I said as much, but didn't explain my reasoning. Maybe it was the Hunt influence shadowing me, but I reasoned, if a man is guilty, he's guilty. No matter if the crime was committed when he was young and foolish or blessed with the wisdom of a hundred decades. GUILTY. Deemed so by a jury of his peers. Whether those jurors sat in two neat rows of six or around Miss Lucretia's kitchen table, it mattered none to me. I thought of Ulysses Hunt. *Kind. Generous. Guilty.*

I leaned toward her. "Who killed my mother?"

"You're hard of hearing, aren't you? I'm not here to spread lies."

"I just want to know the truth, Catty. Put yourself in my shoes."

"Shhh."

I took a step toward her, keeping my voice right where it was, then another step. "No, I'm sorry. I guess you wouldn't. You would simply trust everybody. 'Cause your sweet Jesus would want you to." The heat in my words surprised me.

The slap I got in return hurt more than my face. The door behind me opened. The light from the kitchen showed me a dark heart-shaped face creased and tearstained. I was the one in pain. Why was she crying?

"Catty," Trip said from behind me, "are you all right?" He stepped in between us and pushed me back with his elbow, then gripped Catty by the shoulders.

"Yeah," she whispered. "I'm okay."

The preacher turned on me like a pack of big brothers. "Whatcha done to her."

"Nothing, Trip. Really, he did nothing. We were just talking."

Apparently, I had not moved far enough for him. So he pushed me again, teeth bared, eyes narrowed. I returned the favor by sending a warning jab to his ribs. His face screwed into an even angrier mask and with a meaty right fist he showed me what he meant by "being in trouble with me."

I gasped and stumbled back, coughing and clutching my stomach. "I thought you were supposed to turn the other cheek."

He rubbed his ribs. "You didn't hit my cheek."

There was a quick shuffle of feet behind us. Catty

stepped back, her head in her hands, and looked past us to the open bedroom door. "Grandma."

"What's going on? Isaac, you all right?"

Finally, someone concerned for my well-being. That should have counted for something, but at the time all I could see were Catty's tears, tears of the woman who had shown me compassion one minute, judgment the next. The look on her face—mingled horror, disgust, shame—had more to do with the words I had spoken.

In those few heated words, she'd seen something of the wound deep down in me that I had not shown to anyone, especially not to my former friend turned Christian—Tate Michaels. The fire in those words reflected a mix of betrayal and loneliness that started to weigh me down like nothing I'd felt before. And it could all be traced back to a God who didn't exist. If there was a time in my life when I needed to feel a kind embrace, it was now. But there was none. Except emptiness. A big black heaviness. Where was the so-called compassionate God? I needed healing, not God.

So I turned to Miss Lucretia and did what had come so easily to do with her—I lied.

"I'm fine. Just fine."

the stone in the ring was beautiful. Even in the moonlight it flashed fire. Catty rewrapped it in the denim she'd found it in, then slipped it and the envelope back into the plastic pouch and zipped it, careful to line up the rusty teeth as she pulled.

The pouch then went into the rusty coffee can that had once held the Ross family coin collection. When had Betty Douglas died, she wondered as she smeared the can with Alpo and dropped it in the hole in the ground. Early '80s. Hopefully they were making Sanka back then. Hopefully nobody would notice.

I'm crazy, Catty thought. *I'm crouched here in the dark with dog food on my hands thinking about coffee cans.*

Miss Gladys's backdoor opened. Catty slipped into the shadow created by the low, wide-flung branches of the old fig tree and watched the old woman's granddaughter chase lightning bugs.

Her feet were asleep by the time the girl went back in. Catty couldn't be concerned with that now. She only had about five minutes to cover the can and get back in before the nightly news signed off and Grandma Lu woke up. She had yet to find Mr. Bill. Maybe Crazy Eddie could help.

What can I bribe him with this time?

"I'm crazy," she whispered as she ran across the road, thinking this was certainly not the Christian thing to do.

"Oh, God, please forgive me."

~

I am convinced that some forms of physical pain can be a good thing. Pain of the heart, I'm equally convinced, is not a good thing. It is a bad thing, an evil thing that drives a man to madness quicker and surer than any form of physical torment. Bodily pain can be medicated away. A broken heart cannot.

I applied fresh bandages to the scrapes above my left eye and leaned back from the dresser mirror. A wet washcloth didn't feel like a wire brush today the way it had last night when Miss Lucretia had cleaned me up. I would be my old self in no time. The soreness in my back and shoulder, though, made me feel like someone was kicking me with every step, but that would be gone in a few days.

At least I didn't have a concussion or broken bones to contend with. A blessing from God, Miss Lucretia had pronounced. I didn't agree with her.

I wanted to stay clear of police and hospitals, not having proof of my identity, thanks to my lack of foresight. I was grateful I didn't need a hospital visit. A bill from Washington County Hospital would tip the Hunts to my general whereabouts. That was certainly out of the question, as was staying with these sweet, country, God-fearing people another day.

"Where to now, handsome?" I asked my reflection. I picked up my keys resting in a heap on the dresser, ready to put them in a pocket, before I realized I had no pockets. I had none of my own clothes.

"Isaac," came Miss Lucretia's voice through the closed bedroom door. "Come get something to eat, before Trip eats it all up. Catty made grits and sausage. Pancakes too if you want 'em."

I didn't answer, preoccupied with the decision between a BJ's Restaurant golf shirt and a threadbare Honeysuckle Festival T-shirt and not sure if I wanted grits. Tate had made them once and they made me gag.

"Is he in there?" I heard Miss Lucretia asking, followed by Trip's muffled, "Don't know." The back screen door slammed. It was Catty, I gathered, due to Miss Lucretia asking about me again.

"I don't know, Grandma. Let me see," Catty replied. There was a quick knock on the door and then I was exposed, half-dressed, for all the world to see. Granted they had all seen me last night, but standing there in borrowed drawers, as Trip had called them, bathed in the delicate light of a July morning, I felt ashamed. And so did my audience, at least the womenfolk. Trip's embarrassment, if I could call it that, registered as a raised eyebrow and a grunt between bites.

I pressed the golf shirt against my chest and stepped back toward the dresser. Catty lowered her eyes, blushing. She held a mound of clothes—mine fresh off the line by the look of them—a screen between us.

"Sorry," she said.

"It's okay."

I spoke through the fabric of the shirt as I struggled to get it over my head without causing too much pain. As I struggled physically, I realized that there was another struggle within my gut. Why had I reacted like I had? Blushing and covering myself like a bare-chested teenager. I didn't have anything to be ashamed of. That wasn't how I would have normally reacted. That was how I expected they expected me to react. Who were they making me into? If this was what southern hospitality did to a grown man, I didn't like it.

"I'm decent," I said, stepping forward to take my clothes. "Thanks."

"Let me fold them, at least." She met my eyes then looked away.

"Come eat, chil'ren," Miss Lucretia pressed. "The clothes can wait."

Catty let the clothes fall into my arms. The warmth and freshness of line-dried clothes billowed up at me. "I'm sorry for slapping you last night."

"I'm sorry for what I said." *Am I?* Or was I letting them

"make" me again. Was I losing complete control of myself? "Thanks for doing my clothes."

She smirked and shrugged. "Let's eat."

Trip eyed me like someone who wanted to push me under a moving car. He mumbled "Good morning" and passed the coffee as I folded my legs under the small table.

"Trip says you're leaving today," Miss Lucretia said. The woman's eyes registered an agony that you'd think might come from the loss of the family photos in a fire.

I smiled at her, across the remains of breakfast in Trip's wake, and said, "Yes, I'd better be moving on. I've imposed on you long enough." I wouldn't give her the satisfaction of making me do something I had no intention of doing, and I didn't want to give Trip the satisfaction of appearing to have manipulated me, either.

"Nonsense, baby. You can stay here as long as you need. You don't want to go back to your people looking all beat up. Stay and heal."

Before I could respond, Trip had fished something out of his back pocket. It was a magazine, thick folded in quarters like he had it but relatively thin when he spread it out on the table between our plates. "You wouldn't want your people worrying about you."

I recognized the issue, the Special Edition of *The Statement*, a biannual publication from my alma mater, highlighting special accomplishments and awards of the graduating class. This crumb-strewn table was the last place I expected to see it.

Trip turned to the engineering school section and rubbed his index finger across my photo.

"Nice article." His voice had changed, lost its smooth country edges.

I held my breath.

Miss Lucretia and Catty leaned over Trip's shoulder. They eyed me like I was someone who laced mail with anthrax in his spare time instead of someone who had worked on the landing apparatus team for a NASA Mars Mission Design Project and still managed to graduate summa cum laude.

I exhaled and tried to stay calm. "Where'd you get that?"

Trip ignored my question but drained his coffee cup and wiped his mouth. "My question is why didn't you come clean to begin with. Smart engineer, the son of a rich Raleigh judge. Why come pretending like you're visiting family in Pettigrew? Most everybody figured out who you were after a while anyway."

"I'm not running from the police, if that's what you're thinking. Ricky and Chloe Hunt are not rotting somewhere in a shallow grave." I let out a nervous chuckle.

I kept my eyes down, pushing a biscuit back and forth on my plate, but I could feel their eyes on my neck, roasting me like Sunday's dinner with all their unspoken questions. So I coughed it up, all of it except the part about not taking money or ID when I ran and having to sell my class ring.

"Oh, yes. I knew who you were," Miss Lucretia said after a long pause. "When I saw you 'long the side of the road, talking to Crazy Eddie." She pressed her arthritic fingers against her dark lips and stood. "You look so much like . . . your mama."

She smiled down at me and shook her head. "Then when you came in and ate with me, talking about visiting family, I thought you knew 'bout your mama having passed. I don't know the folks who adopted you, but I thought that they had told you and that's why you were here. Looking at your mama's grave and the house where she died. And I thought that you didn't say anything to me 'cause you was just being private, keeping your business to yourself." Her eyes tearing, she cupped the back of my head with her hand. "Oh, sweet child, I would've told you the little bit I do know if only you had just asked me. When Gladys told me 'bout you coming to her house yesterday, I wanted to run after you then and there. I'm so sorry 'bout how life has turned on you. Sweet Jesus . . . Poor Henry . . ." She covered her lips again.

The phone in the corner rang. Miss Lucretia patted my shoulder, excusing herself, and went to answer it. I continued to play with the biscuit, not feeling hungry anymore, while I watched Trip out of the corner of my eye. Throughout Miss Lucretia's speech, he had been leafing through the magazine like he'd been searching for some little detail he'd seen but lost. Catty had stepped away, backward, and was now leaning on the fridge chewing her bottom lip, glancing alternately at me and at her grandmother whispering to the person on the phone.

After a soft huff, she said, "I guess I'll fold your clothes. We'll need to find you a bag. Maybe I can find my father's duffel."

She disappeared into the bedroom. I chuckled to myself at the thought of having my *own* bag for a change. Yes, that's it. The thing that had been bothering me since seeing Eddie's duffel bag. It was standard Army-issue just like the one I'd seen in Ulysses Hunt's room at the rest home. Old Ulysses' had bulged with unseen contents just like Eddie's had.

Why . . . ?

Trip broke my concentration when he stood and slapped his thigh with the rolled-up magazine. "Isaac," he said with a voice I imagined he used when he preached.

I turned part of my face toward him, fearful I was about to get pounded again. Or worse, sermonized. "Yes?"

Emotion worked across his face. "I'd like to ask your forgiveness for how I treated you last night."

I swallowed the little bit of biscuit I had in my mouth, then faced him.

"I did not act appropriately. I had this information last night. I could have approached you last night about it and not played with you. Seems life's dealt you a raw deal. I'm sorry for that and I'm sorry for the way I treated you."

"Thank you."

"Do you forgive me?"

Why was he pressing this thing? I shrugged. "Yes, I do."

He extended his hand. I shook it.

"Thank you, Isaac." His good ole boy accent was back. "If you'd like, I could take you where you want to go."

I smiled, realizing that I had yet to decide what my next move would be. Where would a handful of Benjamins take me? "To tell the truth, I don't know where I'm going."

He sat and leaned into me. "With your résumé, I'm sure you can get any job you want. You'll need wheels." He pulled the bowl of grits over. "Grits?"

I shook my head. He pushed my biscuit aside with the ladle and dropped a dollop on my plate.

"Sugar."

"Excuse me."

"Sugar, lots of it. That's what makes grits bearable. Butter helps too. Where is the butter?" He pulled the sugar bowl toward my plate and made the white steamy mound into a white sparkly mound, then got up to stick his head in the fridge. "Eat, man."

Miss Lucretia hung up the phone, explaining that she was on her way to see her friend Gladys. She gave me a smile that seemed to say "you poor sweet boy" and left.

With the confidence of a one-legged tightrope walker, I decided to try the grits. *A spoon.*

"Well, if sugar's not your thing, how 'bout some jelly or jam or . . . ?" While Trip rummaged through the fridge, pulling out bottle after bottle of jelly and apple butter, I searched for the silverware drawer. I found a neatly arranged drawer with wooden dividers. Large Army-issue spoons in the far left slot caught my eye, making me think of a certain military man who I still had a soft spot for. I grabbed one and sat down.

Trip had finally finished rooting and sat down next to me, jars of every type of sweet stuff fanned out around his plate. "Oh, my goodness!" he exclaimed and pointed at the spoon laden with grits on its way to my open mouth.

Catty entered with some of my shirts over her arm. "Isaac, stop! Where's Grandma?"

"She went to Miss Gladys's," Trip explained.

"Good. Give me the spoon, Isaac."

Trip slumped over his elbows on the table and let out a deep chuckle.

Catty grabbed the spoon, which was still in my grasp and shook the grits back onto my plate. "Give it!" Her eyes darted to the screen door.

"What . . ."

"Stop laughing, Trip." Catty dropped the utensil in the dishwater standing in the sink to her left.

"Excuse me. Don't know if you noticed, but I was using that spoon."

"Shush. Don't say that word."

Trip was chuckling and snorting, rolling his forehead back and forth on the heel of his hand.

"What word?" I was annoyed, since I had finally started to feel hungry, even for grits.

Trip placed his hand on my shoulder and sputtered, his pursed lips working on a word. He looked like a drunk man in a laughing fit.

"Spoon," Catty whispered, eyeing the back door. She washed the offensive item, dried it with a paper towel, and placed it back in the drawer. "Stop looking at me that way, Isaac. I'm not losing my mind. Contrary to what the occasionally sober-minded preacher here thinks. But I think Grandma Lu is losing hers. I don't know why, but seeing a man use one of those spoons sends her away to a place . . . She starts talking to Daddy like he's still here. I don't like to see her that way."

"She's still grieving your father's sudden passing," Trip offered in a near-normal tone, wiping tears from his eyes.

Catty rolled her eyes and handed me a teaspoon from the right side of the still-open drawer. "And so am I, so you say."

"It's true. Grief is good to a point but *your* grief has become unhealthy. It's the spoons for Miss Luc. And for you it's your father's brand of after—"

She lunged for the preacher across the table. "Shut your mouth, Trip!" Then she shot a glance and a smile at me. "Sorry." She brushed by the table and toward the front of the house, talking over her shoulder, "Then tell me why I'd be willing to give Isaac my father's duffel bag."

Trip waited until he heard a door close and leaned over to me. "Displaced attachment, that's what it is." With that, he stood and cupped his palm over his chin. He squeezed his lips and stared at me like he regretted what he had just said or was about to say.

Before he could say another word, the screen door opened. It was Miss Lucretia followed by the wrinkled, gray-haired woman I'd seen at 65 Water Street. She was carrying a rusty coffee can, the remains of the word SANKA on the side, and smiling at me with pain in her eyes. She had the look of a person struggling to put a good face on with extremely bad news, I remember thinking. Like the look on Chloe Hunt's face when she told me that Mr. Happy was dead.

I regretted having eaten only a bite of biscuit because I had no appetite for anything after seeing the contents of the can Miss Gladys held.

chapter 12

darlene sure was a pretty little thing, Ben Jacob Benson thought as he ran his thumb across the downy hairs on the back of her neck. His wife, Selma, used to be pretty. She used to wear her hair up in a cute ponytail just like the Coke-bottle-figured woman smoking next to him.

"Stop it, BJ," Darlene whined, shrugging Ben Jacob's hand from her shoulder. "That tickles."

"You know you like it."

The blonde rolled her eyes at him. "You need to keep your hands to yourself and your mind on your wife."

The cowboy boots that danced from her earlobes made

Ben Jacob smile. They had been a gift, and he was glad to see her wearing them.

"I *am* thinking of her." He chuckled. "I'm hoping to God Selma don't step out the back door or through them bushes, and find us back here."

She flicked her cigarette to the gravel and crushed it with the heel of her Keds. "I'm just having a smoke, boss."

"Where you going?"

"Back in to do my job. Lena gets sloppy when I leave her alone for too long."

Ben Jacob let her go, lighting up again and settling in against the back wall of his restaurant. He closed his eyes and inhaled the smells of sausage and coffee that drifted through an open window high in the wall and mingling with his cigarette smoke. Sounds from the breakfast crowd would have been music to his ears a year ago. But now he wanted more. More than a successful restaurant, more than the money he earned from managing the Farm. Abraham hadn't been very supportive. That didn't matter. He and Abraham never did see eye to eye on much, especially when it came to the proper use of the family's influence. And he always treated him like a fool. He'd see who was the fool, BJ decided, as he pulled the cell phone from the clip on his hip and punched in a string of numbers.

He took one last drag and crushed the cigarette under his heel as he answered, "Yes, Bruno Lucci, please. Ben Jacob Benson in North Carolina. Yes, I'm with Benson Ridge Farms. He's expecting my call. Yes, of course, I'll wait. Thank you."

He hummed as he waited, reveling in how close he was to

realizing his dreams, of doing his part as a white American male. The heart of the land he loved was being ripped out. Thanks to communist groups like the Workers Party that were running rampant in college towns like Greensboro and Raleigh. Folks were still talking about how the United Front had massacred so many innocent youth in that 1979 incident in Greensboro. To Ben Jacob it was justice, not a massacre.

The disbanding of the Front that happened as a result of the government crackdown after the shootout had meant nothing but more black babies on welfare, more blurring of the lines between race and class. He was tired of standing by and watching the Front and his state go down. He was sitting on a goldmine, he felt: Benson Ridge Farms. The Front needed him now like never before.

"Hello, Bruno. Fine, thanks. Yes, we're getting close. It's my cousin, Abraham. Yes, that's right, you met him once. He's coming around. And you know where he goes, so does the Board. But he . . . well, he needs a little more convincing, you know. And I figured since you were coming, you know, for our fishing trip next week you might consider coming earlier and . . . you know, meet with him again and mention that you were interested in buying. I think he's really close, with the passing of his wife and all. Yes, yes, I know this is sudden but . . . Okay. Oh, I see. Well, once you've cleared it with your father, please call me . . . Thanks."

He hung up and pounded his thigh, feeling a little stupid like he'd been begging for spare change. The Italians had to come, and they would have to pay the price he proposed or else he would never be able to move ahead with his plans for the Front. The Front and the family were destined to be powerful again. Powerful together.

The appearance of Betty Douglas's boy had complicated things in ways he didn't like to think about. That boy was as blurry a line as he'd ever seen. But there were men like Jack Kepler who would help with the Isaac problem.

The bushes to his left rustled. The blond man who stepped out looked dirtier than normal. But then again, Jack always looked dirty to Ben Jacob. Too much time on Water Street, he guessed.

"Where you been?" he asked, lighting up again.

"At the lake house like you told me."

"I checked this morning. You weren't there. None of the beds been slept in. You think I'm a fool?"

"I don't feel comfortable in that house."

"I don't want to hear it."

"I ain't been back to Water Street. You worse than my old man."

"Our problem has to go away, Jack. I'm sure you know what I mean. You know what I wish?" He snuffed his second cigarette on the wall then wrapped his right forearm around Jack's neck and pulled him closer. Jack grinned and allowed himself to be pulled to Ben Jacob's side. "I wish you could keep your zipper closed and your temper in check."

Jack's grin evaporated.

"I need you now like never before. But what do you go and do? Attack an unarmed man. And not just any unarmed man! And not once but twice. Then destroy his car. In broad daylight. With witnesses!"

"Nobody saw the second time." Jack turned his head to the side and grumbled.

Ben Jacob raised his left hand behind his head, as if to slap Jack. "If you knew how to control yourself, you would be of some use to me. But at the time when I need you most you have to be in hiding."

"I can still help you, BJ. The way I figure it, if he hasn't pressed charges yet, then he won't."

Ben Jacob pulled out his pack and shook out another cigarette, rolling it between his fingers for a moment. Jack watched him and waited.

Finally Ben Jacob grunted. "Doubtful. One thing's for sure; he has the ring or else he wouldn't be snooping around the Farm. He's made the connection, but I don't know why he hasn't made a move. We won't wait for that, will we?" He ran his right thumb along the edge of the ring on his finger and tried to make sense of things.

"I can get the Benson ring back for you."

"Not so fast, boy. I want you to follow him. See if he has the ring. If he does . . . You know what to do." BJ held the cigarette lightly between his lips and dug out his wallet. *The boy was too eager.* But there was no one else who would do what he wanted, when he wanted it done, and how he wanted it done. *A little motivation will keep him on track.* "Here. For gas and food. Not women and booze. Discipline, Jack! Don't let that boy outta your sight. Stay outta your daddy's crosshairs."

Jack took the money, looking to Ben Jacob like a beggar.

"Git," Ben Jacob barked. When he heard the prattle of Jack's old Toyota truck fade away, Ben Jacob slipped the unlit smoke behind his ear and pulled the family ring from his finger. He would have to find a safe hiding place later. For now, inside his shirt dangling from a gold chain would do.

The red stone in the large gold signet flashed in the morning sun like a grocery store laser. In the early years, it was a sign of maturity and trust, a symbol of a father's acceptance of his son's manhood. Abraham, being older, had received his ring a few years before Ben Jacob. Ben Jacob had coveted Abraham's ring, anxious for the day when his father would deem him fit to have one too.

In the '70s and '80s, as the government began to take a more liberal turn, the ring had taken on another meaning. It had become a symbol of those faithful to the country's most powerful agribusiness family and all it stood for—commitment to the faith and purity to the race—in the face of a government that sought to dilute and destroy them.

"Too much talk and not enough action," grumbled Ben Jacob as he thought of how things had taken a turn for the worse of late. Many men still wore their Benson rings but they'd all become fat useless slobs like so many swine in the hog house.

"What's the special today, Darlene?" came a familiar voice from the restaurant behind him. Ben Jacob pushed the ring and chain inside his shirt and slipped through the storeroom, then back into his tiny office where he could see the restaurant through a two-way mirror.

"What's he doing here?" he mumbled as he watched Abraham lean over a menu spread out on the counter. Abraham smiled at Darlene and pointed to something on the menu.

"It's all your fault, Abraham," said Ben Jacob to the mirror. "You and that wife of your'n. Letting things slide and slide and slide until it was too far gone. I hate your liberal guts. And now that that boy is back, whatcha gonna do, big man? I'll tell you what you're gonna do. Nothing. You're a poor excuse for the head of the family. A poor excuse for a Benson. Just like Fred Jr."

Ben Jacob glanced to a framed 8"x10" photograph on his wall. It had been taken eighteen years earlier at a family picnic. That had been the last time that all living Benson men had gathered together. Sitting on lawn chairs in the foreground were his father, Fred Sr., and Abraham's father, Karl. The other sons and cousins stood around to make up a group of sixteen men ranging in age from eighteen to fifty-five. Ben Jacob stabbed a finger at his older brother's face.

He heard the jingle of the bell over the front door.

"Well, speak of the devil," he said as he watched his brother walk to the counter and stand beside Abraham. The two men shook hands.

"Well, Fred Jr., what was your excuse? You coulda handled things before that boy passin' fo' white of your'n was born. That Betty girl was as crazy as they came but she won't stupid. Wave enough money in her face and she woulda had an abortion in a heartbeat.

"'Abortion ain't right,'" Ben Jacob added in a mocking voice. "I hate your liberal guts too, Fred Jr." He sat behind his desk, pulled a bag of M&M's and a bottle of corn whiskey from his desk drawer, and propped up his feet. He threw a handful of candies in his mouth and took a swallow of whiskey, then continued to rant at the photo. "Stupid head. Blind idiot. Everybody but you could see that the boy looked more and more like you every day."

He took another swallow of whiskey and pulled the ring from his shirt as he sat back in the chair. He smiled as he remembered how good it had felt to receive his ring the day of the family picnic. And then how good it had felt when the plan had come to him.

"My plan fell through that day 'cause I was depending on you to make your move, Freddy. Everybody was there. Everybody woulda seen that boy with my new ring. Daddy and Uncle Karl woulda thrown Betty and that no-good-for-nothin' son of your'n out right then and there. But you choked. You didn't play along like I told you. What was your excuse that day?"

He threw in another handful of candy. He took a deep breath and closed his eyes and imagined himself addressing the United Front Assembly like his father had done many times. He whispered the words his father would use to close every speech. "Purity, men. Purity. That's what it's all about. If we don't have that, what do we have? Purity don't just happen. We have to take action for it. That is your calling. That is your fate."

A knock on his office door brought Ben Jacob back around. He pushed the bag of M&M's forward and slipped the whiskey bottle into a drawer.

"Yeah?"

"Hey, BJ," Fred said as he opened the door.

"Hey, Fred. Come on in. I was just thinking 'bout you."

Fred raised an eyebrow and sat down in the chair across from his brother. He reached into the bag of candy and pulled out a handful. "Really?"

Ben Jacob tipped his head toward the 8"x10" on the wall.

"Remember that day, Fred? Those were some good times."

Fred shook his head. "Not for everybody, BJ."

"What kind of a fool comment was that?"

"You know what I'm talking 'bout."

"No. Enlighten me."

"I've been hearing a lot about the Front lately. Know anything about that?"

Ben Jacob leaned forward, took some candies, and shrugged.

"Mitchell Highsmith called me. Asked me right out if I would be interested in meeting with him to see how the United Front might help me in my campaign."

Ben Jacob chuckled. "Wonder why he did that? Everybody knows the Front is dead. G-men made sure of that."

"Highsmith's been calling you too. Ain't he?"

"Don't know what you're talking 'bout," Ben Jacob lied.

Fred's eyes narrowed. "And what about this foolishness with Jack?"

"Foolishness. Is that what you call it?" Ben Jacob laughed.

"I don't know what you call it. But some folks might call it assault and battery."

"That's too bad for Jack. How much time could he get for that? In and outta jail that kid is."

"Don't play stupid with me, Ben Jacob. Everybody knows that kid's around here all the time."

"Don't mean I told him to go out and beat up that white good-for-nothin' boy."

Fred stood up and threw the M&M's across the desk.

Ben Jacob held his arm up against the flying candy and smiled. "A might testy, are we?"

"You're the stupidest man—"

"The truth is, Fred, you're the stupid one."

"Shut up."

"You had all those years when he was little. You coulda dealt with him and his mama, but now that he's older it's harder. Nobody's gonna elect a stupid coward for county commissioner. You're a stupid coward, Fred, and you know it. Everybody knows it."

Fred jumped across the desk and grabbed for his brother, sending the bag of M&M's and a stack of papers sailing across the room. Fred pounded him in the chest and stomach. Ben Jacob rolled back, pulling Fred to the floor and sending his chair crashing against the back wall.

The door flew open. "Stop it," yelled Abraham. He pulled at Fred, the lighter of the two. "Stop it." He held his broad palm against Fred's chest. "Just calm down, Fred. Why don't you get Darlene to look at that cut over your eye?"

Fred glared at Ben Jacob and left, slamming the door.

"What was that all about, BJ?"

"Like it's ever about anything different—disagreement over what to do about those blacks. 'Cept now some of them ain't so black, now are they?"

"You make me sick, BJ."

The wall phone rang. Ben Jacob reached around his departing cousin and lifted the receiver.

"Back at you," he yelled. BJ righted his chair, then pressed the phone to his ear. "Yeah, who's this?"

"Hello, Ben Jacob. Did I catch you at a bad time again?"

"Oh, Mitchell. Sorry. No, everything's fine. And thank you for calling me back. We were having a late dinner last night. Selma was sitting right there—"

"I understand. Now, tell me something good."

"Well, sir, I've put some thought to what you mentioned, and I'm all for us working together to start up some meetings and training. I've got some men here, good men."

"Benson men?"

"Well, no. But these other fellas—"

"Ben Jacob, I need to be able to move forward intelligently. With power and influence. The Benson name offers that."

"I understand."

"Not just any snot-nosed yokel in camo."

Ben Jacob clenched his teeth. "I understand."

"Why don't I send one of my men? Excellent marksman and trainer. Preston's his name. You'll know him because he'll be wearing a Benson ring. Is that okay? We're working together and I want us to be on the same page. Don't you? We need to take action, decisive action soon. That's our calling."

"Indeed."

"Anything else?"

Ben Jacob hesitated. His thoughts went to Isaac. Could this Preston fellow help him out where Jack could not? Or maybe there was another possibility.

"Well, there is something. Or I guess I should say somebody. It's a delicate kind of situation with my brother Fred. A little trouble he got into with a little black girl about twenty years ago, if you know what I mean?"

"Hmm. Does this situation have a name?"

"Isaac Douglas. No wait a minute. He came to my restaurant the other day using another name. Hunt."

There was a pause on the other end.

"Mitchell?"

"You said Isaac Hunt?"

"Yes."

"Is he still in Pettigrew?"

"Yes. I've got a man on him. I'm thinking this Hunt boy could help us out, in a way, especially when it comes to getting Fred on our side. And where Fred goes, Abraham might—"

"Tell me more about this boy. Why'd he change his name?"

Ben Jacob smiled. He had something of value to Mitchell. He had the upper hand. "His mama's name was Betty Douglas. Trouble, she was, from day one. But boy was she pretty . . ."

As he went on, his mind went back to a day more than two decades earlier.

It had been a late Friday afternoon. Ben Jacob knew Betty would be home on Friday. All the other migrant workers would be out in the fields, but she, since she now worked at the Benson Ridge homestead, had Fridays off, and would be at her room at the migrant camp.

Ben Jacob had stepped in without knocking and let the screen door slam behind him. Betty was in her light blue cotton dress washing something by hand in a foot tub in the corner.

They were about the same age but she looked so much younger than the other girls his age. So young and tender she'd been when she came to Pettigrew, fresh out of high school, four years earlier with her sickly father.

He had stood in the open doorway and watched the late summer sun gleam on her wet arms. The front of the thin dress was wet and it clung to her ample thighs.

"Get out!" she had yelled.

He had smirked and said, "Why? You didn't mind me coming last time." Ben Jacob still remembered that chilly night. The soft warmth of her skin against his. She had been so trusting then in the wake of her father's death. But now only four years later she'd turned into an ungrateful snake.

"Get out!" She moved to grab a broom in the corner.

"I wouldn't do that if I was you, Betty. I just wanna talk this time, anyway." He looked around. There was a cookstove on the right and a cot and a shabby little chair to the left where she stood next to the tub. Beyond her, the door to a small bathroom stood ajar. A toy truck lay upside down on a tattered rug in the middle of the room.

"Where's the boy?" Ben Jacob stepped forward. "You heard me."

She set her jaw and raised the broom handle higher.

Ben Jacob jerked his head in the direction of the bathroom. "Is he on the toilet?"

"Get out."

"Now, Betty honey, cain't you be nice to me ever once in a while? Fred Jr. says you're real nice to him."

She glared at him. He was enjoying the fire in her gray eyes.

He smiled and walked closer. She stepped back and swung the broom at him. "Get back!"

He lunged toward her and grabbed the handle. "Now, now, sweetie!" He jerked on the handle, she gasped and let go, tumbling against the wall.

"Please don't!" she shrieked and covered her chest with her arms.

"Don't worry none, honey. I just want to talk, that's all." He reached past her, enjoying the way she flinched, and propped the broom against the wall, then he sat on the chair next to the cot. "Well, this is cozy," he said as he brushed his hand over the quilt that covered the cot. It looked too nice for this place, too nice for her. But that was not what he had come for. "Down right cozified."

He looked around the room, searching for hiding places. He lifted a corner of the mattress beside him. Something yellow caught his eye. He sprang to his feet and pushed the mattress over. "Did you steal that too?" He pointed to the yellow satin dress spread neatly over the cot springs. Arms still tightly crossed, she shook her head and pressed her body against the wall.

"You lying." He sprang at her. "Where's the ring, girl?"

"I ain't got no ring!"

"What you ain't got is good sense. You want money for it? I'll give you $600." He pulled out a wad of cash from his pocket. "Just hand over the ring and I'll forget you took it." He kicked the washtub aside and walked closer to her. He pinned her wrists, first the right and then the left, against the wall.

"I ain't steal nothing, Mr. Ben Jacob. Honest." Tears ran down her face. "I'd never take somethin' that ain't mine."

"I'm not leaving here 'til I get that ring, bit—"

The banging screen door behind him cut him short. He released her and turned around. There stood Abraham with two children leaning against him, one a Mexican boy, the other Betty's boy. Ben Jacob struggled to keep his breathing steady.

He threw his chin forward as he faced Abraham. "What you doing here?"

"Hello, Betty." Abraham glared at Ben Jacob. "These little fellas are a little sick to their stomachs. Ate too many cucumbers, I 'magine." He led the boys to the edge of the cot, pulled the mattress back in place, and helped them lie down. "Betty, I hope you don't mind if little Paco stays here with Isaac 'til his mama gets back from the grader," he continued, still glaring at Ben Jacob.

Sniffing, Betty ran a trembling hand across her forehead. "No, sir," she said. "That's fine with me, Mr. Abraham."

"You ain't answered my question, Abe," Ben Jacob demanded.

"Thank you, Betty." Abraham nodded. He turned, pressing his body into Ben Jacob's. His chest muscles were hot and hard. "I don't answer to you, BJ."

━━━

He had the look of a dead man, Catty thought, or a man who had given up on life. Catty had wanted so much to run to him, gather him in her arms, and kiss his pain away. Instead she watched him unfold the letter and stumble into the bedroom, closing the door behind him.

Why had he come to them? Had God sent him? If so, why? To test her? Torment her?

What had gotten into her last night when she slapped him? *I didn't know about the article. And everything else he's been going through*. But she couldn't stand by and let him curse God. That's what he had done. A blasphemous thing. The words had stung her heart and she had lashed out.

"I was right to do it, Lord. Wasn't I?" She tossed her father's tattered duffel bag on the floor and collapsed on her bed. "Oh, God. I'm sorry. Please help him. Heal him!"

Her trembling words crumbled into tears. She cried more for herself than for Isaac. Caught in a web of feelings and faith, Catty teetered between attraction, and the genuine love she knew she should have for his soul. What woman would not be attracted to that muscular chest, trim waist, crystalline eyes? She traced the place where he had laid his head that first night—the night he slept in her bed, his scent mingling with her father's aftershave. No, she could not pray for Isaac in the way her father had taught her.

"Pray without ceasing, Catty girl," he had told her. "Pray for those that love you. Pray for those that hate you. Pray for those that don't know His grace. That is your duty."

She could just say the words, but with what motivation? That he would be fit in every way to be her companion? A man who the church would not frown on. A man who would guide her as a husband someday. That was the truth; to pray anything else would be a lie. She couldn't make him turn to Christ any more than she could make the desire to feel his lips on hers go away.

But why would he even look at her, a poor woman with skin darker than coffee grounds? She was only hired help with a high school diploma. A nobody—to some people.

She couldn't pray. Surely God would not hear the prayers

of one so weak. She would read. Grabbing her book of poems and her keys, she headed to work.

"Oh, Lord. Make him go away." Catty breathed. Still thinking about Isaac, she rattled down Water Street in her rusty, white Cressida.

Her friend Cynthia met her at the cafeteria's rear entrance, crushing a piece of Nicorette between her teeth.

"Hey, girl. I covered for you. Madame Godzilla's on the hunt, though. So I'd lay low for a few if I were you." Cynthia tossed her braids, turning her head to one side. Catty could feel the questions coming.

"I don't want to talk about it," Catty moaned. She tossed her book into the bottom of her locker with a crack.

"What's wrong? He hasn't left yet, has he?"

Ignoring the question, Catty kept her back to her friend. She pulled on her smock, and French-braided her hair. Deep down she wanted to tell Cynthia about the plastic zip pouch she'd found at the old Ross House. She wanted to tell her about the letter, and the Benson ring she'd found. But she knew how judgmental Cynthia would be. With hands on those wide hips, Cynthia would scold Catty like a woman three times her age and, no doubt, tell Catty about some biblical characters who had been swallowed up alive by the earth for deceiving people.

Catty wiped the frown from her face and turned around. "Cynthia. I just need some space. Okay?"

"I'll be praying for you."

"Thanks."

Catty looked past Cynthia's friendly smile to the brown-skinned eighteen-year-old walking toward them on his spidery legs. He strutted like he alone was holding each terra cotta ceramic tile onto the floor and his smile alone was making the stainless steel counters shimmer.

He ran a hand over his afro. Stroking his meager chin hairs—Catty estimated there were no more than twenty in all—he cooed, "Good morning, ladies."

Cynthia rolled her eyes to Catty, turned, and said hello. Catty pushed past both of them. "I'd better get the waffle iron heated up."

"Whoa, wait a minute, Miss Wright. I said good morning."

Cynthia had moved to a rack of pots hanging in the center of the room, shaking her head in warning to Catty. The *tap tap* of their boss's heels in the hallway could be heard long before she appeared. "Madame Godzilla," she whispered.

"That's not very Christian of you, Miss Wright, to ignore a friendly greeting," her coworker taunted.

Catty turned around and crossed her arms over her chest, wondering why only oversexed boys showed interest in her. No men ever had. Certainly never a man like Isaac Hunt.

"Melvin," she growled, looking up from the jeans straining across his thighs to the sneer she was sure he considered alluring. "I would like for you to leave me alone. I've told you before. What part of 'leave me alone' don't you understand?"

Melvin nodded and approached Catty, clucking his tongue until he stood in front of her. His cologne was a bit thick. Catty coughed and backed up a half step. He took her arm and read her bracelet. "WWJD?"

He had nerve, she thought, a man who cussed all the time.

"Forgive me, Lord," she mumbled. Then she pulled back

her right arm and slapped him, thinking as her boss stepped through the double doors at the far end of the cafeteria just how refreshed it had made her feel.

i learned a valuable lesson in Ms. Britters' ninth grade English class. It wasn't what my heavyset redheaded English teacher would have liked—a disdain for dangling participles or a knack for identifying an infinitive phrase. It came in the form of a note from my new friend, Tate. Actually it was a scrap of blue paper he'd stolen, a piece of a correspondence between two pecan-brown lovelies I had had my eye on for three months. He had passed it to me and whispered, "Read between the lines," with fire in his eyes.

"*What do you think about Isaac?*" it started.

"*Too black for me,*" was the response.

The word "black" had been drawn instead of written. What it revealed to me about the inner workings of the young black female mind had been the biggest reason why I had not dated in high school. BLACK: Five hollow letters that jumped out at me and tore my heart out.

In the same way, my mother's words were plain, but they tore my heart out too. I didn't need to read between the lines; taking each of the four pages at face value caused me enough anguish. After reading the first few lines, I lay on the bed and tried to push the tears back. It was then that it occurred to me that I had stopped dreaming of the lilies. In fact, I had stopped dreaming altogether.

My sweetest Isaac, the words you are about to read are so hard to write. They are words from my heart. I don't mean them to cause you pain, but to show you the way to go. I would not be doing my duty as your mother if I didn't tell you these things. I hope you forgive me for not being able to tell you in person.

I am a plain woman and all I've known is simple living, being the daughter of a migrant worker and all. My life has been hard, but God has been good. It is God and His people that have made my life in this town halfway decent. I don't deserve what these good people have given me. People like Olivia Ross, Lucretia Price, and Gladys Ferrel. I pray God bless them real good.

I pray for you a lot. I want your life to be a whole lot better than mine. But, I feel in my heart that the looks the Good

Lord blessed you with may cause you a might of trouble. Many a day, I prayed that your blue eyes would turn brown, and your skin would darken. But I know now that is not God's will. Like it won't His will that I kill you when you were inside of me. He gave you those eyes and that skin. Be proud of them. Don't let anyone make you ashamed of how you look. And never use those sweet eyes to look down on nobody.

My greatest hope and prayer is that you have grown into a strong God-fearing man. And that you have a heart full of love for all people no matter what they look like, or how much money they have.

I have tried to always tell you the truth. But when I told you that your father was dead, I lied. I thought it would be easier to tell you that than to explain why you would grow up in the same town as him and never call him "daddy." It's a complicated mess that cain't be fixed. Honestly, I didn't want you in it—that's why I lied.

And, you must know—I promised him that I would never tell you. We thought it was best that way. By telling you now, I am breaking that promise. But he won't know unless you try to find him. That's likely what you will want to do after reading this letter and seeing the ring. PLEASE DON'T. It is best if you live your life and he lives his. Your father has done some bad in his life, but he is a good man, deep down. He is part of a powerful family.

There was a time when I thought power was good. Now I know I was wrong. The kind of power they have is pure wickedness. God is not in it.

I won't try and fool you. I done made my own share of mistakes. Falling in love with your father was one of them.

Having you was not. I love you, my precious son.
                              Your mother, Beatrice Anne Douglas

I refolded the letter and stuffed it back in the envelope with my name on it. As I stared out at the wash flapping in the sun, I considered the facts. My mother had been a poor woman, but not illiterate. I'm not proud to admit that I found relief in the fact that she could write. And not too badly for a migrant worker.

She'd had friends in Pettigrew. There had been enemies as well. She had believed in God. A fact that did disturb me at first but at least she had not been disingenuous about it. I could respect that.

And last, she had loved me. She had wanted me.

But why had she written the letter in the first place? It seemed obvious that she was not expecting to live to tell me these things in person. Had it been illness or impending harm that caused her to think that?

The ring mentioned in the letter was wrapped in a scrap of denim and tucked in the corner of the plastic pouch. I pushed the lump in my throat down and examined the ring.

A gold finger ring, maybe twice as heavy as my class ring, stared back up at me with its one red eye. It reminded me of something I'd seen in the Louvre. There was not even an inscription, just a jeweler's mark.

Around the deeply set corn design that hugged the stone, the words *Fidèle et Pur* were carved. *Fidèle et Pur?* My French was rusty but I guessed *pur* was pure and *fidèle* was faithful or faithfulness. The translation didn't matter much to me. What did matter was I knew where to begin my search for my father if I ever brought myself to violate my mother's wish.

It took me a little while but I finally pulled myself together enough to reenter the kitchen. But first I stood in the bedroom's cool stillness and listened to a bird's song through the open windows. Someone had started singing softly on the back porch.

The clear tenor produced, "Oh what a foretaste of glory divine."

I slipped my feet into a pair of slippers at the foot of the bed and went to the back porch. Trip jumped when I opened the door. The Bible on his knee fell to the floor.

"Good gravy, Isaac! You like to scared me half to death."

I walked to the edge of the porch and studied the muddy depression around the bottom step. Out of the corner of my eye, I could see Trip watching me like he wanted an update of my mental state.

Finally, in the country accent he dredges up from time to time, he spoke. "Miss Luc left you a plate in the fridge. There's a slice of cantaloupe left too, if you like."

He stood, taking a few steps toward me. "Personally, I don't like the stuff. Yuck." He reminded me of Tigger's response to honey with that ridiculous chin of his.

On a better day, I would have laughed to myself.

"I want you to take me to the bus station."

"Right now?"

I nodded. "Soon as I get that bag Catty promised."

"Don't know where our young Ms. Wright is. Though I'm sure she'd want to say good-bye. Probably across the street with Miss Luc, talking with Miss Gladys . . ."

Trip gripped my bare shoulder.

"I know this has got to be hard for you. Tell you what, go change out of my drawers," he said, pointing at the pj bottoms I still wore, "and I'll pack your stuff while you eat. Then we can go over to Miss Gladys's and say good-bye proper like. Short and sweet, I promise." He gave my shoulder a gentle pat and left.

I heard the screen door close behind me. I pretended to be interested in the squirrel stealing a tomato from the garden. The animal started then scampered along the split rail fence that ran behind the clothesline and shed fence a few yards away, stopping short of a yellow and white flowered vine that covered most of the fence, and nibbled on the tomato. A bright sweet smell drifted to me. The same smell that met me that afternoon I first met Miss Lucretia. There had been a vase of the flowers on the kitchen counter, all wiggling their little yellow and white fingers in a friendly greeting. Now they seemed to be waving good-bye.

Good-bye.

It was definitely time to go. I had found what I was looking for and found what I didn't know I needed until I uncovered it.

My mother had loved me.

That knowledge gave me a deep satisfaction. Though the father question did nibble at me, I could set it aside for now.

I would move on, I decided as I finished my ham sandwich and potato salad. Getting a job wouldn't be too hard. Transportation was a question mark, though.

"Ready?" Trip said.

He walked through the kitchen with a duffel bag over his left arm and a gym bag with an RPR monogram in his right hand.

I nodded. Placing the dirty dishes in the sink, I followed him to his truck, an old Chevy, originally a pukey green, but now milky with oxidation. He tossed the bags in the middle of the broad, sun-roughened vinyl seat and started the engine. I hesitated at the door, listening to the music of a carbureted engine. A sweet sound that reminded me of many happy summer afternoons spent with Granddaddy Ulysses tinkering on some engine or another. He could fix anything with parts to spare. I squeezed the handle and swallowed tears. I missed him. But I missed Betty more. I didn't need this pain. *Stop it!* I didn't want to miss anyone. *Get a job and move on. Forget the past.*

"It's okay. She growls but she don't bite," Trip said, patting the dash. "After you say your good-byes I have to swing by the migrant camp. Maybe even the cucumber grader. I'm looking for my friend Miguel. He said he wanted to visit family in Raleigh if I ever went again."

I frowned.

"Oh, I forgot to tell you. I'm taking you to Raleigh."

He put his green metal whale in gear, and then jabbed a thumb over his shoulder while looking in his rearview mirror. "Looks like your farewell committee is forming," he said, reparking the truck.

I turned and looked. There they were, forty or so dark faces, some from the night before. At least I think they were. It was hard to say. And I'm ashamed to admit that as they swarmed the truck they were all starting to look alike.

Miss Lucretia smiled to me from where she stood at the fringe of the crowd, giving me that sweet little wave of hers. I smiled and waved back, a knot in my throat.

A man materialized beside me and wrapped his knotty white hand around my forearm as it lay across the open car window. His hand was cool and smoother than rose petals.

"Isaac." My name rumbled from his wrinkled throat. He closed his eyes and bent his large head, which was covered with tight coils the color of new motor oil. Then he began to speak.

I squinted as I listened, as if that would help me unscramble the words he spoke. African? I wondered. I studied his features, thick with echoes of the motherland. English words, I realized, poked out here and there.

Lord . . . Jesus . . . grace . . . purpose . . .

But there was something else, something that reminded me of Scotland, of all places. He raised his eyes to mine and continued speaking. They were watery gray, but alive with a blue fire.

I looked to the others around us. Their heads were bowed, bobbing from time to time with an "amen" or a "yes, Lawd." I looked to Trip. His chin rested on his chest but his eyes were half open. He hummed his approval to the words, a grave look on his face.

"They're praying for your journey," he explained, as if he could sense my confusion. "And not just the one back to Raleigh."

What journey?

"Thanks for nothing, Trip," I wanted to say.

The old man stopped and stepped back with his chin high, looking at me through the bottom of his eyes and breathing deeply. The others had erupted in a melee of hand waving and amens.

At a loss for what else to do, I bowed my head to him and said thank you.

Miss Lucretia had pressed forward and was stretching her black arms around my neck, kissing my cheek. Why hadn't I shaved? She was telling me how much she was going to miss me and that I'd better call her every week and start going to church like a good boy.

It was then that I realized that she wasn't there, my dark princess with lips like dates. At that moment, I should have been listening to the sweet old lady who kissed my cheek one last time and then passed food to me wrapped in a small paper bag. But I wasn't. I was looking for Catty in the crowd. *I'm not gonna miss her anyway.*

I regret that longing because I do not remember Miss Lucretia's last words to me. Isn't that how it always is when we sit and talk among ourselves about our departed elders, ruing the day of our selfish confused youth?

The crowd started to drift to one side as Trip backed across the road. Miss Lucretia smiled, stepped back, and waved again.

That was the last time I would see the smile of the woman who had welcomed me with joy and fearlessness into my mother's world.

the red kitchen door stood wide open when Catty arrived at the Benson house. She hesitated with her hand on the cool metal knob of the screen door, a wood and screen contraption that spanked you—just like her grandmother's did—if you didn't go in fast enough. Any other day she would pull the old screen door open, thinking how nice it was that Mr. Abraham with all his money still hadn't lost touch with the feel of being at home in the country, and keeping life simple. Then she'd use her key to open the red door and go into the mudroom to the left to change out of her smelly cafeteria clothes. But the door was open today and there were no sounds. No TV, no radio, nothing. She strained to see into the dining room through the arched opening straight ahead. There were boots there, Mr. Abraham's boots, lying with their toes up, side-by-side and slightly splayed. If she positioned her body just right, she could see pants legs around the tops of them.

She put her fingers to her lips and called out, embarrassed at how strangled it sounded. "Mr. Abraham, are you all right?"

Nothing.

Tears welled in her eyes. Mumbling a prayer, she pulled the screen door toward her. She prepared to call out again but stopped at the crunch of someone walking across the patio behind her. She turned, screaming, like one of those pathetic women in the B-movies, at her barefoot employer in cut-off jeans.

"Wow," Abraham said, pushing a finger in his ear.

"You okay?"

He chuckled, walking closer. "That's the same thing I wanted to ask you. Here, let's go in," he suggested. He pushed the screen door open. "Sit."

Catty obeyed, sinking into one of the padded chairs in the breakfast nook and trembling. He placed the ledger he carried on the counter and went to the pantry, talking as he rummaged. She willed her heart to slow, her breathing to smooth out while she watched the late morning sunlight play across the paintings on the far wall, the ones that always reminded her of van Gogh's haystacks.

"I was working back here under the trees when I saw you drive up. 'Too early for Catherine,' I said to myself." He emerged with a dark brown jug and a box of crackers. "Sorry I scared you."

She tried not to show concern about the jug.

"It's okay."

He set his load down on the table and smiled. "Don't worry, it's just cider."

She blushed.

"Probably the best I've ever made. I don't like to drink it alone. And I don't like to have to wait for Christmas to drink it. I'm a big boy, doggone it."

That made her laugh. He washed his hands and pulled two mugs from the rack over the sink. As he filled the mugs and shook some crackers onto a plate, he hummed—a series of notes that didn't come together into a song really—and glanced at her from time to time. When he wasn't watching her, she watched him, marveling at his handsome head and long fingers. Only the lines on his face and neck told the truth of his age. Especially today, he seemed younger. She half expected him to tell knock-knock jokes, the corny sort that Patrick had been barraging her with lately.

She studied the familiar nose and angular frame of the jaw, toying with how she'd ask the questions that nagged her.

"Young lady, I propose a toast." He raised his mug. She followed suit. "To your health and happiness."

"Thank you, sir." She sipped the strong dark liquid, savoring it like she'd seen wine experts do on the Food Channel.

"Oh, I almost forgot." He pushed his chair back and stood. "I have something for you. I know I said no more gifts, but I don't have the heart to pack these up. Come with me."

She followed him upstairs. Humming, he took the steps two at a time. She hesitated in the hallway outside his bedroom. The door was partially open. She stood there with her hand on her mouth, amazed at the little bit she could see. Abraham pushed it open more and swept his long arm toward the bed like he was Vanna White. He had lain out a dress—the pink and white one that she knew had been his wife's favorite.

"Oh."

"Come on in, Catherine. It's just a dress, not a rattler. I hope you're not offended, but I checked with your grandmother about your size. I want you to have it. I want you to have as many of Olivia's clothes as you like."

"Oh."

She pulled her lips in between her teeth and walked to the bed, thinking her hand would pass through the dress like it was only vapor, only a dream. But it didn't.

"Oh."

"You're welcome, Catherine."

"Oh, yes. Thank you, sir."

His eyes reflected a mixture of pain and happiness. He nodded, turning quickly to the French doors. While he gazed across the backyard, she dared to hold the gown against her body. It would fit, but was she fit to wear it? The questions that had nagged her all night rose like a lump in her throat. How could she throw them at him now? It would be like spitting on the fine fabric that brushed her chin. But still . . .

"Mr. Abraham?"

"Yes, Catherine," he answered, without turning.

"Would you say it's important to always tell the truth?"

"Of course. Is this about your other job?"

"Sir?"

"You're here kind of early today. Did you quit?"

"Well no, sir. I . . . I got fired."

He turned, frowning like her father would have. Catty played with the zipper pull on the dress.

"I slapped a boy who was bothering me. He's been a pest all year. I know I should have found a better way to deal with it, a more Christian way. I tried reasoning with him. But he thought he was hotter than Prince or somebody and . . . well, today I'd had enough."

Abraham turned back to the window, unsuccessful at hiding his amusement. "Sounds like you handled it the best way you knew how."

"Um . . . would you tell the truth, even if it would hurt you or your family?"

His frown was hotter than before, making her want to turn and run, forfeiting all the pretty dresses. "Catherine, you were hired with the understanding that you would not abuse your position or overstep your bounds. I fear that you have overstepped your bounds. Not only in asking me those questions but in suggesting that you know something you shouldn't. I will assume you stumbled onto something or heard something that's making you uncomfortable. I will also assume that you will deal with it by discussing it with God and God alone. I don't want to discuss this any further. And I don't want to have to let you go. If you continue this behavior, you will be fired. Do you understand me?"

Catty cowered in the fire that shot from his narrowed eyes and finally found her voice. "Yes, sir. I'm so sorry."

He slammed the French doors shut and marched past her.

"Sometimes, Catherine, the truth hurts worse than fire."

"I don't know where she got to," Trip said, out of the blue as we edged toward the highway. It was the first thing he'd said since we left Water Street.

Who? I indicated with a raised eyebrow.

"Catty." He shot a crooked grin in my direction. "I was thinking she quit her job at the school cafeteria but I might be wrong. We could turn back around and swing by the high school if you like."

I shrugged and studied traffic whizzing by us while we waited at the stop sign. Trip let out one of his trademark laughs.

"She's not attached, you know, Isaac."

"Is that a fact." I faked a yawn and patted the bandages on my forehead.

Trip smiled and hummed a tune to himself as he drove across the highway and onto the road Patrick had led me down on Wednesday. My throat tightened at the thought of traveling that road again. A Benson Ridge truck chugged ahead of us.

"We'll be driving right by the Benson place. We can stop in to see Patrick. That little head on the passenger side is probably his."

"Yeah, I'd like to see him." *One last time. Forever.*

Trip hummed a little more. "What, is she too black for you?"

"What?"

"Catty. Is she darker than you like?"

I decided not to answer.

"Why do you hate white folks?"

That was a when-did-you-stop-beating-your-wife question if I had ever heard one. I decided not to respond to that set-up either.

"You're a rude so-and-so, you know that!"

"And you'd win the Miss Congeniality Award?"

That made him laugh. "That was a good one." He pulled in behind the stopped truck, pounding the steering wheel and laughing harder. I couldn't help but laugh too.

Patrick bounded from the truck and ran to the house, or should I say mansion, with chunky columns and gables galore. Trip waited until the truck moved on down the road, then he pulled into the yard. Tall trees flanked the driveway like leafy steeples. The clatter of the truck's wheels on a threshold made of metal rollers set into the driveway made Patrick turn around.

"Isaac!" he yelled, throwing his bag to the ground.

I threw open the door before Trip came to a full stop. "Patrick."

The scrawny kid jumped into my arms and hugged me 'til I gagged. His left earlobe was hot and soft against my cheek. I leaned my head into it, pushing down the urge to rub my nose into the light brown fuzz that covered it. He jumped down and started pulling on me. His color was better, I noticed, and he was all smiles and talking nonstop about the new dog he was getting, his swimming pool, picking blueberries.

"Whoa, slow down. I came to say good-bye. I'm going back to Raleigh today."

He stared at me like I had just told him I had run over his new dog. But then he screwed his lips around and grabbed my arm. "Okay. But first you gotta see the blueberries. Big as . . ."

"Patrick," Trip interrupted. "Where's your dad?" He had parked on a bricked part of the drive near the house. Farther away, where the emerald lawn had been worn down to sand, there sat a barn of all things. Red with white trim like in *Oklahoma* or *Bonanza* or something. I expected to see barnyard animals roaming the grounds.

"That reminds me, Trip. Patrick, I need to talk with your dad about my car."

"He's not feeling too good," Patrick said.

"Well, maybe I can call him later."

"Yeah, you call him later. Now, you come with me." Patrick pulled harder.

"You kids have fun. I'll check on big Abe."

Patrick took off running along the drive and down the left side of the house. I followed at a trot, studying the house that grew in appealing fits and starts before me. Chloe Hunt would kill for this eclectic mixture of old and new. I could hear her talking about Arts and Craft and Roman Revival or some such stuff.

I quickened my pace and caught up with Patrick running under a canopy of bright trees that rained shadows along a dirt lane littered with petals. It was cooler there and I slowed. He disappeared around a greenhouse.

What didn't this place have?

"Patrick."

I could hear his giggle and the rustle of bushes. He had slipped down a path, tight with the encroaching bushes. I saw a flash of his T-shirt and then he was gone. I followed the curvy path ten or fifteen minutes before I realized I was lost. Around a bend, it opened up into a field of white wild-flowers.

That's when I saw the woman. From across the field she trembled, or rather the pink and white gown she wore did. The naughty wind dressed and undressed her lithe legs and arms, dark shafts against the pink shimmer of her hem.

A vision?

As I walked closer her song grew stronger and clearer. She stood with uplifted hands and her scarf-covered head back, and singing toward the leaves of the trees above her. Her song was an ancient trembling tune—low and high notes knit with strength and beauty. *Almost Irish.* I could not understand the words but somehow I knew what she was singing about, and that upset me. *How?*

The words came to me inside my head: "Come unto me all you who labor and are heavy laden and I will give you rest."

I couldn't stop them. I covered my ears like I could turn off the words that way, wanting so much to stop them, to run. Not because the whole thing was so strange, but because the words about a God that didn't exist were hitting my chest like the beat of a bass drum. Of all the words to bombard my sleep-deprived brain, why these about God? That send-off with the praying albino had had some kind of effect on me.

Then she turned and looked toward me.

"Catty!" I gasped.

This was crazy. What was she doing here?

My feet had taken root among the daisies. I watched as she walked, floated it seemed, to me.

"Hello, Isaac."

I could only stare and blink. She seemed happier than I'd ever seen her. Energetic. Almost defiant and happy about it. Her skin glowed. Even the sweat on her face was lovely. Those lips, they moved but the words . . . did I hear them with my ears or my body?

"Isaac, did you hear me? I said come into the shade."

I followed her into the shade where she released her thick curls from the scarf, draping it over a log. She swept the folds of the gown around her legs and sat. Vines, much like those on Miss Lucretia's back fence, bathed us with their perfume.

"Thirsty?" She offered me a thermos from a wicker basket behind the log.

I shook my head then studied her lovely bare feet, so lovely I wanted to cradle them in my hands. But the words still rang in my head. "The song you were singing . . ."

She lowered her head. "I was hoping you hadn't heard."

"What—"

"Miss Lucretia doesn't like it when I speak in another language."

I sat, deciding not to tell her that I had heard the words in English, but curiosity tore at me. "What . . ."

There was a little of the wildness, the abandon in her words and her eyes, that I had seen the night before. She had set aside the dutiful, responsible, compliant person and taken up a sail. I liked it, though the actual words rubbed me the wrong way. It disturbed me that I had no idea what she was talking about so I kept quiet.

She stopped and smiled. "You're looking at me like I'm a crazed religious nut."

Had I been that transparent? I smiled at the ground.

"Anyway, contrary to what some folks think, I don't believe it makes me any better than anybody."

I studied the grass some more.

"It's like you and me."

I looked at her, not hiding my frown.

"People would look at us and say you're better than me."

"But I'm not. It's just what I was born with. I had no control over it." My own words hit me like a fist. *I had no control.* I bit my lip. I wasn't going to miss her. And I was not going to miss this place or that crazy little white boy who likes getting lost in the woods. *Get a grip, Isaac. Control yourself!*

Control was the thing I craved. Control over others, what they told me, what they did to me. Real control, I feared, was the thing I would never attain.

It was her turn to study the grass at our feet. I studied her face, the way her lashes curled; her black hands and arms, the way they glinted with a million tiny sequins like dew on the grass. I reached for the dark hand closest to mine. I must have been making her crazy because she stood like she'd been stuck with a pin. I stood up too.

"What are those flowers? I see them everywhere."

She turned to look where I pointed. "Honeysuckle."

"The T-shirt I had this morning. The Honeysuckle Festival."

"Yeah, it's a town celebration every Father's Day. People vote on the Dad of the Year and he's crowned Honeysuckle King. My daddy won the year before he died. It's really hokey, but it's fun. The whole town turns out and it's like everybody buries the hatchet and behaves like plain ole human beings for a change. The honeysuckle's the town symbol."

She spoke fast and almost ran to the vine, pulling off a yellow blossom.

"Come here."

I hesitated.

"It's not poisonous. It's wild but harmless. Some people put 'em in salad."

She walked toward me. "There's something I wanted to ask you. About your parents."

"My parents?"

She played with the petals in her hand and had the look of someone searching for a different subject to discuss. "Your adoptive parents, I guess I should say. The Hunts. Seems like you're running from them. Were they really that awful? I guess it doesn't matter."

I clenched my jaw against the venom that boiled on my tongue. I was about to leave her forever, and I didn't want to part on a bad note.

"I don't mean to pry." She paused, eyes still down, and brushed the flower against her lower lip. "My mother abandoned me and Daddy when I was seven. I remember her leaving, yelling at me from the car as she drove away. 'You dumb, black blankity blank. You'll never amount to nothing.' And that was some of the nice things she said." Catty pursed her lips. "I hated her for years after that. Then I realized how much the hate was killing me, trying to figure out how to make her pay for the hurt she caused me."

She looked into my eyes. "Even if you never go back to the Hunts, figure out how to let it go, Isaac."

Those eyes held too much truth. I couldn't look at them any longer.

"End of sermon. Here let me get another flower. I've crushed that one pretty good." She threw the flower down and got another. "Come here. I won't sermonize you any more."

I grinned and went to her.

"The lowly honeysuckle blossom," she began, pinching the green part away from the yellow petal, "transforms into a sweet treat. Your tongue, sir."

I kept my tongue behind my dubious smile.

"It's harmless," she reassured. She touched the naked end of the flower to the tip of her tongue. "And yummy."

She snatched another flower and pinched it like the first. "Come on."

I bit my bottom lip and exposed the tip of my tongue. *This is crazy.* Her hand started to tremble as I lowered my head. I wrapped my hand around her shaking fingers. Her big brown eyes grew bigger, and bigger still when her fingertips touched my tongue. Was there more surprise or regret in her eyes?

Sweet nectar blossomed in my mouth.

"Yum." I breathed, delighted by the blush I saw growing across her face. "You're beautiful."

She shot me a look of a trapped animal, then looked from the field of white flowers bobbing to our right to the honeysuckle vine sighing to our left, her adorable nose almost brushing my chest. Her entire body seemed to twitch with the desire to run. But she stayed.

"Really," I reassured her.

I lifted her chin, lowering my head. She looked like a beautiful doe, all dressed up and no place to go, caught in my headlights.

"Isaac," came Trip's voice from behind me. "You finished saying good-bye yet?"

with Catty and Patrick's images in
the side mirror waving from the steps of that house like
Jethro and Ellie Mae, it occurred to me that something extra-
ordinary had happened. I had effortlessly found a place of
acceptance—a place where people had taken me for me, not
for what I could give them—and I had left it.

Why?

As much as I hated to admit a weakness, I admit it was
because of fear. What if I failed them? What if they saw im-
perfections and insecurity of this black man with crystal blue
eyes and fair skin?

"Corn." Trip sighed, sticking his head out the window as we turned onto the main road. He took a deep breath. "Benson gold."

The word "gold" made me think of the ring tucked in my jean pocket and wonder if I should stay and look for the man who had contributed some DNA to my existence. In this small town, surely he would have known I was here. It seemed everyone else did. He hadn't made a move toward me so I figured I should keep my distance, and honor my mother's request.

Trip tapped the steering wheel as he drove. For miles, the scenery didn't change. Corn and more corn sprouted from black dirt (not red like in Raleigh) along either side of the narrow road, straight with the gnarly surface of an old railroad tie. Trip pulled to a stop at a Y in the road. He hesitated, screwing his lips and humming. A blue-gray bird, all legs and beak, drifted across our windshield and settled on the left ditch bank like a piece of down.

"Okay. Left," Trip mumbled and turned the truck left.

Cornfields flanked the road as before but then a few hundred feet ahead there was a break—a gravel lot covered with cars and pickups around what looked like a warehouse on thick stilts. Two 18-wheelers idled along the road opposite the building. The drivers, enjoying a break beside their rigs, waved to Trip. Trip smiled, threw them a greeting with a jerk of his chin, and turned left into the parking lot. He killed the engine beside a large sign that read *Pettigrew Cukes.*

"I'm gonna check inside for Miguel. Won't take long but it gets hot quick inside this truck. You're welcome to come inside."

He sprang from the truck and ran up the wide wooden steps that led to the warehouse entrance, two broad steel doors set on a slider. I got out and lingered by the truck.

My curiosity, though, took me up the steps after a few minutes in the sun. Inside, two forklifts traced the rough wood floor between a stack of wooden pallets to the right and the end of a conveyor belt toward the far wall where a person sat packing sturdy boxes with lightning speed while another shoved them onto the pallets. The air was thick with the forklifts' sour exhaust. Large fans set into each end of the long building didn't help reduce the heat or stench. I stood and watched, stunned that I found the sights and sounds familiar.

I strained to find Trip among the shadowy bodies that moved inside and saw his smile among the women—Playtex-clad brown hands sorting what looked like cucumbers as they rumbled by—working the belt, the only well-lit area. A line of large windows stretched across the back of the building like irregular cutouts from a cardboard box.

Trip threw his head back, barking out a laugh that I could hear above the racket of machinery. The ladies laughed in return, some waving a hand at him like they didn't believe a word of what he'd just said but wanted him to continue nonetheless.

Trip moved along the belt, patting backs and waving like he owned the place, then climbed a few steps to where I guessed the conveyor belt pulled cucumbers from a hopper. I looked at his feet among the others on the small platform and figured I'd seen enough of this world. I turned to go, finding relief from the heat on my mind. I heard my name and turned to see Trip, standing on the main floor again between the conveyor belt and me and waving me toward him. I walked to him.

"I want you to meet my girl," he yelled, his mouth close to my ear.

Doubtful, I drew my head back and looked at him. Had his lips just said "his girl"?

"Don't look so shocked."

I followed him across the floor and up the rickety platform steps and shared a firm handshake with a well-tanned white woman sporting a red bandana around her blonde curls. A wooden cross swayed across the front of her T-shirt when she turned to greet us.

"This is Frieda Curts. Soon to be Frieda Curts Robertson."

The blonde giggled and drawled, "Trip! Nice to meet you, Isaac." She said it, using "ah" for the "I" in my name. It made me smile. "Trip's told me nothing about you." She eyed my bandages with pity in her eyes.

Same to you, I thought. He'd led me to think he was interested in the woman I had tried to kiss. Or had that been my imagination?

"I've been busy trying to keep his hide alive."

She smiled, stroking Trip's cheek with powder-covered hands. Her forearms, flecked with paraffin wax, swayed gently. My eyes drifted to the wax vat while Trip retold my accident story to the world. For some reason I couldn't have cared less. Maybe it was the exposed workings of dirty gears and belts just inches from me.

Wax spewed from a vat above the hopper, coating the oversized green cigars stacked more than five feet deep in a truck backed up to the wide entrance. Down on the ground, a four- or five-foot drop down, a couple of Hispanic men leaned against the wooden slats that formed the walls of the truck bed. One gnawed a cucumber absently while the other attempted to make time with one of the naturally copper-skinned women on the other side of the vat.

The woman, a few of her well-oiled curls peeping out from under her plastic cap, ignored the man, then interrupted Trip. "You gonna tell us one of your funny Bible stories?"

"Oh, not today, Shaquana. I'm actually looking for Miguel. We're heading to Raleigh, taking Isaac back home." Trip looked around. "Oh, there he is." He pointed to the gray-haired passenger in a truck pulling up. "Hola, Trip," the man shouted, jumping out of the truck like he had been sitting on springs.

While the two old friends carried on in Spanish, Shaquana beat her eyelashes at me. She could beat the boy out of a man with one bat of those things. I politely smiled and turned to face the main floor. Apparently it didn't matter that I looked like I'd not only lost the fight, but lost it badly.

A rather thick white man with two days' worth of five o'clock shadow waddled to the middle of the open floor. "Break! Fifteen!" he shouted. He held up his hands, fingers spread, as if to say, "I've spoken." He returned to his perch in his office, a box in the corner with Plexiglas windows and a dented AC unit.

The workers fell out of their respective positions like well-trained huskies, some to stand in the line for the soda machine, some to sit in the windows, some to what little shade they could find outside along the edges of the cornfields.

I stepped down to let the ladies on the platform retreat. Shaquana, with her full lips pulled between her teeth, brushed past me and released a puff of a kiss up at my face. I forced myself to smile and glanced up to Trip. He, Frieda, and Miguel had formed a tight knot, laughing with their heads together, so I decided to head for the truck.

"Why you gotta play me like that?" Shaquana growled.

"Excuse me?"

In situations like this—standing face-to-face with an angry black female—I'd found it best to play dumb.

"Didn't your mama teach you any manners, boy?"

I played dumb, but not stupid. "Technically, I didn't know my mama."

"Oh, so you was raised by wolves!"

"Shaquana," Trip said, lowering his voice when she turned. "I think Tyree is trying to get your attention." He pointed to a group of young black men lounging near the front entrance, eyes in our direction.

She turned on me with eyes full of acid, grunted, and left.

Trip chuckled as he climbed down to me. "Thought she was gonna eat you alive, Isaac. I'd hate for that to happen to a wounded man."

Frieda giggled, excused herself, and went to join a group of women sitting on a stack of pallets and sharing a box of powdered donuts.

"Miguel," Trip started, tugging the older man toward us. "This is—"

"Isaac," Miguel interrupted, his eyes instantly smiling and tearing up at the same time. He reached out and took my forearm in his beefy hand. Its smooth coolness surprised me. "I remember you, *mi hijo*. You would have been . . ." He studied the rafters, then let his eyes drift down to mine. "Three or four the last time I saw you. I remember your mother. Sweet woman. After her father passed, me and Mr. Ross, he was boss here for years, always tried to keep an eye out for her. And for you, when you came along. How the years fly. How are you now?"

I smiled politely and told him about my accomplishments at State like I was giving a book report on something I'd read involuntarily. He nodded with genuine interest, his hand still on me.

"Let's go," Trip suggested when I finished.

"No, I'd better not. Mi Miguela, she is due any day now. I'd better not ramble too far from the camp."

"His only daughter," Trip said. "First grandchild."

Miguel flashed a row of large white teeth at me, then slapped his big chest with both palms. "I will let you go, *mi hijo*. Please come back to visit. May through September, we are at the camp. Just down the road a piece." He hooked his thumb over his shoulder. "They call me *El Alcalde*."

"The Mayor," Trip offered.

"It's silly. It's not like we are a town. Just ask for me, and they will know where to find me. I want to tell you so many things, but some things must wait." He had taken me by both my arms this time, holding me back like a life-sized Raggedy Andy and studying the length of me with that funny crying smile teasing at his eyes again. "You have so much ahead of you, Isaac. Godspeed."

With that, we said good-bye and I followed Trip out of

the building. Frieda followed too, slipping her hand into Trip's.

"I'm sorry," I heard Trip whisper to her before swinging his left leg into the truck.

She nodded, biting her bottom lip. "So am I, but still . . ." Her brown eyes flitted toward me. "We'll talk later."

Trip, agreeing with a reluctant nod, started the truck and waved good-bye. He started to whistle, a humorless piercing sound, and pointed the truck's nose toward the road.

"Wait, Trip," came a yell from behind us. It was Miguel. "*Mi hijo*, I must pray for you. For your journey."

Where had I heard that?

Miguel came to my side of the truck, laid his hands on my shoulders, then prayed. All Spanish, I think. No bass drums beating my chest. No words in my head, which was a relief. He and Trip said amen, and he stood back. His scrutiny made me wonder if there was going to be an ambush down the road that he knew about but had sworn not to give away. Waiting politely was killing me.

Finally, he spoke, "You were born here, you know."

I nodded. "Yes."

"Here," he stressed, jerking his wavy salt-and-pepper head to the dusty, smelly building behind us.

My jaw dropped. *Born in a warehouse.* It was like the straw that broke the ol' camel down. I couldn't even wrap my brain around words to begin to form a reply, or ask a question.

"Yep, my wife, Connie . . . " He hesitated, mumbling to Trip, "*La comadrona?*"

"Midwife."

He tried out the word quietly to himself, then continued.

"Connie, she was working the line then just like Frieda does now. I was working the lift, and I saw Betty go down. I called for Connie. The whole grader stopped for the day even though it didn't take you fifteen minutes to come out." Miguel laughed, slapping my chest. "You were an over-achiever even then. Eh, Trip!"

Trip smiled tightly. He continued that annoying whistle.

"You were so pretty. Eyes like your—"

Trip cleared his throat. Out of the corner of my eye I thought I saw him grimace.

Miguel stumbled for words, finally saying, "So pretty. I hope my grandson will be as pretty as you were, *mi hijo*. I will let you go now. Remember to visit."

Trip pulled away, spewing gravel, and throwing a lazy wave in the air. He whistled for the rest of the drive while I grappled with all that I had learned about my mother, a woman who I was beginning to dislike; my father, a man who would let his own flesh and blood be born in a filthy warehouse; and, the town of my birth, a maddening mixture of abject brutality and faceless charity.

chapter 16

who was it that said "A man is a god in ruins"? I didn't feel very godlike as Raleigh's modest skyline rose before us, but I certainly felt in ruins. Without asking, Trip turned right onto Glen Street. I frowned and looked at him.

"What, you don't want to go? I thought you might want to talk to—"

"That's just it. You were making the mistake of thinking again."

"Listen, friend." He spat the words at me as he pulled over. "You don't have to be rude."

"And apparently you don't have to ask me anything. Just assume. We've just spent the last two and a half hours together with less than three feet between us. And all you can do is whistle."

"Does that mean you do not want to see your parents?"

I could only shake my head at his thickheaded attitude. His use of the word "parents" was not helping his case. That word had taken on a whole new meaning for me of late.

"I take it that means 'no.'"

"Listen, Trip. What kind of crazy name is Trip anyway? How am I supposed to trust a man named Trip?"

"And we were just supposed to trust you because your name is Isaac Hunt. Is that it? Three days ago, I came to the rescue of a stranger in need."

"Yeah, let's beat that dead horse some more."

"Then I find out you and Miss Luc had already been getting cozy in the kitchen."

"You make it sound like I attacked her."

"What was I to think? She's so trusting. And a few screws are coming loose. Forgive me, Lord. And she stays with her granddaughter who weighs in around a hundred pounds wet. Most of that is her hair. When I found out you'd been making yourself cozy in the kitchen, that's when I started checking up on you. I have this buddy at State . . ."

"So, you're a State grad?" Eyeing the man's haggard profile, I found it hard to believe he graduated from anywhere.

He gave me a look that seemed to say, "Will you let me finish?"

"He lives here in town. Last time I visited him, I thought I remembered seeing your picture somewhere. Not many men with *your* face. My buddy is a State grad, works as a Research Technician in Mann Labs now. He sees engineering students all the time, especially seniors doing their design projects. Anyway, I described you, and he remembered you. Hard to forget the Mars project. Then he dug up the magazine like nobody's business. I came and picked it up yesterday. While I was here I looked up Judge and Mrs. Hunt's humble mansion."

He paused, yawned, then scratched a hand through his hair. "I didn't do any of this to offend you. My first priority is to protect Miss Luc and Catty. A few months before I came along, they had a break-in. You shoulda seen her, Miss Luc almost rung my neck off hugging me when I told her I'd be her boarder. Help keep the place safe. But life got complicated when I met Frieda. Why am I telling you all this?" He gave a short huff of a laugh and fell silent, rubbing the shiny black knob on the end of the gearshift.

"Listen, Isaac. I'm willing to take you most anywhere. I can let you out here. And you'll never have to put up with me again in your natural born life. You're looking at me like that would not be a moment too soon."

I blew air out through my mouth. What options did I have really? I still had a few things in storage in Raleigh. And I had a few changes of clothes in the duffel resting under my left arm.

Transportation. Money.

Money was the thing I needed most. Had I come full circle? I chuckled to myself as I thought about colorful Buddy Stone and how he'd helped out during my first money problem. I had more than five thousand in a checking account.

All I needed to do to access that account is walk into 1450 Feldspar and get my wallet.

While Trip rambled on about burying the hatchet, my mind traveled down Glen Street. One, two, three intersections and turn right onto Feldspar. Third house on the right, the trendy 1950 remodel, sunflower yellow with Japanese maples lining the circular drive. I could still see the trees in my mind, dropping their leaves like little red fists on my windshield as I sat in my car six months ago rereading the papers I'd received from Stone.

Adopted.

Finally, I had gotten out, grabbing my wallet from the passenger seat and tucking it in my coat pocket.

The house had been empty. Not too unusual on a Sunday night. Movie night out for the happy couple. I remember thinking that it would just make my wait that much more agonizing.

Somehow I had found myself in the hall looking into their bedroom—a tangle of sheets and bedspread spilling from a corner of the bed. Plump purple and green pillows rimmed in lace. Pillows that I would, when no one was looking, lay my little boy's body across and kiss. Especially Chloe's, pretending that it felt like her cheek was against mine.

Their voices at the back door had made me jump. They sounded hollow, distant like sounds from the end of a tunnel.

I'd found Ricky and Chloe Hunt in the kitchen eating ice cream straight from the box, the grocery store bag still clinging to the frosty sides. They were laughing and touching each other like high schoolers. From time to time she would bring her brown forehead to meet his chest and rub her nose there. He would wrap his big yellow-brown hands around the back of her head and run his fingers through her hair.

"You lied to me." My words had come out hotter than I'd expected. "A dying old man is the only one with enough humanity to tell me the truth in this family." I had said it as more of an accusation than a question I wanted them to respond to.

They had just stared at me.

I'd thrown my jacket down, wallet in pocket. "Answer me!" I screamed and added a few curse words. "Who did you adopt me from? I want to know names. NOW!"

Ricky's brown eyes, stretched wide, started to glisten. His broad shoulders melted as he pulled his wife closer to his side. "Oh my God," he had whispered.

At first she had seemed to crumple, then she came to life and sprang at the papers dangling from my right hand.

"What's this?" she had screamed as she scanned the papers. "Where'd you get this junk?" She was crying and screaming coarse words I didn't know she was capable of saying. Mascara was streaking her face as she pushed her tiny nose in my face and bared her teeth like a pitbull. "How dare you do this to me? I'm your mother. You belong to us."

She had continued for several more minutes while the Judge decided he needed to add his bit to the act. The rational side, I'm sure he would have called it. The voice of reason.

"Now, son."

"I'm not *your* son." I had looked him straight on, boring all my rage into his blue eyes. We shared the same eye color, but that's where the similarities stopped.

I remember thinking that there was a man out there who did share the same heavy brows and cheekbones so strong that they seemed to pull the bridge of the nose flat. And I vowed, as I stood there realizing that Ricky Hunt was not my real father, that the man who looked like me would pay for what he'd done to my mother and indirectly to me.

"Isaac," he had continued, daring to step behind his wife who had begun to trample the papers she'd snatched from me. "What's this adoption foolishness. You're our son. You do not have white parents. You're a black man just like me. You like all the things black men like: black women, sports, and the like. You're afraid of all the things black men are afraid of: flashing blue lights in the rearview mirror—and don't get me started on how we need to protect ourselves from some of the same stuff from back in the day on the issue of white women."

I had interrupted his address with a threat that I would see them in court. I had then turned and run, leaving my jacket and unfortunately my wallet, but at least rescuing the crumpled papers. That had been more than six months ago.

Trip slapped his thigh, the noise effectively bringing me back to the present—and our argument. "Enough said," he remarked. "How 'bout we table this one-sided discussion and get something to eat?"

I shrugged.

He mimicked me and did a U-turn. After stopping for gas, and making a call from a pay phone, he drove south along Capital, weaving his way into downtown. He started whistling again, although this time it was a happier tune, as he turned into the neighborhoods that skirted old Pullenwoods Cemetery. *Pullenwoods Subdivision*, the sign read. I'd grown up calling it blackwoods, as did all the kids I grew up with, referring to the skin color of the general populace of the area that we avoided at all cost.

Trip slowed for some black kids walking slowly across the street, waistbands around their knees. A heavyset woman yelled at them from a sagging porch but quickly turned on the charm at the sight of Trip.

"Hey, Mr. Trip."

Trip waved and drove on. The sagging houses turned to neat government-issue cracker boxes. Trip called out Tarzan fashion as we approached a narrow blue two-story on the right side of the street. The dark-skinned man sitting in the swing with his back to us yelled back without turning. He swung his arms out in front of him and lunged forward out of the swing. His music, Mahalia Jackson, was turned up loud.

I frowned as I listened to the song bellowing from his boom box. It reminded me of Margaret Hunt, Ulysses' wife, who would clean house to the same song, singing with the Angel, as she would say.

"Isaac," Trip said as I climbed from the truck, "I'd like you to meet my good friend, Lamont Evers."

I froze, swallowing hard. The dark, large-headed man stepping down to meet us seemed to do a double take too. Lamont Evers, I'd forgotten his name, but his face was unmistakable. "Hi, Lamont," I attempted in a mannish voice, but it came out a bit weak.

"How you been, Isaac?"

"Fine, thanks."

He eyed my bandaged and scraped face and hands. "Don't look like it."

"So, you remember him?" Trip chimed in.

"Yeah," I said.

I remembered him all right. Hard to forget a man who would whisper to you in the middle of engines lab that Jesus was coming back. Like He'd just left the room or something. Tate and I had shared a laugh the day Lamont told us that.

"Yeah," Tate had whispered, "maybe Jesus can give us a few pointers on our Fluids final. He walked on water, didn't He?"

We hadn't given Lamont much respect, to say the least, but he had been a decent tech. Better than most.

Lamont swung his wide body around with a peculiar grace to grab his box from the top step. "Listen, why don't y'all come on back. Nessa is back yonder frying up a mess of fish."

That's what that odor was.

We followed Lamont, through the narrow space between the houses, to his postage stamp backyard. Sweating over a vat of hot oil, the woman I gathered to be Nessa seemed to grow from the bright green grass like two thick tree trunks that joined two feet off the ground by a pair of tight yellow Capri pants. Her right hand was coated in white paste and she was slowly dropping batter-covered chunks from a metal bowl into the oil.

"Isaac, this is my sister, Vanessa Evers."

She twirled a cooking fork in the hot oil, then straightened to reveal her pink and yellow T-shirt that read "You Go, God."

"Hey," was all she said, barely lifting her bang-covered eyes from her cooking.

I nodded a greeting and took the chair offered to me. Trip offered me a can of soda and ignored me for the next half hour, talking nonstop with Lamont about migrant workers.

I listened to the hiss of frying fish and children playing next door, trying to pretend that Vanessa's stare didn't bother me.

I wanted to scream, "My mother was a poor black woman." As if that would validate my existence to her.

Daring to look in her direction, I asked, "Could I use your bathroom?"

She nodded, with unveiled disgust on her curled upper lip, and led me into the house. "Down the hall on the left." And then she threw the empty pan in the kitchen sink and went back outside.

When the back door clicked closed, I moved to the living room in search of a phone. A baby slept on its stomach in a playpen in the corner near the front window. The phone, in the shape of a ten-inch Lamborghini, had been hard to find at first and then a little tricky to open.

I'm an engineer, I can do this.

Finally I had it open, dial tone buzzing in my ear as I sat with my eyes closed listening to the sounds around me. The baby breathing. A fly beating its brains out behind the drawn Venetian blinds. Trip laughing. Passing traffic.

"If you'd like to make a call, please hang up and try again."

I hung up.

"I can do this."

Breathe. Breathe.

I dialed and listened. Three rings, four. Then the answering machine. I hung up. Were they out or just not answering? They went to the Country Club Friday afternoons religiously. But it was after five. Maybe they had gone out to dinner. I could chance going over now or wait until Sunday night when they were out at the movies. Or . . .

The back door opened. I jumped.

It was Trip. I pushed the phone across the vinyl couch, as far away as my arm could reach, and watched him peep in the bathroom. "Isaac, you fall in or something?"

"Kinda hot out there. Thought maybe I'd cool off a bit."

"You do look a little ragged. Why don't you lie down upstairs? The bedroom with the futon is where we'll be sleeping. Uh oh!" He slapped his forehead. "I did it again didn't I? Assuming—"

"I don't mind staying here."

He eyed me with his lips screwed to one side. "And you don't have to eat fried fish. I saw how you looked at it. Nessa's a decent cook. Not like your sweetheart though. Oops! Did I do it again?"

I rolled my eyes and left him chuckling to himself as he went into the kitchen and rummaged through the fridge.

The futon was a little lumpy and short, though it nearly filled the room, but my body didn't seem to mind 'cause I actually fell asleep. I woke to the sounds of a crying baby. I had slept for an hour solid, but it was fitful sleep, filled with honeysuckle flowers that smothered me, while "Come unto me all you who labor and are heavy laden and I will give you rest" throbbed in my head in Mahalia Jackson's voice.

Footfalls on the carpeted steps were followed by a baby's cooing and Nessa's voice, light and playful.

"You a stinky little thing. Yes, you are. But mommy loves you." She reached the top and began to turn into the room across the hall but stopped when she saw me.

"You sleep all right?" she said, her voice still light but more adult, with a little of its original harshness. "You were yelling a little bit. I heard you from the kitchen." She bent her head, her large lips playing with the baby's ear. The baby giggled, shaking her head and beating her mother's wide chest playfully.

My pillow was wet, as was my head. It wasn't all from sweat.

"You washed down with sweat. The towels is in the closet next to the bathroom up here." She jerked her head down the hall. "I better go change this diaper."

I thanked her, stood, and stretched.

She shifted the baby and went into the room across the hall, turning on the light with her elbow. The far wall of the bedroom was plastered with pictures of the baby. Smells from the baby's dirty diaper drifted across the hall. But I didn't leave. I stayed, standing at the one window that overlooked the street, and listened to the babbling exchange between mother and child, the tinkle and rattle of toys.

What toys had I had? What games had my mother and I played? With the memories from the letter in my back pocket, I knew Betty Douglas had played with me. She had wanted me. She had loved me. There was great comfort in those things.

But still I wanted to know, where were my pictures? Where were my memories?

nessa looked down on me, my half-full dinner plate extended toward her, and let out a sigh of disgust. She yanked the plate from me and almost threw it on the stack beside the sink before she returned to feeding the baby.

Trip came to my rescue in between bites from his second plate of food. "Stomach still bothering you, Isaac?"

I nodded. The food was good, in a greasy, salty kind of way. The sandwiches and fruit Miss Lucretia had packed were still holding me.

"Why don't you go lie down for a bit?" he continued.

I stood and was about to say good night when Lamont set his meaty elbows on the table and asked, "You go to church?" He of all people knew the answer to that, or maybe he was thinking that since Tate had made that move to the other side, then I had too. I wanted to tell him that, unfortunately, the charms of Lamont Evers had not had that effect on me. I had not succumbed to organized religion.

"The reason I ask is 'cause our church has a Fourth of July thing tomorrow afternoon. I thought if you was still with us and, you know, if you wanted to then you could come. You know, if you felt comfortable."

I had no plans on staying more than the night. I kept that to myself, and lied. "Thanks, it sounds nice. Well, I'd better get to bed. Good night."

The conversation in my wake switched to church. They seemed relieved that I was gone. Laughing and carrying on like they were on the set of *Good Times*, I thought as I stretched my body, dressed in my own pj bottom, on the futon once again.

The room was hot so I opened the window a little more and looped the curtains up over the rod. Firecrackers, at least I hoped it was that and not semiautomatic gunfire, rattled somewhere across the street.

In the ebbing light, I could see a leggy boy stooped over an overturned bike, trying to get his chain back on. He was frantic like he was trying to beat the world record for putting on a bike chain. Without warning, a stream of water shot him in the behind, from a person out of my range of sight. The boy squealed and abandoned the bike. The shooter, a smaller boy with a super soaker, came running after him, laughing like a madman.

I chuckled and thought of Tate.

"What's the worst thing that could happen to you?" he had asked me once, wetting the tip of his mechanical pencil on his tongue. We were doing a class exercise together minutes before class. One of those spill-your-guts nontechnical elective exercises that I had been putting off, and as usual Tate was loving the idea of making me squirm. He relished any opportunity to catch me unawares and spray me.

"You know, Tate, you shouldn't lick the point like that. You could get lead poisoning or something."

"Ah ha! Death of best friend." He then pretended to write on the form that was spread on the desk between us.

I'd grabbed his wrist. "No! What does this have to do with interpersonal communication?"

He'd shrugged. "Okay, we'll come back to that one. What do you fear the most?"

"Isn't that just like the last question?"

He had frowned at me, pushing imaginary glasses down his nose and wagging his head like the instructor so often did. "Now, now, Mr. Hunt." He then leaned back in the chair and tapped the pencil on his clean-shaven skull, humming the *Jeopardy* theme song with his eyes closed.

"Be quiet." He didn't. I finally said, "I guess talking to a girl with my fly open." I had paused, wondering why Tate hadn't laughed at my joke. Tate was my friend, after all. We'd shared forbidden things—issues of his dad's magazines, and Old Ulysses' cigars. Surely I could tell him the truth, show him the moldy, ragged underside of lifestyles of the moderately rich and slightly famous. So, as I traced my thumbnail over the word carved in the desk, I told him about the time I'd been left in the house for a whole weekend.

We had just moved to Raleigh. I was thirteen. Those were the days when Richard Ulysses Hunt was not the humble judge that he is today. His superior, a big white bully of a man, had called and extended an invitation to a party in Asheville. No big deal, I had thought when they told me Friday morning before school. I'd been to posh parties before where I was the only child. I knew how to be invisible.

I returned that afternoon to an empty house. It was eight o'clock before I found the note on the fridge saying that they would see me Sunday night (sorry, no kids). There was food. There was juice and milk. There were clean sheets on the bed and videos. But no one to hold me when the bumps in the night scared me so bad I peed in the bed. No one to hear me cry or answer my prayers. Not Ricky. Not Chloe. Not God. Maybe it was then that I stopped believing in any of them.

Shaking off the memories, I turned away from the window and sat hard on Lamont's futon. My search for love had taken a funny twist. Had I really found it? I guess for the simple fact that I was asking myself that question, I had not yet found it. Not like I'd envisioned deep down.

"Is this all there is?"

I lay back and tried to sleep, tried to push the memories into the dark crevices of my brain. Two or so hours of fruitless effort later, the door opened.

"Hey, dude." Trip staggered in like he'd had a little too much. Except in his case it wasn't wine or beer; I didn't smell anything on him. "You still awake?"

"You look drunk."

"Drunk! Yeah, man. Drunk on life. Everlasting—"

He belched. Rummaging through his gym bag, he pulled out a thin sleeping bag and threw it down on the patch of floor between the futon and the door. He tramped around in a circle like he was doing a Mr. Happy, getting-ready-for-bed impersonation.

I chuckled. "What are you doing?"

"Trying to figure out where to put my head. If I put it down toward the end of the futon where your feet are, then I'm going to get it in the nose when you swing them big size thirteen to the floor when you go pee tonight."

"Don't worry, I don't plan to get up in the night."

"Good." He emptied his pockets on the little cloth-covered table near the door, then tossed something metallic, a quarter maybe, onto the dresser. He started to undress, so I turned to the wall. "Did you get your money?"

"My money?"

"Yeah, that roll of cash Miss Luc fished out of your wet socks."

"Yeah, I got it." It was with the letter and the ring under my pillow.

"I shoulda mentioned it before now." He was standing at the windows with his hands on his hips. Firecrackers sputtered down below. "Crazy kids. What did y'all do for the Fourth?"

I didn't want to tell him we usually traveled abroad. What good Americans leave the country for the Fourth? Last year we had watched fireworks from the Eiffel Tower. "Nothing much. Usual stuff."

"We'd always go to the little mountain town where my parents grew up and watch the fireworks. It's like you hear 'em two or three times in the valley." He scratched his bare chest and turned around.

"Want to know something?"

I shrugged in the dark.

"My real name is Rupert Percival Robertson Jr."

I bit my bottom lip, but my chuckle escaped.

"Go ahead, you can laugh."

I did.

He chuckled and flopped onto his sleeping bag like it had more than a thin layer of carpet underneath. "Okay, you don't have to be so energetic about it." I could hear the humor in his words. He was smiling in the dark, I figured.

I brought my glee to an end and apologized. He went silent. I followed suit, listening to his breathing even out and deepen.

Sleep was finally gnawing at the edges of my consciousness when Trip spoke up again and brought me back.

"It was good to hear you laugh." It sounded like something an old man would say. He made a big fuss of fluffing his pillow. "You probably think I laugh too much. 'Well, son, I tell you, life for me ain't been no crystal stair.' Did you have to learn that one in school?"

Why was he quoting Langston Hughes? I thought his words were starting to run together. The fake country boy accent was gone. I imagined I heard a little West Coast between his words. He continued. "I did. Not in school, though. My daddy, Trip Sr., made us learn it.

"Isaac, man, I look at you and I try to figure you out.

Why are you chasing this rainbow? Truth be told, you have everything I've ever wanted in this earthly life. Education. Money. Power. I try to make up for it with my exceptional charm and razor-sharp wit." He dryly chuckled. "Take Frieda for instance, you'd think 'nice girl.' Not a care in the world." He paused. I could hear him sniffling. When he spoke I knew why.

"She was raped a few weeks into the growing season. One of the Farm hands— After the attack, she broke off our engagement without telling me why. A few weeks ago, she miscarried. I didn't even know she was pregnant. She broke off the engagement so people wouldn't think it was my baby. She didn't want me to lose face in the community. She's been through so much and yet she was thinking of me. What a woman! I love her so much. She's the best thing that's happened to me in my whole pathetic life. Besides Christ, that is.

"Why am I telling you this rambling tale? When I first came to Pettigrew and met Frieda, I thought it was because of her that God led me there. But now I know that it was because of you."

He paused, sighing.

"I know you've got to go back to find your father. I won't waste my breath trying to talk you out of it. Truth is, he needs you more than you need him."

I propped myself up on my elbow. "What are you saying?"

"Go find him."

"You know who he is." It was more of a statement than a question. I didn't hide the shock in my voice.

"Yes. I promised him I wouldn't tell you. So, if you find him, it'll be God's doing and not mine. Go, Isaac. Go or you'll never know the kind of love a man can have for another human being."

chapter 18

jack woke to a knock on his truck window, just inches from his slumping head. He jumped upright and looked into a young woman's black face made up with lots of sparkly pink lipstick and blue eye shadow.

"What you want?" he barked, rubbing his eyes, determined not to show how much her sudden appearance had scared him.

"What *you* want, handsome?"

"Huh?"

She pushed up her bosom toward him and stretched her arms apart, placing one hand on the door handle and the other on his antenna. "Want some company maybe?"

Jack rolled the window down and gazed at the sweat glistening across her ample chest. He thought about the possibilities just for a moment. BJ would never know.

I ain't spent but $20. Just gas and food.

He glanced up the street to the house, the sky blue one with the preacher man's truck in front. There would be time enough for fun later, he reasoned.

"Naw, sweet thing." He judged her to be around sixteen. "You better run on off home to your mama. I'm working right now." He bit the inside of his bottom lip as the girl turned. Then an idea came to him how she might help him. "How long you been here?"

"Looking at you sleep, you mean?"

"Naw, around these here houses?"

"Why I wanna talk to you?"

He grinned and slipped his fingers in his front pocket, discreetly peeling off a couple of twenties from his money wad. "This here if you tell me the truth."

Her eyes shifted from Jack to the money. She licked her lips. "Since it turned dark. 'Bout eight hours. But I left one time, you know, on business." She grinned. "Why?"

"That house with the beat-up green truck in front. See anybody come out since you came back?"

She looked at Jack, eyes narrowing. "You the police?"

"Naw!"

"That blue house?" she asked, looking up the street. "Nobody's left that I know of. Who you looking for?"

Jack ignored the question. "Here's a twenty. The other one's yours too if you keep watch for me while I go to the

McDonald's back yonder and get myself a big cup of coffee."

He winked at her.

She batted her eyes and said, "All right."

He'd keep an eye on that stranger, Jack figured, one way or another. BJ would be proud of him, being so clever. He could see the girl, perched on the curb where he'd been parked, in his rearview mirror. Her long legs, looking like twisted wisteria vines in the streetlight, were calling his name.

Another day, sweet thing.

How could he have been so stupid, Jack wondered as he pounded the steering wheel. Not only had that girl disappeared with his money, but the truck was also gone.

"Stupid. Stupid. Stupid."

He pulled into the spot where the preacher's truck had been and held his head like it hurt. If only he could remember the stranger's name. Ben Jacob had said it, hadn't he? He was hard to miss with those bandages and that truck.

But maybe he hadn't left at all. Maybe the preacher had left.

"Yeah," Jack whispered, trying to convince himself that he hadn't messed things up too badly. The steady click of someone in heels running toward the truck interrupted his reasoning.

The girl was back, slapping his window and panting. "Hey, I saw him leave . . ." She paused for air. "And then when I didn't see you I started running to Mickey Dee's.

Then you came back, flying like Five-O was on your tail. I was waving . . . " She mimicked her wave.

"Wait. Stop. Who left? What'd he look like?"

"It's hard to see in this light."

Jack grumbled. The first of dawn was bleeding above the tree line. "You coulda seen a'plenty. Cough it up."

"You cough it up, Mr. Cash."

Jack pulled out the twenty.

"I had to run like . . ."

Jack teased another twenty from his pocket and held it against his knee with the other. "Talk first. Pay later."

"Well," she started, eyeing the money. "He was kinda tall and cute. Looking 'round like somebody was gonna jump out the bushes. Didn't see me, though. I was hiding—"

"Was he white?"

"He was black."

"Black?"

"Yeah, you could tell. You know, 'bout the mouth and nose. He was a black man, all right. I mean, even though his skin was white as yours."

Jack scratched his chin hairs and thought. "Which way'd he go?"

She pointed in the direction he faced.

"Did he turn left or right at the stoplight?"

"You didn't ask me to 'member all that. When I saw him leave, I took off for you. Give me my money."

"Just quiet down, sweet thing." He said it like he was beginning to think of her as anything but sweet. She reached through the window and grabbed the money. "Hey!"

He watched helplessly as she ran, across the path of an

approaching truck, and between the houses on the other side of the street. The driver of the truck, an old Chevy with a milky green paint job, slammed on brakes and stared at Jack like he had two heads before gunning it down the street.

Jack yelled again and jammed his truck in gear. He would not lose this man again, whatever his name was.

*

"That was Jack!" I yelled, one eye on the rearview mirror.

I shook my head but the truth couldn't be denied, particularly truth that was following me in a beat-up Toyota truck.

"If only I knew where I was going. All these one-way streets. Why am I talking to myself?"

It had been a long time since I'd been anywhere near blackwoods or the Pullenwoods Cemetery. But I did remember a rundown country club nearby. I'd participated in a charity golf tourney as a freshman.

If I could just find the club. If I had paid more attention to the path Trip took to get here. If I hadn't been so scared of blackwoods at night, I could've left earlier. If I could just lose this maniac.

"If . . ."

When I looked back the truck had stopped, as if the word "if" had had some power over it. In my rearview mirror I watched Jack jump out and pound the hood of his smoking truck.

i would plead not guilty to grand theft auto, I
decided as I spied on 1450 Feldspar Lane from behind old
Widow Goble's bushes, hoping she didn't put in her hearing
aids before 7:00 a.m. I hadn't really stolen the truck, I amused
myself further. Trip had set me up. He'd deliberately separated
the truck key from the others and tossed it on the dresser in
plain view, later ordering me to search out my real father.

In a twisted kind of way, maybe the joke was on me. The
old green truck was a grizzly to turn, having no power steering
and a shocking habit of stalling at long lights. I'd found myself
playing a balancing game with the gas and brake pedals to

keep it alive. Ricky Hunt would fall out laughing to see me in the heap of metal on wheels. He'd fling one of his favorite sayings at me, "Pride, my boy, comes before the fall."

But it wasn't pride that had me crouching in the bushes watching Trip park a late-model compact across the street, pick up the paper in the drive, and skip to Judge and Mrs. Hunt's front door like a long-lost son happy to be returning home. I knew there was something fishy about him.

Me, proud? The son of a migrant worker, born in the dirt. What did I have to be proud of? Achievements for the NASA Mars Mission? Graduating summa cum laude? Hardly. Those were things they wanted me to achieve. Things they made me do. Another setup. Maybe it was foolishness or even the beginnings of madness, but surely not pride.

"Now, Chloe." Trip sang as he left carrying an envelope under his arm. "Don't start lunch without me."

There she was—the woman who'd always insisted that my friends call her Mrs. Hunt—waving from the front door in rollers. I used the binoculars I'd found in Trip's glove compartment to look at her. She looked happy, almost too happy. A barrel of a bare chest appeared behind her. Large caramel hands caressed her neck. I followed her gaze up into Ricky Hunt's face. He looked too happy too. Like he was relieved or at least not worried in the least bit that he had an adopted son at large. Possibly dead. Did they care? Seemingly not.

Had they set me up as well? Had they put Ulysses up to telling me, pretending that he was delirious? That was far-fetched.

"This is too crazy." *And it's making me crazy.*

I watched the loving couple kiss and close the door. Their

presence in the house was going to make things complicated. I didn't like complicated. All I wanted was to quietly retrieve my wallet and a few of my things and disappear into the sunset like a mild-mannered bad guy.

"Isaac, is that you?" came Mrs. Goble's voice from behind. I turned and caught a branch across the face. "Easy, honey." She'd always called me honey and it irritated me, mostly because the way she said it never had any sweetness in it. She patted her blue hair with a hand brown with age spots and leaned over me with her coffee breath. "Whatcha doing in my hydrangea, honey?"

I was glad I'd taken the time to peel off my bandages. "Morning, Mrs. Goble. I was . . . To tell the truth, ma'am, I was spying."

She wrinkled up her already wrinkled white face and grunted. "I don't blame you, honey." She cast a disapproving glance toward 1450 Feldspar and invited me in.

I stood in shock for a few seconds. "Thank you."

In the nine years that I'd spent on Feldspar, I'd never seen the inside of the woman's house, a spacious Tudor that Chloe had slobbered over as she ate breakfast many a morning.

"Have you eaten?"

I shook my head. From the dining room I watched the aged body move at a snail's pace, gathering coffee cup and saucer, fixing a plate of eggs. I set the binoculars on the floor under my chair and passed the time studying the spines of the endless stacks of *National Geographic* on the dining table.

After what seemed like a couple of hours, she placed eggs, toast, and coffee before me, then sat and watched me.

"Thanks."

She adjusted her hearing aids.

"So, you're on the lam?"

She had one of those classic New York accents. New York born and bred, I figured, only lowering herself to come to North Carolina at her husband's insistence to jump on the burgeoning Research Triangle Park bandwagon. I'd never known the late Mr. Goble. She'd talked of him before at Community Watch meetings Chloe had hosted. He was a genius before his time, according to her. He was a drunk, according to everyone else in the neighborhood.

I caught myself wondering about her motivations. Why had she stayed? Particularly in a neighborhood that was slowly being populated by nouveau rich buppies. Stability for her two snobby kids, maybe. But what about her? What did she want in her old age? What were her regrets about choices she'd made, opportunities she let go by?

What do I want in life?

"Pardon the mess. I'm packing."

"Packing?"

"About time, huh?" She chuckled in a way that was not funny. "My kids want me to move up North. Long Island. So I've been packing like a madwoman. Want some magazines? No, I imagine you wouldn't. On the run like you are."

She shifted the stack between us to the floor and continued. "You know I figured you'd take off before now. The way they treated you. Like a dog. No, worse than a dog."

The phone rang and she excused herself to answer it in the kitchen. I finished eating and stood to stretch. The chirp of a bird drew me into the next room. A bright yellow collection of feathers hopped around a large elaborate cage. Half-packed boxes crowded the small room. TV in the corner, armchair beside the cage.

I had decided it was time to leave the widow to her packing when a small box marked "art supplies" caught my eye.

Who had been artistic in this family? The only color I'd known from her kids were the names they called me.

I lifted the flap and saw boxes of pastels and tubes of paints. The thick dark bristles of a used brush poked up from a corner, reminding me of a certain sweet country girl with dark wild hair.

"You want 'em?"

"Ma'am?"

"You paint, don't you?"

I shook my head.

"Funny, I could have sworn . . . Anyway, they were my late husband's. Can't believe I kept them all these years. You can have 'em if you want. Take up a new hobby. You're young. Lots of life ahead of you. Lots of possibilities. Me?" She shrugged and rummaged among some boxes.

My hand lingered on the brush. *Why not?* I picked the box up.

"There you go. Good for you. Mr. Goble would be happy. He would have liked you." The way she said it made me think she thought his affection would had been ill-placed.

I smiled. Thanking her, I turned toward the door.

"Won't you stay longer? You look so tired. And those scrapes."

It was her loneliness talking, I figured. "No, I'd better not stay any longer. I—"

"Don't worry, I won't tell 'em."

"Ma'am?"

"About your being here. It's our little secret." She winked at me. "Here, take a few bananas off my hands." She shuffled back into her kitchen, returning with a grocery bag full of something. Out of respect (or dread), I just thanked her without looking. She showed me to the door.

"Be safe, honey," she said, adding with her head turned to one side like she'd just made a discovery, "You're not a bad kid, are you."

Not sure how to respond and certainly not about to share my true thoughts, I simply smiled and said good-bye. "You're not too bad either, for a white lady."

It was just getting dark by the time I returned to Feldspar Lane. I parked Trip's truck a few doors down from the front of house 1450. I sauntered through the side courtyard via Chloe Hunt's Japanese garden. I walked with the confidence of a burglar who had just placed half a dozen unanswered calls to the residence.

The key still fit. That was a good sign. But the walls in the kitchen were a different color, and the family photos had been removed from the hallway. I couldn't spend time speculating on such; I had to pack a bag and find my wallet and my gun, a Glock .40 caliber.

The door to my former room was closed but not locked. I drew my hand back from the knob to find a fine black powder on my palm. Someone had been dusting for prints.

There was a similar treatment on the three tennis trophies on my dresser.

My long-lost wallet was on my dresser—everything intact. I stuffed it in my back pocket and walked into my closet. Into the biggest gym bag I could find, I crammed some clothes, especially cold weather things, then slipped my favorite leather jacket over my shoulders. I turned next to my gun safe, dialed the tumbler without thinking and pulled out the pistol, stuffing it and a couple of extra magazines of ammo into my bag. The gun was heavier than I remembered. Next I swept my eyes along the bookcase, a built-in deal that ran the length of my closet.

Which books?

All my collection of Hughes's poems, of course, and *Raisin in the Sun*. And maybe . . .

A noise near the back of the house made me jump. I slapped off the light, almost peeing on myself in the process. I felt silly when I realized the voice I heard was from someone leaving a message on the answering machine.

"Hello, Mr. Hunt," the drawling voice began. "This is Ben Jacob Benson again. Seems like we've been playing phone tag forever. Don't mean to be a pest but your deadline for forwarding the money into my account is close of business Monday. I'll be away for a couple of days for the holiday but please feel free to reach me at the family lake house."

He left a number and hung up. I wrote the number on a scrap of paper and slipped it in my bag. Might come in handy later, I thought.

Who exactly was Ben Jacob Benson? Didn't matter much. He was a Benson and he was trying to get money out of

Ricky. Scenarios of blackmail and scandal whirled through my frenzied brain as I grabbed my stuffed bag and slunk back to the truck. I decided that moneygrubbin' Benson was the first person I'd see when I arrived in Pettigrew.

I made good time getting out of town, since the bulk of the holiday traffic was west of town trying to find a parking spot to watch fireworks at the fairgrounds. Dark clouds were gathering up ahead. Hopefully I'd beat the storm. When I leaned my head out the window to let the wind beat through my hair I could see the beginning flash and fizzle over the fading sun. I lifted my arm in a salute and reached in my bag for another banana.

"Good-bye, Raleigh."

His hideaway under the stairs had gotten smaller. So small in fact that he had to crawl out to turn around. That was silly, Patrick thought as he scampered across the tiles in the entrance hall and slipped into the pantry for another drink box. The house hadn't shrunk; he had gotten bigger.

"You grow quicker in the summer," his mother had told him. "It's like magic, that's why when fall comes none of your clothes fit anymore."

She had been joking, he realized. She'd had that little twinkle in her eye like she was pulling his leg. Fall would be hard this year. She wouldn't be here to take him shopping. Everything would be different. So much harder.

"We'll survive, son," his father had told him just this morning. "We need to do the things we always did. She'd be happy to know we went on with life, tucking a little bit of our memories of her in between the pages."

Like the way she always did rose petals, Patrick thought. And the way she would always help him find a neat hide-away on stormy nights. They would snack, and she'd read to him until he fell asleep.

Thunder shook the kitchen as he shut the pantry door behind him. He ducked down and squeezed his eyes tight against the flash of light, then raced back with an armful of food to his nest beneath the stairs. He pulled the small door shut and reached for his flashlight. It let out a weak pop when he pushed the button. No light.

"Oh, man. Not again."

Thunder rumbled again followed by a bright ribbon of light under the door. He didn't want to go back out. As he sat in the darkness trying to screw his courage back on, he heard voices.

"You could have waited 'til morning to tell me this, Ben Jacob. Or you could have called."

Daddy talking with Uncle BJ.

"The phones are out. I was just over at the grader when this mess hit, so I figured I'd just drop in on my way home. Maybe even wait out the storm a little." Patrick could hear his uncle's boots on the tile.

"You're dripping everywhere. Take off your coat and come in my office."

"I'll meet you there in a minute. I need to visit—"

"There's nothing in the kitchen or the pantry."

Daddy sounds tired.

"What, you drank it all?"

"BJ, what is this all about anyway?"

"The ring."

There was a pause. Patrick held his breath and pushed his ear closer to the door. His father sighed heavily. "What about it?"

"You know what she did with it?"

"It was just a cheap copy. I let the boy have it. Why make a scene over it after your little stunt?"

"Where is it now?"

"She gave it back to me."

"Liar! Why'd you copy it?"

"Why'd you steal it to begin with?"

Another thunderclap and bright flash. Patrick covered his ears. There was some more talk but Patrick could only hear snatches of it like cap gun bursts above the lingering thunder.

Then with only the sound of rain pelting the front door Uncle BJ asked, "Did he see you? He came by here, didn't he? What'd you tell him?"

Patrick could hear his daddy breathing heavy. He must be leaning against the stairs.

"Why don't you go to—"

Uncle BJ spoke. "Spitting Benson image. Your cute little housekeeper won't no angel, you know. I wish she'd just killed that baby like I told her. Him being in Pettigrew, asking questions just complicates things for us in a bad way, you know. We've got to do something 'bout him. He might favor us but he ain't *us*."

Patrick heard his father breathing heavier now. He

shouted something Patrick couldn't make out. But his curse could be heard above the thunder.

"Get out, BJ! I don't want to see your sorry hide 'round here—"

"You can't do this to me. I'm blood kin."

The front door opened and slammed. Patrick could hear Uncle BJ pounding and kicking, but his father had locked it already.

chapter 20

with the driving rain that hit around
Finleigh, I started entertaining the thought of stopping at a
hotel instead of going directly to the migrant camp. I pulled
into the parking lot of Finleigh's only hotel, Finleigh Arms.
The neon "no" on the vacancy sign was flicking like it couldn't
make up its mind. I parked, hoping against it.

"Good evening," said the front desk guy, who reminded
me of the Michelin Man.

What was he smiling about?

"Do you have a room?"

"I'll have my sister, Vera, check."

He yelled over his shoulder to a pasty woman with a two-foot high bouffant. From where I stood, I could just see her through the open door of a back office. She was crouched over a computer keyboard.

"It'll just be a minute," the man said.

He tapped his fingers on the counter to a song on the radio and studied me. But I didn't mind much; I was more disturbed by the sign above his head that read "Come unto Me all you who labor and are heavy . . ."

I didn't finish reading. I'd had enough.

"Wait a minute. Where you going? Vera's not finished checking yet."

How long could it take to check in a hotel with a couple of dozen rooms? My hand was on the door when he asked, "Have you heard the good news?"

"What?"

"God so loved the world that He gave His only Son—"

I was in the truck, though the door was not yet closed, and backing out before he finished his sentence.

"Wait!" he yelled. He chased me across the parking lot, yelling what sounded like, "God bless your journey."

God was beginning to be a nuisance. It wasn't God that I needed unless, that is, He could drive like Richard Petty in torrential rain.

Thirty-five miles to Pettigrew, the sign read.

I'd driven over seventy-five miles in this downpour. Surely I could make another thirty-five miles.

A few miles outside town traffic slowed and came to a stop. Just the thing I needed in a truck that stalled during long idles. A couple of blue lights were already flashing up ahead and an ambulance was coming up from behind me, sirens blaring.

I pulled over with others in front of me and let it pass, thinking all the while that I felt the truck sinking into the soggy shoulder. Maybe this was my sign to wait things out in Finleigh. I was just about to turn around when a white car in front of me pulled off and turned left onto a road I hadn't seen before. The green street sign read *Old Pettigrew Road*.

Did that mean it led to Pettigrew? Some curvy backroad way. I would take a chance on it. I put the truck in gear and followed the white car.

Years later when I would tell this story to Christians they would tell me that that car had been sent by God. They would get that spooky look in their eyes that entertained me more than it irritated me and say that maybe it had even been driven by an angel. I'd smile politely and think about the guy that saved my backside that night, my aromatic *angel*.

The driver curved this way and that like he wasn't bothered by the rain in the least. At a crossroads he hesitated.

Great, the blind leading the blind!

It wasn't too late to go back but maybe, just maybe, I was just a few miles away from a connection back to the highway. I pulled around the car and turned right. It was an easterly kind of turn, toward Pettigrew, I reasoned.

Two wheel revolutions later I was struck from behind. Just a hard enough bump to send the bald-tired truck skidding, but not enough to harm me bodily. The truck stopped moving, its tail in the ditch. In the taillights, I could tell that it was a shallow ditch, not the drainage ditches that ran through Benson Ridge Farms.

The driver of that car had set me up, I thought. I was a sitting duck. Lost and loaded with a wad of cash. I tried my door. It was stuck. I smelled gas.

"Great!"

But surely the gas wouldn't catch on fire in the rain. A frantic Latino man, his brown face dripping with rain, appeared to my left. I screamed. He screamed.

"*Usted se arde.*"

"What?"

"You're on fire, man! You better get out!"

No kidding!

I followed his wide-eyed stare to the rear of the truck. Flames were starting to lick up above the rim of the tailgate. While he yanked on the driver side door, I tried to get the other door open. No dice. I tried to roll down the windows. Nothing.

"I'll be back," he yelled, vanishing in the darkness.

I stretched out on the seat and started kicking at the driver side window. I ran my hand under the seat for something hard and heavy enough to break the window. Where were those binoculars? My hand hit a book. Its paper cover was soft around the edges as were the pages. For a split second images of Margaret Hunt's Bible flashed through my mind. Hers was leather-bound and bigger than my little arms could hold for too long, but the pages were butter soft.

Now I had a more pressing issue: flames licking up around the edges of half the bed of the truck, and choking fumes.

I raised the book in my right hand and yelled to the ceiling, "God if You are real, where are You now?" No answer but the growing roar of fire above the tinkle of rain on the roof.

"Just let me burn. Who am I anyway? Just the son of a poor black woman. Nobody. You don't care about me." I yelled through the tears that had been burning my eyes since I first saw the flames.

My life was certainly shaping up to be a very wild ride, but I didn't want to die, not yet and especially not by fire. I threw the book across the dash and covered my face with my hands.

"You don't care!" I screamed and pounded the back window, warmed by the flames. The smoke sent me into a coughing fit. I pounded 'til my fists stung and collapsed to the seat across my bags.

"Come."

I looked up to see who had spoken. My Latino friend was not around. The voice had come just as clearly as if it had been him yelling from the closed window.

"Come."

There it was again. I held my breath and looked around like a confused child.

"Who . . . ? Where . . . ?"

Silence.

Had I imagined it? Was this some sort of neurosis that comes from dying by fire?

Breathe. Breathe. Listen. Think.

"Come," I found myself mumbling in the hot truck cab, "unto Me, all you who labor and are . . . Come unto Me . . . Come unto . . . Oh, it's no use. I can't remember. God, if this is some kind of joke, it's not funny. I'm flunking this test. I can't crack the code. I don't know the formula. I thought You were supposed to be about love."

"Hey, man, back up." My Latino friend held a large stick. "Cover your face."

I turned to the side and balled up, covering my body with my leather jacket. When the glass pellets stopped falling, I threw my stuff out and piled out into the Latino man's waiting arms without a thought about how crazy I looked.

As he picked up my stuff and led me to his car, a white compact a few yards back, I remembered that stupid gun. I could've used it to knock a window out. I climbed into his compact, numb and ragged, and looked at the flaming truck, surprised that I'd been in there.

"You all right, man?"

I think I nodded.

He drove on for a few miles, apologizing over and over for not finding a stick fast enough and chattering on about how the fire looked. All I wanted was quiet. Nothing but pure silence so I could process what had just happened. Had I actually talked with God? Had He actually talked to me?

"Anyway, my name is Julio."

"Isaac."

"Where you going, man?"

"Pettigrew."

"Like, you going to First Street or Freeman?"

I turned and really looked at him for the first time. His young round face glowed green in the dash lights. He had the beginnings of a beard and a big smile and he smelled of tortilla chips. "Do you know the Mayor?" I asked.

He frowned. "Of Pettigrew?"

"No. From the migrant camp. Miguel . . ." I suddenly realized I didn't know Trip's friend's last name.

He chuckled. "Oh, *the* Mayor. Yeah, I know him. You want me to take you to him. Sure, man. No problem, Isaac."

He opened his mouth wide and laughed. "This is so weird, man."

"What?"

"Like, the Mayor, he is my father-in-law."

chapter 21

she was soft and warm and tiny. Too tiny. Miguel had thrust her against my chest and wrapped my uncertain arms around her swaddled body.

"She is beautiful. Yes?"

I nodded, looking down on the tiny head, covered in slick black curls. Her beauty—simple, pure, and strong—was startling. To hold a day-old life in my arms just hours after almost losing my own was blowing my educated mind. I realized with this new individual squirming in my arms, life was more than a wild ride. If that's all it was, then why live? Why didn't I die as soon as I was born? Why bother with the dreams and ideas, the loving and hating, laughing and cry-ing if it was all for nothing?

Where was the meaning? I had asked myself that ques-tion so many times before. But it never occurred to me until that moment just how much an answer, a real, concrete, un-deniable answer was crucial. How could I take another breath without knowing the answer? How could I hold this baby, this tiny life, without knowing why *I* lived? I felt like a fraud in the face of truth.

I wanted to scream.

Julio had stepped forward and slipped his warm hands under the baby.

"Here, let me take her, man." He leaned in, tears glisten-ing at the corners of his eyes in the light of a single lamp, then whispered, "Man, it tears you up, don't it. God is so good." He joined his wife reclining in the bed, kissing her softly on the lips.

God. God?

"Connie," Miguel spoke up, grabbing my elbow and pulling me from the small bedroom. "Fix Isaac another plate. Come in the kitchen."

"No," I said weakly, smiling to the round woman push-ing homemade tortillas around a flat cast-iron skillet with her fingers. Her black eyes seemingly saying in a polite perky way "I know what you did last summer." "I couldn't eat an-other bite. Thank you. I'd like to lie down."

Connie gave me a knowing nod. "Of course. Yes. Yes." She wiped her hands on her apron and led me out the front door, along the breezeway. She stopped at the next door and pulled out a key. "You can sleep with my boys. Oh, wait here."

I stood by the door with my bags, listening to the sounds of sleep through the heavy wood. Connie returned with sheets and a towel and unlocked the door into an apartment, similar to hers and Miguel's, littered with sleeping bodies it seemed.

She grunted. "My darling boys. You will meet them in the morning, when they are at their best. You will sleep in the back room with my youngest, Paulie. Not so much noise." She chuckled.

I followed her, careful not to step on fingers or feet that dangled from the pull-out sofa, to the back room and waited while she put sheets on a small metal-frame bed. A lanky boy, a little bigger than Patrick, breathed deeply on a cot in the corner.

When she handed me the folded towel, she smiled up at me. "You try and get some sleep, *mi hijo*." Her small rough hand on my cheek surprised me. I hadn't expected it or seen it coming in the dim room. "You have had a rough night. God bless you."

With that, she left.

I collapsed on the bed, stuffed the pillow in my mouth, and cried for what seemed like a couple of years. Tears at first, then dry sobs when there was no more water left in my head. I sat up and slumped against the bare wall, spent to the core.

My eyes hurt. My throat hurt. But there was a deeper hurt, more serious than physical pain.

And in truth, I realized I seriously didn't want to fill it this time. I wanted it to go away. The question and the hurt it always brought.

I needed something. A distraction, a diversion. But there was nothing. Nothing but a strange boy, a bed, and darkness.

The Glock.

I pushed the thought away as quickly as it came. How could I think of the gun? Things weren't that bad. I hugged my knees and rocked until I could see a sliver of purple sky in the tiny rectangular window high in the far wall.

In a ragged voice I asked, "What is the answer?" Then I finally drifted for a few minutes, into the beginnings of sleep.

"Jesus."

That single word brought me back with a start.

Who said that?

I wanted to scream.

I looked at the boy on the cot, spread-eagle, drool trailing from his open mouth. He hadn't spoken a word.

"Come."

I heard the command as clearly as if I had said it myself; as plainly as I'd heard it in the burning truck.

I started whimpering like a scared child. I knew the answer.

ben Jacob Benson owed him money for unusual wear and tear on his truck, Jack decided. He'd march into BJ's and demand it. That's what he'd do, as soon as he found the stranger again and got the ring from him. BJ would be impressed then, maybe so impressed and happy that he just couldn't keep from throwing boatloads of money at Jack.

He seemed to have a liking for Water Street. Miss Lucretia's.

He pulled off Main Street, a few blocks short of BJ's, circled around behind the high school and football field until he connected to Water Street. No one seemed to be stirring at

Miss Lucretia's, a good sign. Her granddaughter's car was gone, a very good sign.

He stepped over a foot tub of water under the pear tree in the side yard. There was a three-legged stool and a bucket of greens next to it like someone was about to clean them but stopped short. Maybe the granddaughter, he thought, had started but then had to rush away for something, which meant she'd be back real soon. Well, what he had to do in the house wouldn't take long. He went around to the back door and entered, not bothering to knock.

"Catty?" He heard the old lady's voice from the front of the house. Jack let a small smile creep across his thin lips and pushed the door closed before moving toward the old woman's voice. "Catty, honey?"

He stepped through the kitchen, sure she'd not even heard his boots click softly against the soft yellow linoleum tiles.

"All right, old biddy," he growled at her as the TV flickered colors across her dark face. "Where is he?"

She threw up her hands and screamed, though not too loud.

He shouted, "Shut up!" anyway and took one big noisy step into the center of the room. "I said where is he?"

"I don't know what you're talking about," she whimpered, shaking so much that the snapshots in her lap cascaded across the photo albums on the couch next to her.

"Don't play games with me, old woman."

"Get out," she shouted, louder this time. Then she screamed.

He lunged for her and pushed the books and pictures to the floor, then brought his knee up and pressed it and his rough hands against her chest.

"You want to scream, do you?"

She trembled and whimpered.

"Now you were just telling me where your boarder got to. Right?"

She swallowed and drew a ragged breath. "Our Father who art in heaven . . . ," she whispered.

"What!" He drew his open hand back to slap her.

"Thy will be done on earth, as it is in heaven—"

Jack let his hand find its target, but it didn't bring the satisfaction or desired effect. He bit the inside of his lip without meaning to and staggered back, frowning down on the babbling woman.

"Stop it, old bat!" The taste of his own blood was souring the whole thing.

"Forgive us our trespasses as we forgive those who trespass against us."

"Trespasses! Ha!" He turned to go. "You just watch yourself when you go outside tonight. I'll be there, watching and waiting. He's coming back. I can tell by the way you're protecting him. I'll catch him 'cause I'll be waiting. You hear?"

The old woman was still lying back, bent at the waist in a funny angle, babbling to herself about God and Jesus. He could see her anger, her disapproval. It was freaking him out.

"You . . . you just wait," he added and ran out.

There wasn't enough of Crazy Eddie to fill a New York minute, as Old Ulysses used to say about people who were as skinny as a rail. But Crazy Eddie sure could pedal a ten-speed.

And it didn't seem to matter that it was loaded down with my stuff and me.

"Where'd you get this bike?" I asked as we neared the Benson house.

"Funny. I know you been gone a long time, but it seems like it was day 'fore yes'tidy the last time I seen you. But I could be recollectin' wrong. That was back when I was crazy."

I laughed and let it go. It really didn't matter where he got the shiny red bike. We'd ride off in the sunset, carriers of all our worldly possessions in bags and partners in robbery. For all I knew, Crazy Eddie could be my father. That thought made me laugh harder.

"What's so funny?"

"Nothing, Eddie. Just drop me off here."

He kept pedaling like he hadn't heard me. I tapped his bony shoulder. "Eddie. Stop here! Eddie!"

He stopped with a jerk, sending me stumbling back onto the bags crisscrossing my back.

"Why'd you call me Eddie?" he yelled.

I got up, more than a little irritated. At least there was no traffic. "That's your name, isn't it? Or did it change in between the migrant camp and here?" I got up and dusted myself off before tossing my two bags onto the newly mown shoulder of the road.

"Folks 'round here call me 'Crazy Eddie' not just 'Eddie.'"

His tone had gone squeakier than normal, and he had a look on his face that was somewhere between annoyed and pleading.

I was confused. "Well, what do you want me to call you?"

He stuck his lips out and looked up, the pupils just about disappearing into his eye sockets. With a nod, the lips went in and the eyes came back down. "Mama said you can call me Eddie."

I swallowed the chuckle. "She did. You didn't have to call her?" I pointed to his bag.

"No. I ate the phones. Easier that way."

"Oh." I slapped him on the back and set his bag in the basket in the back. "You're all right with me, Eddie. Thanks for the ride."

"You're welcome, Isaac, my man. Homeboy. Homeslice. Homey . . ." He rode away, babbling 'til I couldn't hear him anymore.

The Benson house was just as impressive as before, maybe more so now since I had a recent picture of the Hunt home in my mind to compare it to. No one answered my knock on the front door, so I walked around in search of another entrance.

At the side of the house a black man with a salt-and-pepper moustache hopped down from a tractor mower and called to me. "Hey." He took off his work gloves and goggles and walked closer. "Who you looking for?"

"Hi, my name is Isaac Hunt." I extended my hand. He shook it with a funny look in his eye. "Do you know if Mr. Benson is around? I'd like to talk with him about my car," I lied. In truth, I didn't know how the gun was going to play into my face-to-face meeting with a Benson man, but I could have cared less for that beat-up Saab. I thought of Catty's words about forgiveness.

Justice. That's what I needed. Not forgiveness.

"Not here. Left on business," the man told me. "Took Patrick with him." He raked his brown eyes over me as he talked, occasionally wiping sweat from his wide forehead with a dirty rag. He frowned when his eyes fell on my left hand. "Where'd you get that ring?"

"My mother gave it to me." I'd almost forgotten I'd put it on this morning. It was a little loose on my thumb but I wasn't wearing it as a fashion statement.

"How about Ben Jacob Benson?"

The man's demeanor shifted into caution mode. "Don't live here."

That's okay, I thought. I had his number.

He drew a breath, and a look of an idea come full circle flashed across his face. "You're Betty Douglas's boy. The one what had a run-in with crazy Jack."

I nodded.

"Sorry 'bout that. He needs to be put away. Sorry 'bout your mama too."

"Thank you."

A younger black man walked up with a weed eater across his shoulder. His dusty 'fro poked out from under a ball cap. He eyed my ring, blurting, "Did I hear you ask about BJ Benson? Check their lake house. Hey, Uncle Ned, I thought you said we'd be finished 'fore 9:00." He swung the weed eater to the ground and dusted grass from his cuff. "It's quarter 'til. I'm finished with the back, so I'm outta here. I didn't wanna work on the Fourth anyway . . ."

Ned dragged his palm across his face and sighed. "Excuse me, boy, *I'm* talking to this young man here."

"Whatever," the boy said, mumbling something that

238

sounded like, "How'd he get that ring? Looks like BJ Benson's."

Ned's eyes narrowed. He pulled his gloves on. Smiling tightly, he said, "Well, we'd better get back to work, Mr. Hunt. Fifteen more minutes 'fore I lose my help. Nice to meet you."

I thanked him and hit the blacktop once again. I was bothered in a small way by the reaction to the ring. But I had a few things to bring closure to before I chased down the Benson man who had given my mother the ring. Had someone in the family killed her for the ring? That disturbed me. Had that man sent Jack after me? That disturbed me even more. I was at a loss as to how to proceed.

Since neither Benson man knew I was coming, I figured they would stay put. At the moment, I had the overwhelming need to speak to a white man, one Rupert "Trip" Robertson. But first I would make a stop at my mother's grave.

Down the dirt road that Patrick had shown me days earlier, the blue house seemed to smile in a lazy summer kind of way, classical music spilling from its open windows filling the moss-scented woods. There was a rusty white Cressida parked around the far side. Catty's car, if my memory was right.

I smiled and climbed the steps slowly, then stooped and dug out a small flowery box. At my insistence, a curious Miguel had found me some wrapping paper with flowers on it. I'd only had enough paper to wrap the chalks. I would just let her go through the other things later and take what she liked. The door opened behind me. I turned and stood, hiding the small box behind my back.

"Hello," I said. She looked prettier than I remembered, standing barefoot in a paint-smeared, oversized white oxford, blue T-shirt and jeans.

She smiled through her shock. "I didn't hear anyone. I was just going to my car. How'd you get here?"

"Long story." I pulled out the gift and stepped closer. "Happy Fourth."

She giggled. "I've never gotten a Fourth of July gift before." She took it into the house, smoothing her fingers over the paper. I followed, inhaling the smells of oil paint and turpentine.

An easel with a blank canvas on it stood near the open window where a book on oil painting was propped open on the sill with a rock. On the card table under the window I spied a couple of leather-bound books, classics by the looks of them, and a vase of white flowers on crumpled red velvet.

Her subjects.

She drew a breath at the contents of the box. Dust from a million Technicolor diatoms danced between us. Chalk dust. What memories did it dredge up for her?

The smell of chalk recreates a strong memory for me. The hairs on the back of my neck stand. My normally dry palms run with sweat. My breathing quickens. I'm somewhere between fainting and flying. But then I remember the brush of a nose against mine, I calm myself and replay the kiss—my first kiss—delivered to the little yellow-headed girl that sat in front of me in fifth grade.

With dust-covered hands, she had slapped me hard on both cheeks to let me know just how much she appreciated my forwardness. "You lied!" she screamed, tossing an eraser at me. She ran crying from Mrs. Bedford's classroom. I had not lied. I genuinely did need help with my vocabulary list, but who could resist that hair—dressed in long honey-colored gloves, smelling of her mother's musk oil. Needless to say, she had not kissed back.

The lips of Catherine Wright, on the other hand, moved with a zeal that surpassed my own. Their owner, clutching the used artist's pastels from the late Mr. Goble, eased her heels to the floor and lifted the opened box to her nose, shifting the colorful bits from side to side. She inhaled deeply and glanced at me like a woman who had been caught being real, then wiped tears from her eyes with her pinkies. How could I not love a woman who would cry over used chalk? She'd shown me a little corner of her heart—where she probably kept memories of pressed prom flowers and love sonnets. Had she just placed me there? Or was I reading too much into this delicious exchange?

She pulled on her safe, dutiful granddaughter mantle again, and walked to her easel near the window to stroke the empty canvas like she had been planning to do that all along. I smiled and followed, hoping to see Catherine Wright again.

She placed the box of pastels with the paint tubes and brushes in an old wooden shoeshine box and looked at me again.

"I'm sorry," she whispered.

There, in her eyes I still saw a little bit of her bare soul, melted by tears, fired by the sunlight slanting through the window.

"That's not what you say when someone gives you something."

She covered her half-grin with a trembling hand. "Thank you," came her muffled whisper.

"And I thank *you*, Miss Wright." I touched the hair that radiated from a bandana, dark and thick like molasses. "For sharing your talents with me."

How she challenged every stereotype I'd ever formed about poor black women. She had no idea what she had given me. And I didn't have the words to explain. I felt myself on the verge of more emotion than I was willing to share. Despite our disagreements and the turmoil in my life, I could not deny the way this woman filled me, thrilled me.

Molasses was definitely sweeter than honey.

chapter 23

"so cough it up, Georgie Porgie. What happened to my truck?"

Trip jumped from the top step to the ground, trotting alongside me as I walked across the deeply shaded yard.

"Sorry about your truck. How'd you find me, anyway? Miguel call you?"

He nodded. "And Julio told me about how he 'rescued you.' His words. I figured you'd walked back to Water Street, maybe stop in on the Bensons or here. I'd hunt you down either way."

"You set me up." I had an overwhelming desire to ask

him about his visit to Ricky and Chloe's but I held my tongue.

He shrugged. "I'll miss that ole green bucket. It had an endearing way of stalling at lights."

"I'll pay—"

"Don't worry 'bout it. I'm just kidding."

He nodded toward a brown compact on the other side of Catty's. "Got a loaner from Lamont." He walked away, past the cars.

I followed. "I really am sorry."

"And I really am not pressed about it. Drop it, okay?" He turned and looked me in the eye.

We were standing before the cemetery, light playing across the freshly mown grass around gravestones like feathers in the breeze.

Trip continued, his voice soft and strange. "Mortality reminder. Being in that temperamental tin can of mine with fire licking up around your ankles had to be pretty scary."

I gritted my teeth against the memory.

"I'm sorry that happened to you. But I'm glad you're okay."

"Thanks."

We stood in silence while a blue jay chattered overhead. Through a break in the trees overhead I saw two hawks circling. Hot air pushed through my hair.

"You probably came here to spend time with your mother. Don't let me hold you up. I'd like to talk with you when you're done. In the meantime, I'll put your stuff in my car and then have a little talk with Catty. She should be done crying by now. How come I don't have that effect on women?" He smirked and left.

Past all the Ross graves, I followed the short trail that Patrick had led me down that rainy day to my mother's grave.

The brambles and weeds around the headstone had been cut back recently from the look of it. I pulled the envelope from my back pocket and sat down, hugging my knees to my chest, and read her letter again.

She had loved me.

"I love you too, Mama," I whispered, pressing the pages against my lips. "I don't want to disappoint you, but I've got to find out more. I need to find him. I need to know . . ."

I watched the light warm the stone in the ring. It glinted along the crevices along the band. I needed more.

"I'm sorry, Mama."

I found Trip posing for Catty on the front porch. She was sketching a caricature of him.

"Not bad," I said, peeping over her shoulder. She'd even smeared a five o'clock shadow across his ridiculous jaw. "But don't you think that chin should be longer?"

"Ha. Ha. Ha. Draw him next, Catty. Man with one eyebrow."

She laughed in that cute snorting way of hers and tore off the sheet with Trip's face. I covered my face with my hands.

"Okay, okay. I won't do it."

"Well, we'd better get going, Miss Catty. See you and Miss Luc tonight. I'm grilling my famous Trip burgers."

She rolled her eyes and twirled an index finger in the air. "See you tonight, Isaac."

I smiled and waved good-bye.

"It's okay to blow a kiss. I won't look," Trip told me as I folded my body into Lamont's car.

"You never quit! Where are you taking me?"

"I was hoping you'd tell me."

"Take me to the lake, wherever that is, and don't ask why."

"Why?"

I glared at him.

"A man can try. At least let me ask you a few questions while I drive."

And boy did he ask questions. From my GPA to my favorite *Columbo* episode.

Swamp, thick and smelly, engulfed us on either side. Stout heavy-bottomed trees stood like scaly old men in the black water. Skiffs of green slime floated here and there. Another weird blue-gray bird watched us for a moment before taking flight.

"Why are you grilling me?"

"I want to know the mind of Isaac Hunt. What's made him into the man who he is."

I could tell him that it was more of a who and not a what. "Writing a book?"

"Why does he hate white people so much?"

Not that again. "I don't—"

"You know, all this time I've been trying to not take offense. Being a white person and all."

"What are you talking about?"

"Then I realized that it's not really me that you're angry at as much as it's a black thing that I'll never fully understand. But in a crude way I think I do understand."

The landscape around the straight road had widened out and was much drier. In the distance, across flat green tables of grass there were houses and what I figured to be cows looking like monopoly game pieces.

I sighed and tried to get lost in the landscape. Trip continued, despite the fact I hadn't looked him in the eye for more than fifteen minutes.

"It seems to me that you hate having to justify yourself, prove yourself as a black man every time you're around darker-skinned black folk."

He was quiet for a few minutes. I guess it was the dramatic pause during which I was supposed to applaud him for his brilliant psychoanalysis.

He took a breath and continued. "I'll bet Catty is an anomaly for you. Did I use that word right? Anomaly. You're having a great effect on me. Increasing my vocab." He chuckled.

"Anyway, I'll bet you never really had a girlfriend. Rejected by white girls 'cause you look black. Your features, I mean. Then on the flip side, you were probably rejected by black girls 'cause you look white. It's gotta be maddening. And then to top it off, there's the nagging realization that there's a white man to blame—not just in your distant ancestry, back in slavery days when Massa raped your grandmama's grandmama kind of thing, but in your recent past. With all that bugging me, I'd hate white folks too."

He took another breath like he was going to continue.

"Please, stop!"

"Sorry."

"Why is it you're always right, *Reverend* Robertson?"

"I didn't mean to come across that way. I was just trying to be helpful."

He drifted off and started doing that annoying mournful whistle.

"Please!"

He stopped, pulling into a gravel parking lot with a small house to one side.

"Welcome to Finleigh State Park. The lake's down that gravel road there." He jerked a thumb over his shoulder while he parked the car.

As much as I hated to admit it, I didn't want to see him go. I still needed to ask him something.

"Well, you getting out or did you change your mind?"

"I um . . ." I fiddled with the door handle. "I want to ask you something."

His eyebrows went up. He killed the engine and jumped out. Smiling, he chirped through the open window. "Let's walk."

We walked side by side along the gravel road just big enough for one vehicle at a time. Cool winds sighed in the feathery green branches overhead. The smell of the swamp was here, but it was more of the perfume of the place rather than the stench of water that had stood too long.

As we walked I thumbed through a dirty park brochure I'd rescued from a puddle, troubled more with my own words than the words on the pages in my hands.

The path opened up to a large gravel circle, a turnaround from the look of the wheel patterns. There was a boat ramp and a pier beside it. As we neared the pier, I glanced around at my surroundings thinking how much it looked like places described as bear country on a National Geographic Channel program I'd seen. A mile or more down the left bank, the flash of large paned windows above the tree line distracted me for a moment.

Trip waited until we were standing on the pier to ask me. "Is this about God?"

I shot a look at him, embarrassed by my own indecision and vulnerability.

"Well, Romeo, I was sure it wasn't about me. What would you be struggling with about me? I figured it was about the one thing most sane people struggle with all their lives." He paused. "Sometimes there are no words."

I frowned and sat down on the rough sun-bleached planks. "Does God . . . Does He appear to people?"

"In bodily form? No, not since Jesus walked the earth. And then only in a limited fashion. God didn't show all Himself to everybody all the time. You're frowning. Don't worry, sometimes I don't understand Him either, and this is my business, or so they tell me.

"Bottom line: I believe He *shows* Himself to people in a way. Did He come to you in the fire?" Trip crouched beside me and touched my arm.

I did all I could to hold back the tears and shook my head. My voice came out small and tight. "In the bedroom at the migrant camp."

I took a long breath and retold all my run-ins with God since the prayer meeting at Miss Lucretia's. Trip nodded, tears building in his big brown eyes, and said, "I knew He was pulling you. I just didn't know when you would answer.

That's why I 'set you up,' as you called it." He pulled his lips together in a tight smile and stood.

I stood too. "What do I do now?"

He looked out over the twinkling water like he hadn't heard me, or had no intention of answering.

"Has He ever come to you like that?"

He shook his head, tears flowing freely now. "Not exactly."

"What am I supposed to do, Trip?"

He smiled and faced me. "I don't think this means you need to join a monastery or go to divinity school."

"Well, what then?"

"Would you say you've come to Him and given Him all your burdens?"

I hesitated. What kind of question was that? "I think so. I don't know how."

"Would you say—"

"Trip, whatever's been happening to me, it's like nothing I've ever experienced. If I lived to be 150, I'm sure I would never experience anything like it. I can't even start to tell you how it felt to be touched by a hand, held by arms, that I couldn't see."

I was crying now, making an awful blubbering spectacle of myself at it. And it didn't matter because Trip was blubbering too. I covered my eyes with my hand and screamed. "Jesus Christ!" The words came out with the force of a curse, but for once in my life I was far from it.

We were quiet for a few minutes. I didn't feel like talking anymore, but something told me Trip still had the capacity for further gab. I heard him take a breath.

"Yep. He's a big God. Bigger than any hurt. Bigger than any disappointment."

"Bigger than hate?" I asked, my face still covered.

"Especially hate."

Trip hugged me, not the awkward kind that I always got from other men, and prayed. I don't remember the words. But the prayer left me feeling included and unjudged like never before. When he released me and stepped back, explaining he would leave me to myself for a while, I was shocked to notice how white he looked. White, not just color of skin and angles of his nose, but in the extreme opposite of everything I was. He was a white man, and he had touched me deeply. For all that he'd done for me, I wanted to discredit him and shake him off like an old shirt, but I couldn't any more than I could shake off my right foot. Knowing that made me mad and confused.

I watched him as he strolled back up the gravel lane, head hung, then turned my back on him, studied the lake and thought.

God was big, I'd agree with Trip on that. And He was also crazy. Why was He picking on me?

The crunch of gravel and the rumble of a diesel engine a few minutes later made me turn. It was a shiny blue truck pulling a trailer with a camouflage painted johnboat on it.

The driver backed halfway down the boat ramp beside the pier and jumped out to unhitch his boat with *Johnny Reb* scrawled on the side.

"Morning," he said, an unlit cigar clenched between his teeth.

"Good morning." I watched him jump in and pull the

boat to a pylon where he tied it off. He was a short round man, maybe twice my age, and obviously a local by his drawl. It took me by surprise to see the flash of red on his right ring finger.

I froze and stuffed my hands in my jean pockets, hoping he hadn't seen my left hand.

"Nice day for being out here on the lake."

I smiled and nodded, not taking my eyes from the far bank. He followed my gaze.

"You looking at the Benson house?" he said, the cigar wobbling from one corner to the other. "Right purty. 'Course they got the other one over on Benson Ridge Road." He hopped onto the pier, pulling his truck out of the way.

I wasn't there when he returned with his fishing gear. I had broken into a sprint, chased by opportunity. Or stupidity. Only time would tell.

chapter 24

abraham smiled down on his younger sister Elise as he rolled lemons on the counter. How long had it been since he had been with her at this very counter rolling lemons? Since Mama died. That would have made it more than five years. So many years that he'd forgotten why they'd stopped coming to the beach house as a family.

When she had finished filling all the pitchers with water and looked up at him, he kissed her cheek.

"What was that for, Abe?"

"Sticking up for me, like you always did."

"I thought that was your job, big brother."

"It was until you came along. You were always a spoiled little thing."

Elise pushed him aside with a shove that reminded him of their mother and divided the lemon juice among the pitchers. "Was not," she pouted.

Abraham slumped against the counter and sucked what was left of the pulp from a lemon half.

"Stop that, Abe, it'll give you a stomachache."

"Bossy."

She stuck out her tongue at him. Abraham tossed the mangled lemon aside and chuckled, turning to look out at their children playing football on the beach below. His two other sisters and brothers-in-law lounged on towels nearby.

"Why did we all stop coming on the Fourth?" he said, not really expecting an answer.

"Too crowded. Look at all those kids. There are ten kids, not counting you."

One less person now that Olivia's gone.

Abraham pushed the thought away. "Anne and Jed only have the one kid. And now that Karen and Bradley live in Manteo, space isn't really a problem. And on top of that when I come, you and Bob don't stay more than a few days. That's what you get for marrying a corn farmer from Iowa."

She glanced up from her stirring. "Now, Abe."

"Okay, I'll drop it."

He watched her shuffle things in the refrigerator to make room for the lemonade. She pulled out a crockery bowl covered with plastic wrap, then looked around like she was expecting to be caught.

"I guess we'd better eat this." She set the bowl on the

254

counter in front of her brother. Abe looked down at the fluffy white contents. "It's taking up too much room, you know. Can't have that."

Grinning, he grabbed the spoon she offered. "Nope, can't have that. You know, Samantha's looking more and more like you every day." Abe watched his oldest niece tackle Patrick, her long blonde braid flapping wildly like a horse tail, as two kids turned into a pile of laughing children.

Elise smirked. "Poor girl."

"She's gonna be a knockout at State next year."

"I'm glad Patrick's back to his old self. And so are you."

Abe sighed. He placed the spoon on the counter.

"Had enough, already? What's wrong? What did I say?"

"Nothing."

"Oh, Abe. It's gotta be hard for you being here. The only one here without—"

"A spouse?"

He sighed again and walked across to a wicker rocker. Elise joined him, perching on the table as she wiped whipped cream from her lips.

"I'm sorry I brought it up."

"Don't be. I miss her, sure. But . . ."

He leaned forward, studying her hazel eyes and strong cheekbones—undeniable marks of a Benson. Should he tell her all the things he'd kept hidden all these years? Things not even their parents spoke of, though Abraham suspected they knew but didn't voice out of respect for their eldest child.

"A man does a lot of things in his life he's not proud of," he could hear his father saying. "Some he had to do out of loyalty. Some he had to do out of saving face. God knows and He understands."

He didn't agree with his father. Many of the things he'd been called on to do for family or pride were wrong. They haunted his dreams and plagued his thoughts.

Henry Wright knew, but he was gone now. Should someone else know? God knew all about them, Abraham was sure of that, and He would send His judgment soon. Maybe losing Olivia was part of that judgment. Maybe losing Benson Ridge would be as well. Maybe even losing his own life. Yes, it was time someone else knew the secrets.

Elise leaned toward him and placed her small thin hand over his. "What's wrong, Abraham?"

He rubbed a rough hand over his face. "What if I told you Patrick was not my son?"

She turned her head, her short blonde curls falling to one side, revealing the few silvery wisps that she kept tucked behind her ear. "What are you saying?"

Abraham lowered his eyes. "It's not like he looks like me."

"Don't talk so crazy. 'Course he does. He's got Olivia's coloring. But he's got your bones, same mouth. He's gonna grow up big and tall just like his daddy."

"Calm down, Lise."

Her reaction to his question had told him more than her words. She wasn't ready for the truth.

"Well, what were you saying? Abraham, what's going on?"

He stood and strolled out onto the deck.

"Abe, talk to me." She stroked the small of his back.

Abraham gave her a smile, drew her close to his side, and

watched her husband climb the boardwalk from the beach. "In time. I will in time. Bob," he called to his brother-in-law as he released Elise and stepped in front of her. "How is it you kept your wife from doing her duty as a sister?"

"Abraham." He heard his sister's warning growl.

The shorter man approached, showing his teeth in what could have been either a smile or a grimace. "How's that, old man?"

"She's always taking care of everyone. That's how she is. It's her nature."

"She's a grown woman. She can make her own choices."

Elise pulled on the back of Abraham's T-shirt as he stepped closer to her husband. "Left to herself it would have been her choice to keep Patrick for me while I pulled my mind back together. But she's a dutiful wife first and foremost, isn't she?"

Bob's blue eyes narrowed. "You Bensons think you own everything and everybody."

Abraham brushed past him on his way down the boardwalk, yelling over his shoulder as he left, "Don't we?"

During my first year at State, I had walked into Chloe's prizewinning kitchen from a hard morning on campus and found an undergarment on the counter.

Amazingly, my shock at seeing that temporary undergarment and all that it implied was mild compared to the shock I got at seeing Trip leaning against a woman who was leaning against Lamont's car, their lips fully engaged.

To his credit, the woman turned out to be Frieda. And also to his credit it did seem to be a good-natured kiss with only a touch of recklessness. And while his palms were pressed against the windows of the car, hers were only exploring what was left of his hair.

They started at the crunch of my feet on gravel and blushed as bright as me.

"Sorry," I mumbled.

Trip cleared his throat and fumbled with his lips like they were just a set he had borrowed and he was trying to find his. Frieda brushed at her blouse, then turned all the way around and greeted me. "Hi, Isaac." I was starting to like the way she pulled out the "I" in my name. She smiled and walked toward a bike propped against the back of the car.

I nodded to her and tried to conceal the thrill of having caught The Saint at something naughty.

"Trip," I started. He eyed me with a warning. "When you're through—"

"I'm through."

"Oh, okay. You sure?"

He ran a hand over his stubbly chin. "What do you want?"

"I need to get something out of my bags."

He mumbled something and threw the keys at me.

"Thanks."

"Keep 'em. Frieda and I will be at the pier." They laced fingers and walked up the lane I'd just come down, Trip pushing the bike by the handlebars. "Take your sweet time," he yelled back, a smile playing at the corners of his eyes.

I would take my sweet time all right. But that was all of

the plan I'd worked out in my mind. If you could have called it a plan. It involved a gun, a ring, and the father I'd never met, to my knowledge. But what did I want from him more than to hear him confess that he'd raped my mother and killed her when she had become a problem. That's when it occurred to me that he might have wanted me dead eighteen years ago and still wanted me dead. Maybe that was why Jack had been shadowing me.

However it played out, I hoped God would stay out of it.

I tucked the Glock in my waistband and pulled out my T-shirt to cover it, then slipped the car keys behind the visor.

The Benson lake house, I figured, was easily accessible from land. I hoped to find a trail through the dense woods that edged the park. I set out across the picnic area dotted with the same stout-bottomed trees that I'd seen in the swamp on the drive over. Children playing hide-and-seek, and joggers with dogs crisscrossed my path as I trekked across the well-used campgrounds.

Beyond the campgrounds I was forced to hop a drainage ditch. The gun shifted a bit, so I took it out and carried it in my hand, thankful that I'd left humanity behind me. And so it seemed, as I neared the woods, like I'd left civilization behind as well. The mosquitoes were still just as prevalent, but the air was heavy and cool and still, making me think of a graveyard. The moist, dark ground kept my footsteps like mementos of my passing. I wanted to stand and admire the gnarled massive trunks that stood all around me like old resting choir boys sighing a mournful hymn, their rough knees drawn up to their chests.

Then I turned, looking for a path of least resistance

against the briery underbrush and for the first time saw a large yellow house, two story with wraparound porches on both levels. The lake shimmered in the background through the green lace of a line of trees. Even from the distance, over a hundred yards away, I could make out the large white columns like polished teeth against green-shuttered eyes. It was an old plantation house, I guessed. An assortment of sun-bleached outbuildings squatted around the big yellow house like ugly servants.

This was what was left of the former Finleigh Rice and Lumber Plantation I'd read about in the park brochure. It was evident that Eustis Carmichael Finleigh, benevolent rice and lumber magnate from Somerset, England, had, like the brochure stated, indeed lived for the betterment of this dark earth I stood upon and the thousand or so dark bodies that he populated it with.

At that moment I realized that I hated him and I hated what blood of his flowed in my privileged high yella veins. Looking at that house did nothing to quell my hatred for another privileged couple who lived in a bright yellow house back in the state capital and dared call themselves my parents.

seeing the collards, still speckled with Sevin and starting to curl from being left in the heat all day, made Catty furious. Why couldn't her grandmother finish anything Catty asked her to do?

Just one simple thing!

She ran some fresh water from the spigot and washed the greens quickly on the back porch before putting the broken leaves into a plastic grocery bag. She'd finish the job later, she thought, as she pushed the bag into the bottom drawer of the fridge.

Her temper had calmed a bit until she saw the photo

albums and pictures strewn on the floor near the TV. She stomped her foot and scooped up the mess, then let it fall from her arms to the couch.

"Grandma!"

No answer. At least the TV was off. She hated the thought of her grandmother sitting at home watching soaps all day long while her granddaughter was out earning a wage.

"Grandma!"

Catty started shuffling the pictures, pushing them into stacks like so much paper. One picture caught her eye and made her cover her mouth.

Isaac.

In the picture, he stood with his arm around Patrick. She recognized it as one of the Polaroids that Trip had taken. Isaac was smiling but in his eyes she saw sadness.

So much sadness.

But he had been happy today when she saw him. When she kissed him.

She pressed trembling fingers against her lips and tried to push the forbidden happiness aside. His lips had felt just like she'd imagined. Nothing like those of the other boys. He was nothing like the others, not in the least. He was a man, only two years older than her, but so much more mature.

Where had life taken him? She wondered. What places had he seen? What had he done in the world? What had she done in comparison?

Nothing.

Her ingratitude shamed her. "I'm sorry, Lord. Thank You for all You've given me. How could I be so ungrateful?"

And lustful.

Noises from her grandmother's bedroom brought her around. Had the old woman taken a nap, she wondered.

"Grandma, is that you?"

She pushed her grandmother's door open and gasped. Pins of shock stabbed through her body as she rushed toward her grandmother's crumpled body on the floor.

"Oh, Grandma. What happened?"

She cradled her grandmother's body, turning her over with very little effort. A trail of blood, now dried, had carved a ghoulish half-grin from her grandmother's mouth to her right ear. Her eyes fluttered and she tried to speak, producing only a whimper instead.

"Don't talk. Oh, Grandma." She drew her to her chest for a brief hug. "I'm so sorry. Let me get you up on your bed."

Laying her on the rose-colored comforter, Catty felt her clammy forehead. How long had she been like this? Catty brushed the dark circle on her grandmother's left cheek. Was that a bruised cheek?

Her grandmother mouthed something, lifting a hand to her mouth.

"What is it? Water? Okay. But first I need to call 911. Then I'll get you some water."

Catty made the call, feeling like she was standing outside her body. She filled a glass, spilling a little when she tripped over the braided rug that she'd been meaning to mend.

Had the ragged rug caused her grandmother's fall? She had been such an awful, selfish granddaughter.

"Here you are." She pressed the glass to her grandmother's lips, supporting the back of her head. "Easy, now. Enough?"

She placed the half-empty glass on the night table and knelt beside the bed.

"Catty," her grandmother whispered.

"No, don't talk. Save your strength. The ambulance should be here soon."

"No, honey. I need to tell you something."

Catty started to complain, but her grandmother continued. "The house is yours if you want it. Your Uncle Dexter owns it now, but he knows that it's yours if you want it."

She didn't like where she thought this was leading. "Grandma—"

Miss Lucretia swallowed and went on in a raspy voice. "Trip can stay on if he marries Frieda. Stay as long as they please. It's a good place to raise chil'ren."

"I don't like to hear you talking this way."

"I know, child, but it's okay. I've had a good life. This old building is a leaning. It's time I moved out."

Catty gagged at the tears that swelled in her throat. She knew too well what her grandmother was alluding to and she didn't want to hear it.

Where's that ambulance! If we lived on Freeman, they'd be here by now.

"No, Grandma. It's not time for anything like that. I'll tell you what it's time for," she paused to wipe tears from her eyes, regretting all the time she'd spent washing collards and mooning over Isaac's picture. "It's time I asked you to forgive me for being such a disobedient granddaughter. I'm so sorry, Grandma, for being so mad at you, and for being so spiteful and going behind your back to paint at the old Ross house, and—"

"Hush, child. I ain't finished."

"But Grandma . . . I'm so sorry."

She buried her face in her grandmother's side.

"I know, honey, and it's okay," she said, patting Catty's hair. "I forgive you. I want to ask you to forgive me. For holding you back, clipping your wings. You and me, we're two different women but children of God, all the same. Forgive me for treating you like you was less. I want to leave this earth with no regrets. I'm holding nothing against no man."

A cough shook her weak body. Catty sat back on her heels and reached for the glass of water.

"I forgive you, Grandma."

Miss Lucretia took a little more water and smiled at her grandchild. Catty frowned as she listened to her shallow breathing. Catty closed her eyes, praying quietly. She rested her forehead on the bed and her hand on her grandmother's stomach.

"Thank you, Catty. Give your father's clothes and spoons to Isaac. They suit him. Let Trip know I'm grateful for all he done for us. I love him like my own son. Tell him I expect him to keep an eye on you. I expect him to make sure you keep your mind on your painting and the Lord and not on Isaac Hunt."

Catty stopped praying, shocked and embarrassed.

The older woman chuckled. "Didn't think I noticed, did you. I ain't blind. He's got a long way to come, honey. Don't rush it. Listen to the Lord."

Catty watched her grandmother close her eyes and lay still for a long time, breathing like she was counting each breath. Catty was counting—counting and straining to hear the siren.

"Now sing for me. 'Amazing Grace.'"

Catty covered her face with her hands and wept. How could she sing? She couldn't even talk without crying. She buried her face in the comforter, wailing.

Miss Lucretia hummed a few broken notes of the hymn. "Dear gracious Father," she said, "have mercy on us, most holy Lord. I come to You now, O Savior, as humble as I know how, beseeching You on behalf of this sweet child. My precious Catherine. Bless her, O Lord, with Your grace and Your wisdom. Keep her in the hollow of Your hand."

Catty heard her pause, and cough, like she was clearing her throat to continue praying. Anticipating the need for water, Catty sat on her heels again. She stopped short. Miss Lucretia's body no longer needed water. She was gone. Only the shell remained—looking like "amen" was poised on its smiling lips.

Catty wiped the tears from her face. She stood back, eyeing the body that once belonged to her grandmother, the woman who had taught her to jump rope, sew, and cook.

She drew a breath, looked toward the ceiling, and sang the last stanza of her grandmother's favorite song. "When we've been there ten thousand years bright shining as the sun, we've no less days to sing God's praise than when we first begun."

⸺

I did finally find a trail. But I had to go past the big yellow house to get to it, down the *Bee Tree Trail*, the rough wooden sign read. I imagined the sound of whips on black backs and the roar of the overseer over the cry of mothers being separated from their babies. I pulled on all the strength I had not to shoot out every valuable leaded pane of glass in that stinking house.

Walking the trail was like traveling through a mosquito-lined tunnel of vegetation. What little light that reached the green interior was weak, making it appear at least late afternoon, if not early evening. I wished for a flashlight and, of course, a big bottle of DEET. Before long I was running full tilt, the pistol held out to my side like I was in a Bruce Willis movie. Smiling at my own sick humor, I hoped that in the movie that was playing out around me that the black guy would not get killed first.

I glanced at my watch. I'd been running for almost forty-five minutes and still no house, but I could make out a dirt road curving toward the trail through the thinning underbrush. With a thick fallen limb, I whacked back the veil of briers and jumped across the ditch that separated the woods from the road. The familiar stutter of an old truck made me jump back seconds later.

I crouched low to the moist dead leaves and waited, grateful that my shirt was dark blue. I was not too surprised at the sight of Jack behind the wheel of the truck, the same beat-up Toyota that had almost run me down in Raleigh.

He was singing along to a country song on the radio so he didn't seem to hear me when I hopped the ditch and trotted behind him, careful to keep my distance. The road curved, but I could see the eaves of a house through the trees and lots of windows, so I waited until I heard him kill the truck engine and slam the door shut before I jumped the ditch again into the cover of the woods.

I followed the curve from the relative safety of the edge of the woods. It was slow traveling, but I was grateful for the dense, albeit prickly, cover. A dead log overlooking the house provided a good perch while I sat and watched Jack unload groceries.

There were no other vehicles, but there was a freestanding carport to one side with a boat trailer under it. Jack had parked his truck between the carport and the house and was using a side door. Easy access to the kitchen, I figured. The front door of the house, an alpine cottage monstrosity, opened to the main road, the dirt road that I'd just run down.

If Abraham Benson was in the house, he would have driven his own truck, I guessed. Which meant I'd have to return to my perch and wait for him. But in the meantime, I could take care of Jack the Menace, as Trip had called him. He'd surely been a menace in my life.

I stood and checked my pistol.

But what about Patrick?

What if he came with his dad? Surely, Abraham wouldn't bring him. The boy seemed so innocent. He wouldn't know anything about any of this. He's treated me with kindness and compassion, nothing like what Jack, probably under orders from his boss, had shown.

My thoughts were taking me in circles, dulling my sense of danger and my awareness of the sounds of the woods. So, I didn't turn around at the approach of my attacker. And I most certainly didn't feel the ground when I fell out cold.

chapter 26

buster Conley, who'd graduated a year before Catty, and his Uncle Royce had come in the ambulance, only to try vainly to revive Miss Lucretia. They pronounced her dead. Catty had told them that before they entered the house, but they had a job to do, she figured. All the same, she had stayed on the porch, sitting in the glider, holding Miss Gladys's hand, and listening to the passing cars and the scrape of metal on metal as the glider moved back and forth.

Life goes on, Catty reasoned, one way or another. She stood, thanked the men for their efforts, and signed some forms without really looking at them. As she watched them leave, glancing at the handful of neighborhood folks gawking by the roadside, she found herself wondering how many people had gathered when her father died. Who had signed the forms for his mangled body?

She would need to make a few calls to arrange things for the funeral and burial, and she wanted to be alone. She knew what to do, having helped her grandmother just over a year earlier make arrangements for her father. "I can handle it from here, Miss Gladys. Thank you for coming. You can go home now."

"Stop talking crazy, Catty girl. You go lay down. I can handle everything." Miss Gladys patted her back as they walked into the house. Catty lowered her head.

"Thank you."

She closed her bedroom door behind her and sank to the rag rug she'd made in Home Ec, longing for comforting words and the strength of two arms around her. She couldn't remember all that her grandmother had told her. It was too much.

Her thoughts drifted to Isaac. She closed her eyes and forced herself to think of heaven. In a loose expression of the ache she felt in her heart, she talked to God and fell asleep.

Movement on the porch woke her.

"Catty—" Trip called. "Oh, hello, Miss G." Catty heard him drop something heavy on the floor outside her door.

"Afternoon, Mr. Trip," said Miss Gladys, heaviness in her voice.

"What's the matter? Where's Catty? Miss Luc?"

He walked toward the back of the house. "Have you seen Isaac?" His voice, much louder than Miss Gladys's, carried throughout the house.

Catty stretched and stood, straining to hear the conversation in the kitchen, but only hearing Trip's response.

"No! How? Oh, my God. Where's Catty? How's she taking it?"

She heard his footsteps approaching at a trot. Her bedroom door flung open, filled with Trip Robertson, his minister face intact.

"Oh, Catty girl. I'm so sorry," he cooed in his minister voice and wrapped his arms around her, pressing his scratchy cheek against hers and letting their tears mingle. She didn't mind one bit.

"Take the Top Lake Road," Abraham had told Trip. "Look for a white handkerchief tied to a tree. He's lying about twenty paces from that tree into the woods near a log. Come quick, I don't know how BJ's gonna react if he sees him."

Trip had never been to the Benson lake house, and in his haste had assumed that since it was easy to see from shore, then it was easy to find in a car. It was getting dark and he hadn't found the house. Panicked and lost, he pounded the steering wheel as he stood idling at a crossroads. He should have confirmed things with Catty before he left. Or Miss Luc.

He pounded the steering wheel again at his slip of memory. Including Miss Lucretia Price in his life was a habit he would find hard to break. They were like night and day, he thought, but he had loved her dearly. He wept, remembering what Catty told him concerning Miss Luc's last words about him.

"I love him like my own son."

"I loved you too, Miss Luc." He sighed and wiped his face on the back of his hand. "Which way, Lord? Which way would Miss Luc have gone?"

She would have known all these crooked curvy roads, he figured, like the back of her wrinkly hand. She probably would have followed the breeze coming off the lake.

He put Lamont's car in park and got out. It was going to be a moon-poor night, just a sliver smiling above the darkening treetops, not enough to help him find a man lying in the woods. He studied the road to the left, then the one to the right, and prayed more for Isaac than for his own direction. In his mind, the spirit of man or the spirit of godliness would triumph tonight. For Isaac's sake, he prayed that the spirit of man was weak in Isaac Hunt tonight.

A loud noise split the darkness to the east. Gunshot or backfire? Trip tossed his body into the car and raced eastward.

~~

Birds circled overhead. Not like buzzards in a desert or bluebirds that danced around Wile E. Coyote's head but white graceful birds. I was lying on my back watching the birds and enjoying the sun on my body. Was I naked? The birds turned into flowers—floating white flowers with long graceful petals dipping from above, caressing me.

Then there was a tall tree with one limb, and one single white flower hanging from the limb. I found myself trying to calculate the tensional force on the limb. It was frustrating because I had to make too many assumptions and there weren't enough equations.

Someone was calling my name. A woman. Was the test over already?

I pulled my eyes open to look for the woman and realized I had been dreaming. And by the way my head was hurting, I wished that the dream had never ended.

Damp and stiff, I pushed myself up, propping an elbow on the log, and felt around in the darkness for my gun. I found it tucked under the log. Surely it hadn't fallen there by accident. Maybe I had kicked it in my fall. Doubtful, but surely my attacker wouldn't have put it there. What kind of crazy nut was he? Of course "he" could have been a she. Bottom line, though, was who would want to knock me out and run away, leaving me armed and unbound?

I sat up, glancing at the lake house while I checked for the magazine. Still loaded. Of course it was still loaded.

No other vehicles were in sight. The pedestal lamppost on the far side of the garage was the only light. I crept down to the dirt road and checked my watch. I'd been out more than seven hours. A lot could have happened in seven hours. A person can set up a very elaborate trap in seven hours. A handkerchief was tied to a tree limb near where I'd just taken a seven-hour nap. Was that part of the trap? A marker for an accomplice to find me? I decided not to wait and find out.

From where I now stood, just across the road from the front door, I could hear yelling coming from the front of the house, I judged. With half my face tucked inside my shirt, I slipped across the road, ducking beside the far side of Jack's truck.

I could hear the voices better now.

"You've lost your mind, BJ!" yelled a man with a mild drawl.

"Shut up and turn around," hollered another man, his accent thicker. "'Fore you end up like those two."

BJ—at least, I guessed one was Ben Jacob Benson. Who was the other man? I inched to the front of the truck and eased my head out like a turtle. A wide stone path ran from the carport to the kitchen with a smaller path joining it from the back of the house.

"I'm not that stupid."

"Ain't you? I'm 'bout to sell Benson Ridge right out from under you."

"I spoke with Lucci. Your so-called deal is off. Ben Jacob, put down the rifle."

Great, he has a gun. Paranoid, I checked my Glock again. *Still loaded.*

"Shut up and turn around, Abe."

Good, the other man was Abraham Benson. And hopefully there was no one, a seven-year-old boy for instance, cowering in the corner. I tiptoed to the back corner of the house and pressed my back against the shingled wall.

"Give up this craziness, BJ. If you kill me, you won't get far. Trip Robertson is on his way. Isaac Hunt is somewhere out there in the woods with a gun."

BJ snorted. There was the tumble of what sounded like wooden poles falling. I took a step closer, trying to hear.

"When are you going to finish this deck, Abe?"

"Never mind the deck. What did you mean—"

"That night I came to your house during the storm?" He

274

laughed again. "I was talkin' nonsense. I didn't sleep with your precious Betty, Abe. That was someone else's doing, if you know what I mean." He chuckled.

If BJ wasn't my father, surely it wasn't the man with the johnboat. A taste like battery acid rose in my mouth. There was no way out now.

"And the fire?"

"Well, I did tell the truth 'bout that one. It was an accident that she died, though. I didn't mean for her to die. She deserved it though, being so pigheaded."

That was enough proof for me. I rushed forward.

"Shut up, BJ," Abraham yelled.

I could hear the rapid scrape of heavy boots on wood.

"Look now, I'm tired of you telling me what to do. You turn around. Stop right there! Don't come no closer or I'll—"

The shot made me jump a foot off the ground. There was a pause or maybe just me holding my breath. Then . . . the noise of a large somebody almost falling. Next, someone shuffling to stay upright, but failing. Finally, muffled moaning.

Someone was running, Ben Jacob I guessed, over wood decking. I heard the tentative rumble of an outboard motor. It sputtered and stopped.

The stepping-stones along the back of the house were uneven, and I stumbled as I ran, banging my elbow and knuckles a couple of times. I was crazy to be running with a loaded gun, but sense was taking a backseat to logic. My mother's killer was trying to get away. But there was the Benson on the deck to contend with first.

As I neared the corner I could see a deck lit with a single floodlight, nose-high, with no railing. The wood was bright new; several pieces of railing were stacked farther out in the yard. A large pair of boots, sole-first, stared me in the face. I was about to push them aside and throw my leg onto the deck when I realized they were attached to a body that had moved. I eased back and listened to the big man pull himself upright.

He staggered, clutching his side, along the boardwalk and toward the end of the pier. My eyes followed the foot lighting to the end of the pier. I could see BJ kicking the motor of the johnboat. I pushed my gun onto the deck and started to pull my upper body. I froze. This time at the sight of two white men, naked, bloody, and suspended by their hands from a tree limb that arched the deck.

The two Benson men at the end of the pier were fighting, in and out of the water. The rifle that had been fired earlier was nowhere in sight.

Unnoticed, I pulled myself onto the deck and scrambled to the first man, a round man with several unlit cigars stuffed in his mouth. He was dead. His face had been lashed, maybe with the knife at his feet. I recognized him as the man with the johnboat earlier in the day.

This was no way for a man—white or black—to spend his last moments. I used the knife to cut the rope. His dead weight fell over my left arm. I eased him to the ground, staring at the pile of humanity as the other body bounced like a morbid yo-yo on the branch overhead.

Why?

What had he done to deserve this death? What kind of man could do this to another?

I picked up my pistol again, ready to rush and shoot the

fighting men at the end of the pier. A moan coming from the other man, bloodier than the first and far skinnier, stopped me. At least he was still alive.

I pushed the gun into my waistband and used the knife again to cut him down. His blood-matted hair fell over my shoulder when his hands were free. I eased him down against the wall of the house and sat back on my heels.

He was trying to open his eyes, mumbling something I couldn't make out.

"It's okay. Don't talk."

I looked toward a half-open door a few feet away. Maybe I should call 911, I thought. The fight was still raging behind us, in and out of the boat. My guts were churning with adrenaline.

The man mumbled again.

I stood and made motions for the door. "Shh—"

But he continued with what sounded like, "Your name?"

"What?"

His eyes fluttered and opened. Through bloody lips he said, "What's your name?"

I stumbled back in shock. "Jack!"

The man I'd just cut down was the man who'd been trying to do me in. He'd been hunting me like a dog, and he didn't even know my name. I pulled the Glock from my waistband and stepped toward him, aiming at his head.

"My name is Isaac Hunt."

chapter 27

when my only pet, a wire fox terrier
named Mr. Happy, was run over, I was playing in the All
Conference Tennis Final. I had lost, with nothing to show for
my efforts but a tan. I came home to Chloe Hunt crying on
her antique French davenport, went into the shed and got
the shovel, scooped up Mr. Happy's guts and dumped them
in the trash.

Contrary to what Chloe thought, I was close to the dog. I
missed him. A few days later when the dump truck came I
did wish I'd put him in a hole in the backyard. But it was too
late. He was a good dog, faithful as all dogs are I suppose. He

knew things about me nobody else knew. Not even Tate. But he was just a dog and there was no sense crying over him.

Jack Kepler, on the other hand, was beneath canine on my scale. I would have no second thoughts for him. People would say I had executed him, one shot in the head with his hands tied behind his back. His big eyes watered when I pressed the muzzle to his head. I didn't care what people would say.

"My name is Isaac Hunt," I repeated.

"Isaac!" someone screamed in my right ear and grabbed my right hand.

I turned. "Trip!" I elbowed him.

He was breathing like he'd just run all the way from town. "Isaac, He chose you."

"Huh?"

"He chose you, Isaac. God chose you."

"Trip, please. No more—"

"How could you just throw it all away, like this? He's been pursuing you. 'Come unto Me all you who are weary and heavy laden and I will give you rest.' Shooting Jack won't lighten your load, Isaac. You think it will solve things. Make things even? It won't."

He pressed his hot forehead against my ear and hissed, "You don't know how many times I've wanted to put a bullet in that head too. The woman I want to marry almost gave birth to his child. Killing him won't make things even."

"He owes me."

"Owes you?" he mocked. "You owe God more. If we're talking 'bout giving people what they deserve, then God could put a million bullets in your skull and you'd still come up owing Him." His voice cooled a bit. "It's not about anybody owing. It's about you answering Him—choosing freedom, forgiveness. Choosing Him, and turning away from the way you were so you don't have to get a single bullet for all the mess you done in your life. Freedom. Put the gun down, Isaac."

I watched the blubbering face of Jack Kepler. He owed me. "It's not that easy."

"No, it's not easy. Forgiveness is never easy. It's like saying, you should get a bullet in the head but I won't do it 'cause you don't owe me nothing. Letting it go and never bringing it up again, that's not within a man's power, Isaac. It's in God's power through His Son, Jesus. You know that power don't you, Isaac? The power that can fill a room and answer all your questions with one word."

"Oh, God," Jack moaned.

I knew that power. But . . .

"Stop, shut up."

"That power can direct your choice right now. It can help you stick to it, never regretting it."

"Shut up!"

He backed away from me and shook his arms over his head Rocky-style. "To hold a man's life in your hand, with the power to end it, and giving it back to him instead. That's forgiveness, Isaac. God offers that to you. Will you take it?"

"Trip! Shut up!" I turned the gun on him.

He extended his arms, palms up, like the picture of Jesus I'd seen over Margaret Hunt's piano in Richmond. "Will you take it, Isaac?" He stepped toward me. I always hated to see that picture of Jesus—those empty white hands reaching toward me, offering me what? Nothing? When she died I was happy when Ulysses took it down.

But when Trip stepped toward me with his arms out, offering me . . . What was he offering me? Jesus? How could he offer me the Man who had come to me at the migrant camp like he was Jesus' agent or something? I still wasn't sure what to make of the power or the Man who had brought it but one thing I knew, Jesus was a free agent.

"He loves you."

"Oh, God," Jack again groaned.

How could Jesus love me? I was planning to kill at least three men tonight. I stared at the weapon hanging from my tired fingers. Trip cried. Jack wept behind me.

"He loves you," Trip repeated. He stepped closer, slipping the gun from my hand. "Both of you. Freedom."

"I'm sorry," Jack wailed. "Oh, God, I'm sorry. Isaac, I'm sorry. Preacher, I'm sorry. I'm so sorry."

I faced Jack. He was lying on his side, sobs racking his body. Sorry?

He continued wailing. "I'm sorry for what I done to Frieda. I'm sorry. I'm sorry. Oh, God, I'm so sorry. How could He forgive me, Preacher. How? You're crazy. He's crazy if He'd let me into heaven. I deserve to go to hell. Shoot me! Please, shoot me." He looked at me like I had the key to his success. "Please."

I stooped by his head, suddenly realizing what Trip was trying to tell me. I placed a hand on Jack's head and looked down on the white man who had pursued me like an escaped slave.

"No," I said. "You're free. I forgive you."

You're free.

At that moment I realized how I could be free as well. Free and forgiven.

⸺

I squatted there on my heels, with Trip sniffling at my back and Jack blubbering on the ground. What had been happening to me? I figured that Jack, a white man who had pursued and tormented me, had done so out of fear and hatred. Hadn't I been operating under the same MO? We were both guilty, regardless of the crime. Justice called for both our deaths. Why were we still alive? Why had the One who could take our lives given it back instead? What kind of God would give a man like me this indescribable thing that filled my entire being and compel me to forgive? It didn't seem logical but it felt right. Was I still sane?

Then, like a breeze hovering over me, I could feel Him again. *No. Not here. Not now.* No more crying. I wasn't ready for this, for Him. But maybe . . . *Yes. Yes, God.*

I was at a loss for words and feeling. I suppose we were all lost in our own thoughts and prayers, of sorts, so we didn't hear the approach of Ben Jacob. But at the sound of him cocking his rifle, we were all very much alert.

"All right now, up against the wall," he ordered, shoving Trip toward the house while he eyed me. "That was right touching, fellas. All the God and Jesus stuff. Didn't know whether to cry or throw up. Glad you finally put that pistol down, though. Didn't want to have to shoot you in the back." He let out a laugh that evaporated as quickly as it came. His face, disturbing with cheekbones shaped like my own, settled into a scowl like he smelled something bad. He kicked my gun off the end of the deck and stepped toward me. BJ Benson wasn't a big man, a few inches taller than me, but not overly bulky. He carried his upper body like a child pretending to be big. And I thought the ponytail ruined his effort at machismo or maturity.

"Isaac Hunt," he growled. He stood in front of me, the muzzle of the rifle inches from my stomach. "Good to finally meet you. 'Course worthless Jack here's been feeding me info but it's nice to finally see you face-to-face. I believe you have something that belongs to me. A certain ring." He smelled of whiskey and cigarette smoke.

My stomach sank as my index finger went to my thumb. The ring was gone. Had my attacker taken it? Probably so, which meant that the murderer standing in front of me had not clubbed me earlier. A small consolation.

"I don't have a ring." I fought the urge to shake off the mosquito extracting a pint from my wrist and held out my hands, palms down.

He glanced at my hands and then back up to my face, eyes narrowed. "What'd you do with it?"

"I don't know what—"

He let go of the rifle for a second and slapped me, back-handed. "Where is it?"

I clenched my teeth against the sting and glanced at Trip, a few inches to my left, wondering if I got BJ to slap me again if Trip would have the guts to grab the rifle. I looked into the enraged colorless eyes in front of me, racking my brain for words of greatest hate.

Trip spoke up. "Why do you want it?"

"None of your business, Preacher."

"Let 'em go, BJ," came Jack's weak voice from the ground.

"And why would I do that?"

"They don't know nothing. You don't know that Isaac really had one of the Benson rings to begin with."

"Shut your trap, boy."

BJ turned his attention back to me. "Now, what'd you do with it?"

I studied my trembling pants legs and braced for another slap.

"I'm a reasonable man. Most and gen'ly. But tonight, it's different . . ." He raised his hand to slap me again.

"BJ," Jack tried again, "if you don't let them go, I'll tell them why you want the ring."

BJ's hands snapped back to the rifle and brought the butt down across Jack's ear. "If you won't hard of hearing before, you is now. Shut your mouth or I'll do it for you."

While he hovered over Jack, who had fresh blood flowing across his face, I glanced around for the knife. Where had I left it? He spat on Jack's face and looked at me.

"See I don't even care for my own kind. Just think how much I care for you, black boy." He swiveled closer and continued. "You might pass as white in some circle in Raleigh, but you still black to me. All it takes is one drop. One drop."

The knife?

I had cut Jack down and set it down beside him. Then Jack had scooted back across the floor to the wall. It had to be under him.

BJ had backed up and was keeping an eye on us while he

glanced in the direction of the boat from time to time. Out of the corner of my eye, I watched Jack. Had he planned to use the knife on me as I held the pistol to his head? Was he planning now to use it on BJ? Jack looked up to me.

"The knife?" I mouthed when BJ's eyes were on the boat.

Jack nodded toward his bound hands and then from me to BJ as if to say, "Distract him." Bound and beaten, he was a madman to think he could attack an armed man. But what did we have to lose?

I cleared my throat and spoke up. "That one drop that I have in my veins makes me better than you, BJ."

He marched toward me, threatening to strike again. Out of the corner of my eye, I hoped I saw Trip lean forward, ready to strike BJ.

I continued, almost sticking my jaw out so he wouldn't miss. "And that's what you're afraid of isn't it. The truth about black folks. We're stronger than you. And even that one drop of black blood in me, makes me better."

"Shut up, boy." He raised his rifle.

"At State, I worked on the NASA Mars Project Team that designed the landing gear for the Mars Module. I graduated summa cum laude. I'm better than—"

He lined up the sight. "I said, shut up."

Come on, Jack.

I saw BJ's finger moving the trigger. I closed my eyes and held my breath. Trip yelled and pushed me to the right. I felt Jack's body against my left leg. A shot rang out. I heard BJ fall.

A shot?

Like a fool, I stood there feeling for bullet holes on my

face and chest while I stared through blurry eyes at the body twitching in a pool of blood at my feet.

"Hey, Trip," came a familiar husky voice from the dark corner I'd climbed up from earlier in the evening. "Y'all okay?"

He stood head and shoulders above the edge of the deck no more than fifteen feet away, but I could barely make out his features. I didn't need to.

"Yeah, we're doing fine, Abraham," Trip offered as he walked toward the voice. "You don't look too good."

There was a groan and the snap of tree limbs.

"You've been shot!" Trip said. He jumped off the edge of the deck. "And you're soaking wet." I watched his shadowy form struggle with the large man sprawled across the bushes. "Isaac!" He shouted back over his shoulder like I should've read his mind.

In truth, I was scared. Not of what the big white man could do to me, but of who he was. In my mind, I knew what he looked like. Like an age-stiffened switch, that voice had turned on something in my brain. I remembered a burning house. I remembered my mother's scream. I remembered I knew this man—the man who had pulled me to safety, the man who scared me to death.

chapter 28

i could do nothing but sit there. Sit there and try to make sense of this crazy day while I pressed an old hand towel against the hole in the shoulder of a man who'd been on my list of people to kill today. Sit there and piece together the bits of eighteen-year-old memories that were drifting back to me because of this man. Sit there and try not to think about who he might be.

His eyes were closed now. In fact, I hadn't seen them open since I had helped Trip pull him from the bushes and spread him out on the kitchen floor.

From where I sat on the kitchen floor I could see half the

living room. The farthest wall of the living room was all glass, floor to ceiling windows except for a sliding door. There were no curtains on the rods so there was no missing the burlap-covered lump that was the body of the other man I had meant to kill today.

And then, huddled in a half-naked ball on the flagstone hearth in the living room, was number three on my list. Jack Kepler. Pitiful and trembling, he had reluctantly allowed Trip to clean and bandage him a little before retreating to the cold fireplace. He glanced over his shoulder toward the kitchen and pulled into a tighter ball when he saw me, his arms folded tight.

I could hear Trip's voice on the phone in a bedroom down the hall. Most of the words came to me like whispers in the wind, but I could tell he was all business now. None of that hee-haw local-yokel talk he used with me. I pulled out the words "gun" and "kidnap." I heard my name as well as that of Abraham Benson.

Abraham moaned and shifted a little under my hand.

"Who are you?" I asked the big man spread out beside me.

Floorboards creaked behind me. I turned to see Trip.

"The ambulance and the police are on their way." He stood there looking at me. "You know who he is. Just as sure as you know his name. And your name."

"But—" The fear was there again. I couldn't explain it.

"But?"

"But there was another man. I remember, or at least I think I remember him coming around at Christmas to give me and my mother fruit and candy. He gave her a yellow dress that she kept under the mattress of her bed. His name was . . . Frank?"

I strained to see his face in my mind. He had the Benson face—the set of the eye, the line of the nose—just like my own face.

Trip shook his head. "There's no Frank Benson. There's a Fred, though. Lives in town and calls himself a candidate. But he's not your father no more than he is a politician, Isaac. That man on the floor is your father. And you know it." He rummaged through the cabinets. "I need some coffee."

He pulled a jar from a cabinet and examined its brown contents. "From what Miss Luc told me, people used to think Fred was your daddy for years. Maybe he thought so too. Maybe that's why he was so nice. I don't know. But after your mother was killed, he sort of slunk back to his hole and never showed another black person any kindness ever again.

"I'm not saying this man bleeding here on the kitchen floor is candidate for head choirboy or nothing, but he was real. Always been real. From what I can tell, he's tried to be the same man to everybody. Now if you remember him being so hateful and ornery that no boy in his right mind would pick him for a daddy, then you can bet your last buffalo nickel that he was hateful and ornery to every little boy. Illegitimate offspring or not. Nothing personal. I need coffee."

He ran water into a pan and rinsed out three cups. He was getting on my nerves. The last thing I wanted was coffee he made.

"Where's Jack? Jack, where are you, man? We need to make a toast. Jack, come in here."

A toast?

"Isaac," Trip continued from the living room. "Where's your gun?"

"My gun?" I'd lost track of it.

"I found it." Trip had returned, pulling Jack along by the wrist and looking down the barrel of my Glock. "Have a seat, Jack." Trip pulled out one of the four chairs around the small wooden table across the room. "Have you fired your gun, Isaac?"

I shook my head.

"I don't want to sit in here."

"And I don't want to hear it." Trip smiled and pressed Jack into the chair. The little plastic flower arrangement in the center of the table toppled over. "There. Comfy? I don't know why but in spite of all the mess that's happened today, I feel hopeful. And you want to know why?"

He passed me the gun. I took it and placed it on the floor beside Abraham. Trip smiled wide and spread his hands out, palms up. Jack kept his chin tucked into his chest and plucked at the plastic flowers on the table. "You two. My two new brothers. So, we make a toast."

"A toast?" I asked.

"Yes. When a little bitty baby is born into this mess of a world, people celebrate. Pass out cigars, send gifts. The whole nine. You two have been given a new life, a new start. Like little babies. So, we celebrate that. It is a gift from God. A second chance. Freedom." He measured instant coffee and sugar into the cups lined up on the counter. "Oops. You two take sugar, I hope. I like it sweet myself. Cheer up, fellas. Look, the way I see it, we're family. And each of us brings something the other needs to the family. That's part of God's plan. Just like it's no accident that your parents are who they are, Isaac. Betty and Abraham. Ricky and Chloe." Trip stopped short, his sweeter-than-Saccharin grin melting into a frown. "Isaac, what have you done with the gun that quick?"

"The gun? What's with all this talk about my gun?"

"Well, perhaps Jack can enlighten us about the necessity for the gun."

Jack's eyes darted to Trip and back to the tabletop.

My thoughts went to the sadness in his eyes earlier and the relief at the thought of having a bullet in his head. "Were you going to shoot yourself?"

Jack continued to stare at the table.

"Nope," Trip volunteered. "Not even close. Tell us about the others, Jack. How many others were coming tonight."

Jack shot Trip another glance. "Just one other that I know of," he mumbled into his chest.

"No, Isaac. Jack wasn't going to kill himself. At least not with your gun. He was going to use your gun to defend us against this man. Someone Ben Jacob invited. What's his name?"

"Highsmith, I think."

"We appreciate your willingness to put your neck on the line for us, Jack, but chances are there's more coming than this Highsmith. I have half a mind to leave. If only Abraham—"

His face drawn, Trip turned his attention once again to the cups. He gave each a stir and placed one cup in front of Jack and one beside me. Then he leaned against the counter, silently blowing across the top of his cup and staring at the opposite wall.

I didn't like this sudden turn to silence. His monologue was beginning to wear on me a bit, but it was a might more comforting than the thought of actually having to use my gun on someone.

"What about this toast, Trip?"

"What was that, Isaac? Oh, yeah. The toast." He cleared his throat and stepped to the center of the small kitchen. "To family. To forgiveness. To freedom." He lifted his cup, a small smile pulled across his face as he looked to the ceiling. "To kings and priests."

I frowned up at him.

" 'To him who loves us and has freed us from our sins by His blood, and has made us to be a kingdom and priests to serve His God and Father—to Him be glory and power forever and ever! Amen.' "

We each stared into our cups. In the silence I could feel Him again. My heart quickened at the notion that He would touch me again. Part of me was afraid of it—that it might make me cry like a baby as I had before. Part of me yearned for more of it like a drug. I closed my eyes.

And then He said my name. "Isaac."

I caught my breath and opened my eyes. Trip smiled down on me. Had I answered God out loud? The wail of sirens ended the moment.

"The cavalry has arrived," Trip said, rushing for the kitchen door. He pushed the door wide and placed one foot on the first step.

"Preacher."

With one foot outside and one inside, Trip turned toward Jack. "Yeah."

"They're gonna take me away. The cops. As soon as they get in here. I might never see you again, so I gotta ask you this right now."

Trip stepped back into the kitchen. He lowered his long chin and lost the accent. "Yes?"

"Just how does this forgiveness thing work? Do I need to ask God to forgive me for every single thing I done? Like one by one?"

Trip nodded. Doors were slamming outside. I could hear people running across gravel outside.

"If you know it was bad, confess it to God and He will forgive you."

Jack stood up and started talking faster. "And how 'bout the folk I done the bad stuff against? Do I need to ask their forgiveness too?"

Trip nodded, words forming on his lips.

"Well, what if I cain't get to that person?"

There was commotion all around—the sound of a helicopter far off, people running along the deck, searchlights from outside flashing through the living room.

Jack explained. "Well, that's kinda what I thought but 'til I can get 'round to see her, maybe you could get word to her, that I'm sorry and all for hitting her so hard."

Two men in blue-gray shirts brushed past Trip and made a beeline for Abraham. A policeman followed and took a strategic spot along the wall while he eyed Jack and Trip.

"Who, Jack?"

"That old lady you stay with."

Trip lunged for Jack. "Miss Luc! You hit her."

"You did what?!" I just about jumped over the EMTs working on Abraham.

The policeman, a well-built man a little shorter than myself, reached for Trip. "Sir, control yourself."

"You don't understand, officer. The woman he's talking about is dead."

"Dead? But she was still alive when I left. She was praying. Honest."

I stood there, mouth open.

"I'm telling you, Preacher. She was breathing when I left. I didn't kill nobody," he told the police officer. "There's a lot you can take me to jail for but murder ain't one of them. I didn't kill her, Preacher. You gotta believe me. I'm sorry for hitting her."

Dead. Tears welled in my eyes. I thought of Catty. Poor Catty. I wanted to be with her. *Dead.* I wanted to hit Jack. I moved closer toward him.

"I'm sorry. I really am."

"Sir, calm down."

"How many times do I have to ask you, Preacher?"

Trip shook his head. He threw up his hands. I could barely hear his answer. "Only once. I forgive you."

I pushed forward ready to strike. "What!"

The light scent of flowers surrounded me. "Excuse me, sir," came a female voice from behind. There was a light touch to the small of my back. I turned and looked down into a nut-brown face of a medium-sized woman with blue eyes and a big gold badge pinned to the lapel of her light brown pantsuit. The letters FBI stood out. "May I?" she made a motion with her hands like someone parting clothes on a rack. I stepped aside.

"Evening, Trip."

"Not a happy scene, Charise," Trip said.

"Never is when I show up. Could give a girl a complex."

The FBI agent paused to glance at me and then at the man on the gurney. She cleared her throat. "Special Agent Charise Blue."

"Isaac Hunt. But of course, you probably knew that."

She flashed a wide-eyed grin at me and turned to Jack. "And you are Jack Kepler. We would like to speak with you at length. Officer—" She leaned forward to read the officer's badge. "Officer Brown. How 'bout that. Brown and Blue. Good thing it wasn't black. Black and Blue. But we won't go there, will we? Officer, can you see Mr. Kepler to your car?"

Officer Brown nodded. He began cuffing Jack's hands behind his back.

Jack screamed and wrenched free. "Not until he says it."

The agent rolled her eyes and finished the failed cuffing job with a quickness that surprised me. "Who says what?"

"Isaac," Jack said. All eyes turned to me. Even the EMTs, poised for exit with Abraham on the gurney, were looking at me.

"Tell me you forgive me."

"What is this, Burger King? Have it your way, today. I don't think it works that way. You can't order me around."

"Isaac," Trip interrupted.

"Stop. I don't want to hear it. She's dead. She was old. Old people are weak. He hit her. He might as well have beat the life out of her. He killed her, Trip. Simple as that."

"Isaac," Trip and Jack said at the same time. Trip with his hand on my shoulder; Jack kneeling at my feet.

"Look at me," Jack said. "I ain't nobody special. I ain't trying to order you around. I'm just trying to do things right. Trying to do things different than the way I used to. Like the Preacher said. A new life. New start. Please, I'm begging you. Forgive me."

"Isaac," Abraham spoke from behind me.

I froze. Trip squeezed my shoulder. He smiled. I didn't.

"Isaac."

I held my breath and turned around. Abraham's clear blue eyes met mine without flinching. A smile creased the edges. He cleared his throat.

"It's the right thing to do, son."

I melted. Lost in the warmth of his eyes.

Before I knew what had come over me I had turned back around and told Jack I forgave him.

The EMTs took my father away. The policeman took Jack away. Trip and Agent Blue wandered to the living room where other agents and police were meandering about with fingerprint powder and cameras.

Desperate for quiet, I sought out the bathroom. I locked myself in it. The hard cool rim of the bathtub was less than comfortable, but I didn't feel like being picky. And I didn't feel like being bothered.

I sat there for several minutes with the side of the pink bathtub against my back, thinking—or more like trying to think.

What had started all this death? Had it all started with my birth? With my existence? "Illegitimate offspring," Trip had called me. My mother dead. Miss Lucretia dead. Ben Jacob Benson dead. Who else was dead? My mind went to Ricky and Chloe. Were they? I found myself hoping that they weren't. What if . . . ?

I shook my head at the mere thought. No!

There was a knock at the door. A light knock. So light that at first I thought it was just someone moving something around in the kitchen. But then the knob rattled.

I struggled to get up, stiff from the floor.

"Yeah, wait a minute," I said.

"Isaac, is that you in there?" a man said from the other side of the door. I stopped short, my fingers inches from the knob. For the second time in one night, I heard a voice from my past. A voice from a man I was sure I would love forever, a man who had died months ago.

I opened the door and stepped back.

"Hello, Granddaddy."

i don't like games. Especially those that called for pretending I was somebody else. What was the point of it?

It was just that thing, the pointlessness of it all, that I considered as I looked across that threshold at an anything-but-dead Ulysses Hunt.

"Why?" I said. Other words were churning inside me. Hateful words. Words that would hurt him like he'd hurt me. But all I could manage was "why."

He just stood there, his hands out to me, looking too much like his son Ricky. I didn't need Ricky and I didn't need him.

I pushed past him. He touched my arm. I pulled away.

"You lied to me. 'A lie is a lie is a lie. No matter how pretty you tell it or how long you live it, it's still a lie and in the end when it's brought to light, it brings misery.' Do you remember that little bit of wisdom? You knew about my mother all along."

"Yes, I knew. And about Abraham as well." He let his head drop. I turned away from him. Half a dozen people stared back at me from the kitchen. Trip and the FBI agent were among them. I wondered how long they'd been watching us.

The old man behind me continued to talk. "Yes, I lied. I've been lying most of my adult life, Isaac. And I'm tired of it. It's my job. Isn't that right, Charise?" He chuckled a little and shrugged.

I couldn't stand to look at him anymore. I studied the green shag under my feet.

"I lied about my illness. I faked my death. But I haven't lied about everything. I do work for the government." He lowered his voice and stepped toward me. "And I do love you."

I walked away from him. "When can I leave, Trip? I'd like to see Catty."

Trip shook his head.

"Isaac," Ulysses called after me. "You can't go."

"What do you mean?"

"Your life's in danger."

"Look, I don't want to play this game anymore. I want to leave."

"Your mother took a risk when she started working with us."

302

"What are you talking about?"

"It was a big gamble. But she had guts. She did it to save your life. After she was killed I vowed that I would do whatever it took to keep you alive."

I couldn't believe my ears. Here was the man formerly known as my grandfather looking and talking like the man from U.N.C.L.E. I turned to Trip again.

"Listen to him."

"Who are you?" I asked him.

"I'm Trip, Isaac. No spy stuff. Rupert Robertson Jr. Migrant worker. Preacher man. I just happened to stumble onto a few choice bits of intel, shall we say, about the Bensons. Everything's gonna be okay. Listen to him. Let's just go into the living room and—"

Agent Blue and her cronies started walking toward the living room. Ulysses touched me from behind.

I pulled away from him, shaking my head. I had to get away. Where was my gun? I scanned the kitchen table and countertops as I walked toward Trip. "Who else is in on this craziness, Trip? Who else is working for them?"

"Isaac, take it easy." He reached out and grabbed my arms. "Take it easy, man. I'm not working for them. No more than Miss Luc was or Catty or Miguel."

"Catty?"

"I wouldn't be surprised if she or Miguel knows some of the same stuff I do. The thing is I figured I had the least to lose. I went to Abraham, that's when I found out about the information he had been sitting on, eating at him. He pointed me to Ulysses here."

Ulysses was standing beside me now. For a brief second

he looked at me like he used to. I half expected him to pull some chocolate kisses from his pocket and slip them into my hand. But that was what he would do if we were in Richmond. But we weren't in Richmond anymore. Nothing and nobody was familiar.

"Isaac, man, Ulysses was right. Your mother was plenty gutsy. She was coming against the Bensons at the height of their power. She did it for you."

Agent Blue was back in the kitchen again. She was leaning over the table, spreading several manila folders out. "Come and see for yourself, Mr. Hunt."

I could see the corner of my mother's photo peeking out from one of the folders. And next to it was a folder with Ricky and Chloe's names. I should have known they were involved too. Liars from day one. I stayed where I was.

Trip continued. "She didn't want you to get hurt or killed. The man who started the fire that killed her is gone. But there are a lot of other crazies out there. Filling the emptiness in their hearts with hate. Just like Jack had. 'Cept some of these men know what they're doing. Men like Mitchell Highsmith, the man Jack said Ben Jacob was waiting for."

Agent Blue interrupted. "Ah, Mitchell Highsmith. That's his real name. He also goes by Michael Schmidt—" She flipped open a file.

"And Mick Smith," Ulysses interjected.

My mouth dropped open.

"He has two wives to whom he is currently married and three children by at least two women in as many states. But we don't want him for bigamy or for being a Class A deadbeat dad. We want him for a thirty-year-old murder of a young, black Chapel Hill man who was just trying to educate his community about biases in government." She tapped a thick stack. "With the information your father turns over to the Justice Department, we will be able to reopen that case. And as a little fringe benefit we'll be bringing down the infamous leader of the United Front."

I looked to Trip.

"Hate group," he whispered.

"Quite the understatement, Mr. Robertson. Highsmith was last seen in Richmond. At the old folks' home your grandfather was faking Alzheimer's in for a few months. This is the woman who we believe to be his current wife. You may have *seen* her there. This photo was taken over two years ago."

She held up a grainy 8"x10" photo. There was the man I knew as Mick Smith being kissed by the woman I knew as Rose. It was not the kind of kiss a daughter would give a father. He was anything but handicapped with his tennis outfit on, racquet in hand.

I felt sick.

I wondered just how much the Agency knew about me and Rose. What did they know about me and Eva? What did my granddaddy know? I pushed those thoughts aside.

"Why are you telling me all this?"

"So that we can better protect you."

"And so I can work for you."

She hesitated.

"Son," Ulysses interrupted, "some of us believe Highsmith wants to kidnap you. Hold you as long as it takes to squeeze every shred of evidence out of us."

"Wait a minute. You said he was last seen in Richmond at the rest home. That was months ago. You don't know where he is, do you?" I looked at the grimacing faces around me. "And I'm supposed to draw him out. I'm supposed to be some kind of bait in this crazy game of yours."

"Isaac—" Trip started.

"No."

"Son, it's too late to turn away. Some people are in too deep. Ricky. Chloe. Trip. Abraham."

Great, Ricky and Chloe again. My head pounded. I would have screamed if I thought it would have helped.

"People could get killed, son."

"Where's Patrick? And Catty?"

"They're okay," said Agent Blue.

"How do I know that?"

"You're right. Eric—my phone," she called out.

Eric, a thin pasty guy with square glasses, appeared. He handed the phone he was dialing to Agent Blue.

"Thanks," she said to him. "You're absolutely right, Mr. Hunt. I wouldn't trust a black woman with blue contacts either. Heaven knows what issues she's got."

She spoke into the phone. "Hello, Stevens. Blue here. May I have the pleasure of speaking to Prince Patrick?" She covered the phone and whispered, "Of course, I don't call him that to his face. Hello, Patrick. This is Miss Charise. How are you doing, darling? Great. I have someone here who's dying to talk to you. Oh, I'll give you one guess. His name starts with an 'I.'"

I could hear a squeal from the phone. Agent Blue held the phone back from her ear and shook her head. "Wow," she mouthed and handed me the phone.

"Hey, Patrick."

"Isaac. I knew it was you. Wow, where are you? Are you still in Pettigrew? Have you seen Daddy yet? Did you know I got a dog?"

I swallowed the lump in my throat and chuckled at his enthusiasm. "A new dog. That's great. Yes, I'm still in Pettigrew. And yes, I've seen your dad."

I wondered how much he knew about me.

"What are you doing up so late, Patrick?"

"It's not late. I just ate breakfast. Anyway, I'm not supposed to tell you where I am. I better go now. My tutor's coming. I miss you."

I'm not gonna cry. I clenched my teeth.

"I miss you too, buddy. Bye. Bye." I handed the phone back to Agent Blue.

"And now for Miss Catty. Eric, has she been relocated yet?"

Eric shook his head. "A little bit of a stubborn streak in that girl. Apparently, her grandmother just passed away. We've got the house guarded in the meantime."

I turned away. No tears.

Blue started dialing. I held up my hand to stop her.

My voice came out small. "I believe you."

"Good." She shuffled her files together and handed them to Eric. "Whew, two a.m. I don't know about y'all but it's way past my bedtime." She faked a yawn and gave her people several orders before turning back to me. "Get some sleep, Isaac. We've got a busy day ahead of us."

Mitchell Highsmith put down the *News and Observer* and stretched his arms wide. He allowed himself a wide yawn—his young proper-mannered wife having stayed back at the hotel—and turned on his laptop.

He would sit and write on his computer until the call from Pettigrew came in. The newspaper said one thing, but he needed firsthand news from his men there. People had faked their deaths before. One couldn't be too sure.

The waiter came and he placed his order for breakfast, farm-raised egg on toast. He loved the way the whites stood up firm on the top of the bread.

He leaned back to look around the stubble-faced kid with the pad standing next to him. Where was that pretty waitress he'd seen last week? There she was seating a couple on the balcony.

"Will that be all, Mr. Highsmith?" the boy asked.

"Huh? Oh, do you mind if I move out to the balcony?"

"Oh, no, sir. It's such a nice morning, isn't it, Mr. Highsmith?"

A little fog was rolling in from a stand of willows beyond the clay courts to his right. Several geese were just now signaling their ascent over the clubhouse.

"Yes," Mitchell agreed, "a fine morning."

"And such a great view," the boy added as he left.

Mitchell nodded, eyeing the waitress. She smiled and nodded at him as she walked closer. How young was she? Rose would kill him.

He folded his laptop and tucked his racquet under his arm.

"May I help you with that, Mr. Highsmith?" she asked.

"Oh, no. I've got it. Just moving further out. Such a nice morning."

"Yes, it is. Working so early, sir?" she asked, pointing at the laptop.

"All work and no play. Working on my memoir."

"Oh, a memoir. Surely you're not old enough to write one of those."

She laughed. He liked the way her yellow hair bounced when she did. He put her around twenty years old.

"Older than dirt, young lady. Older than dirt."

She tucked her pad in the apron cord pulled tight around her small waist and folded her arms across her bosom. He watched the thin gold bracelet dangling from her wrist. No other jewelry, he noted. Her name badge read *Heather*.

"Just what do you do, Mr. Highsmith?"

"Now that's a personal question, Heather. I didn't think y'all were allowed to get personal."

"Course we can. Who told you that?" She leaned in and whispered, "We're supposed to 'get friendly, but not too friendly.' So my supervisor says. It's good for membership, she says."

He nodded. "I see. Well, I motivate people for a living."

"Hmm. Like a motivational speaker?"

He nodded. "More like a life coach."

She frowned.

"For instance, how many days of the week do you work here?"

"Every morning 'cept Sundays."

"What? No schooling?"

She grinned. "Afternoon and night classes."

"Good for you. Ever notice anything about who comes here every day?"

She looked around her and shrugged.

"Ever see any . . . How do people your age say it nowadays? People of color?"

"Oh—" She turned her head to one side.

Is she buying it?

"No, I guess not, Mr. Highsmith."

"How does that make you feel?"

She stared back, eyebrows raised, lips poked out.

"Comfortable? Happy?"

She shrugged.

"You could bring your friends, your grandmother here even and not be afraid that they'll meet anybody that will make them feel uncomfortable or unhappy."

She drew her arms in tighter. Her eyes grew a little wider. Was he losing her?

"You've made a choice for them. And you didn't even know it, did you, Heather? You're looking out for them. For us. You're a leader, aren't you?"

She smiled, then laughed, tossing the hair again. *Eating it up.*

"What kind of courses are you taking? Business, I bet."

"Yeah, how'd you know?" She glanced over her shoulder. "Listen, I've got to hustle. Thanks for talking with me."

He fished out a business card. "I'd love to have you work for us. We need bright young people like yourself. Too many old minds make for an ineffective company."

"The Benson Group," she read. "Thanks, Mr. Highsmith. I'll check you later."

Just as he had found a table near the balcony his phone

rang. He placed his laptop down and answered it, walking away from the couple chatting nearby.

"The newspaper story is legit," came his man's voice. "He's dead."

"So, you've seen the body?"

"No, sir. His wife confirms it, though."

"I don't need sobbing widows. I need a body."

"Yes, sir."

"Anything else?" He hoped there was.

"Preston's dead. I've seen his body. Sliced up pretty bad. Whoever did him was pretty sick."

Mitchell Highsmith winced. Preston had been a reliable source. Didn't sound like something the Bureau would do.

"Anything else?"

"Well, sir. There's Bureau everywhere."

"Tell me something I don't know."

"There's Blue and Hunt. And—"

"Have you seen the boy?"

There was a pause. "Not since he left Raleigh."

"That's not what I wanted to hear."

"I'm almost certain he's in the middle of all those agents. I just haven't seen him with my own—"

"He stands out like a sore thumb. White skin. Blue eyes. Looks like a Benson. Anything else?"

The man chuckled. "Here's the good news. About two this morning Kelly was able to unscramble a little bit of a call. A boy named Patrick talking to someone named Isaac about a dog. Just a few seconds of it."

Mitchell hummed satisfaction. "Locations."

"Nada."

Mitchell cursed.

"But she's almost certain it was Bureau."

"Anything else?"

"That's all, sir."

"Nothing more about Abraham?"

"Resting at home. House guarded, 24-7."

"Good. Double watch on him." Movement on the courts caught his attention. A single man, dressed in white and carrying a red racquet, stood at center court. *Good, he's here.* "And remember, I need proof that Ben Jacob Benson is dead. Proof."

"Yes, sir."

Mitchell watched his waiter approach. The man still stood at center court.

"No more crying family members. I need a scalp today."

"A scalp, sir?"

"You know what I mean. Proof! Firsthand proof."

He hung up as his food arrived.

"Will that be all, Mr. Highsmith?"

"Could you send my friend down on the court a little something? Coffee and a Danish, maybe. I'd hate for him to play on an empty stomach. Put it on my bill."

"Yes, sir."

He'd have his breakfast and confirm a few things with his men in Raleigh before he met the man at center court. There were a few more points to clear up about Ricky and Chloe Hunt before he talked with the man in white. If his men had done their jobs correctly, maybe there would be no need to talk with the man down there at all.

Unlikely, considering the mistakes his men were making lately. Miracles can happen, he thought, chuckling to himself.

the morning light brought me no joy. The bed had been hard, as had the pillow. And standing against the far wall watching me wake up was the last person I wanted to see at first light. Ulysses Hunt.

"Good morning, son."

"Don't call me that."

He lowered his head. "Isaac, I wanted to talk with you before Charise got ahold of you." He took a couple of steps toward the bed. I turned my face to the wall.

"What I did was necessary. The secrecy, the lies—all part of my job, like I said earlier. But I did it because I wanted to protect you. I love you like a son. Nothing can change that. If I had every year to live with you again, I would do it in a heartbeat. You'll always be a part of me. I'm sorry for the pain I've caused you. I pray one day you can forgive me, trust me again."

"Trust?"

He cleared his throat. "Your mother was a strong woman. A brave woman. I am proud to have been her handler."

"A handler? Is that what you are? And I'm sure she was a valuable asset to her country, and you'd expect nothing less from her offspring, illegitimate though I may be."

He was quiet so I turned over. His tears caught me off guard. I buried my face, fighting my own.

He cleared his throat again. "I loved her like a daughter. Part of me died when she was killed. I vowed I would protect you with my life. If I lose my life doing that, it will be a small price to pay in return for what she gave me as her friend."

He cleared his throat once more and left.

I let the tears out. I felt stupid for doing it, like a little kid afraid of the dark. But in that moment everything felt like darkness again. Deep cold darkness.

"Oh, God. Help."

Someone knocked on the door.

I put the pillow over my head and steadied my breathing.

"Isaac?" It was Trip. The door opened. "Hungry, man? I scrambled some eggs. Made some toast and coffee. It's not as good as your honey would have made, but it's edible." I heard the sound of a plate being placed on the nightstand. He was chewing.

"Wake up, before I eat it all."

The smells reached me through the pillow. I was hungry. There was no denying that. But I didn't want him to see that I'd been crying.

"Go ahead," I mumbled.

"Yeah right, and have you snapping at me all day. I'm praying for you. I'll bet Catty is too. God is in control. You have to believe that. He is bigger than all this craziness. For some reason He's letting it happen to us. To you. You remember how big He is, don't you? Like you were telling me just yesterday at the lake. Can't believe it was just yesterday.

"We got word that your daddy's back at home. Resting fine. Isaac—"

I felt his hand on my shoulder.

"Never mind, I'll save it for later. Enjoy your breakfast."

He patted my shoulder and left the room.

"Good morning, Trip," Agent Blue said from the hallway. "How's our prince this morning?"

"Well, I feel—"

"No, not you, silly man."

She lightly knocked on the door. "Prince Isaac. I mean, Mr. Hunt, might I come in?"

I dried my face with the bedsheet and sat up.

"Sure."

She stood near the foot of the bed. "Morning. Did you sleep as rotten as I did?" She smiled at me and perched herself on the corner of the bed. The brown pantsuit she wore last night looked almost freshly pressed. "Please eat."

I took the plate in my lap and started eating. Trip was right. Catty's would have been much better. Just seeing Catty would have been much better. Holding her . . .

"Good. I was beginning the think you were on a hunger strike."

"Now there's an idea."

"Ah. Spicy. And you haven't even pumped your veins full of caffeine yet. Isaac, you're going to see a lot of me over the next forty-eight hours. You'll probably see me from time to time for the rest of your life. The next two days will be intense. In a few minutes we're going to go out there and plan some heavy-duty cops and robbers kind of stuff. Real guns, real bullets, and real Kevlar. Our target is Mitchell Highsmith. Not Isaac Hunt. So, if I hurt your feelings, don't take it personal. We may push you around like brussels sprouts on Thanksgiving but that just means we care. Simple fact is we've got a man to catch, and you're our bait.

"I want you to stay with me. No snide remarks. No attitude. No renegade stuff. Trust us. Do what we say. We're with the government, and we're here to help you. I always like saying that."

She stood up, tugging at the hem of her jacket, before taking a few steps toward the door. She turned around, standing like she was posing for a sales catalog. "You're probably thinking, How can I trust this woman, I barely know her and she knows all this incriminating stuff about me? Trust me, I don't know more than I need to know. And besides, if I screw up, your grandfather will hunt me down. And yes, this is as close to bedside manner as you get from me."

For all her tough talk, Agent Charise Blue had at least one soft spot—young love. With her permission I was allowed time with Catty.

"Fifteen minutes," Eric said, glaring at his glow-in-the-dark watch. He opened the back door of Miss Lucretia's and let me walk in. As I shut the door, he stepped back into the deeper shadows of the back porch with the other agent there, guns pulled.

Another armed man sat in the kitchen. But he wasn't relaxing. He had been expecting me. Expressionless, he nodded toward the closed door of the room I'd slept in.

I entered without speaking, without knocking.

Catty was lying down on the floor. The smell of oil paint filled the room. An easel stood in the corner with an empty canvas. Brushes and a loaded pallet lay on the dresser nearby.

I eased myself to the floor beside Catty. She was asleep. So beautiful, peaceful. I longed to kiss her face. To feel the warmth of her lips against mine.

She stirred and opened her eyes. "Oh."

"Hello."

"Oh, Isaac." She threw her arms around my neck. "It is you. I thought I was dreaming. Isaac, Grandma Lu is dead."

"I know, Trip told me."

Her sobs rocked me. I wrapped my arms tight around her and cried too. I cried like a baby. For my own mother. For lost years. For fear of my life. For Miss Lucretia.

She let go of my neck and wiped her face on her sleeve before laying her head in my lap. I smoothed her hair in the silence. There was so much in me that I wanted to tell her. I didn't know where to start. I didn't know how to put words to it all.

How could I tell her about trying to kill Jack? What words could I use to explain how I knew God was in me now but at the same time wished He wasn't. I felt crazy and guilty and scared. But at least I didn't feel the empty darkness anymore.

"When do you leave?"

"You know?"

"The man in the kitchen told me. Something about you helping them catch a man who killed a preacher in Chapel Hill a long time ago."

I nodded. "We're leaving tonight. They want me in Raleigh before first light. Seems like we do everything in the dark."

"Then it'll be over." It wasn't a question, and I was glad it wasn't because I couldn't have answered it. I had no idea when this would end. Chances are, it wouldn't ever.

"Grandma wanted you to have Daddy's clothes. And the spoons." She giggled and took my hand, her smooth knuckles gliding against mine like a salve.

I laughed too. "Oh, yeah. The spoons."

There was a knock on the door, and the man from the kitchen stepped in the room.

"Two minutes?" I begged.

He nodded and backed out of the room.

"Catty." I looked at her, trying desperately to remember every part of her face. Trying desperately to remember the words I'd practiced. How she challenged every stereotype I had about southern black women. How she satisfied me just by holding my hand. "I . . . You're an amazing woman."

She pressed a finger to my lips. "Kiss me." I did.

We left at midnight. Most of the agents had left hours earlier. Or so it appeared. I imagined many more in the woods much like it was in the swamps I had traveled through to get to Miss Lucretia's.

Faithful and multitalented Eric drove the car. It was a dark sedan, the only car left besides Trip's.

Trip was with him. "Well, Isaac," Trip said, "Godspeed. Remember, God is in control. Whether you feel it or not."

"I thought you were going with us."

"Nope, this is where I get off. Don't worry, I'll be calling you. Don't think you'll get away without being in my wedding." He gave me a hug and a Bible, then left without another word.

"Mr. Hunt," Agent Blue said from the front seat of the sedan. "Get in, please."

I had the entire back seat to myself, so I stretched out and allowed myself to drift off. I woke to the crashing of waves.

I sat up and smelled the ocean. It was still dark. I strained to make out my surroundings. No houses. No streetlights. "Where are we?"

Eric opened my door. "Get out, Mr. Hunt."

I looked around in vain for Agent Blue.

"What's going on?"

"Get out."

He looked harmless enough, but I didn't want to test my theory. I got out.

"Can't you tell me—"

He pointed to the line of dunes along the road, the sand the color of pencil lead on this moonless night. I held my breath as I made out the form of Abraham Benson, arm in a sling, coming over the rise.

"Five minutes," Eric instructed with a glance at his glowing watch.

I nodded and stumbled forward. I waited for the fear to come, but it wasn't there.

He was breathing hard when I got to him. He frowned as if he was trying to figure out what to say. Just like I was.

"We've got five minutes. I guess more like three now." I attempted a laugh.

He smiled. "I know. That's what Charise said." He glanced around. "Wherever she is. Isaac, I wish none of this has to happen."

"But it does. I understand it now."

"I'm sorry."

I nodded. All of a sudden he was this big friendly lion. Approachable, but a lion nonetheless.

"I had all this sentimental mess I wanted to say but now—"

He stared at me for a few seconds. "You have your mother's eyes—well, not the color, but they remind me of her. She would be proud of you. You don't talk much, do you?"

I smiled.

"Day before yesterday I wanted to kill you."

"I figured as much. I was the one who hit you in the woods."

"It was you. Because you suspected I was out to shoot you?"

"Naw. Well, sort of." He laughed. "But mostly to save you from running into my cousin."

"It still hurts."

"What?"

"My head."

"You're welcome, young man."

He laughed. I liked his laugh and his sense of humor.

"I'm sorry," I said.

"For trying to kill me? It's okay. You're off the hook."

"And you're off the hook too."

"For hitting you on the head?"

I laughed. "No. Well, I mean, yes. But mostly for saving me from the fire."

"You remember that? You were so young."

"I didn't remember until I saw you again, and heard your voice."

"Sorry I couldn't save Betty. I'll never forgive myself."

"And thank you for sending me to live with the Hunts." There, I said it. In a crazy mixed-up kind of way I was grateful for having spent the last eighteen years with them, given the alternative, that is. His inactivity and the Hunts' secrecy was like being hit over the head—saving me from something worse. I had to be grateful for that. Lumps and all. If only Chloe and Ricky had been more loving.

"You're welcome, son."

Agent Blue came up the dune behind my father. I turned to see Eric coming up the dune behind me.

"What should I call you?"

"Call me Abraham."

Ricky Hunt looked older than I remembered. His hair was much thinner on top and there was more gray in it. He smiled at me as I approached his table outside the restaurant. It seemed to be a genuine smile.

"Isaac." He stuck out his hand.

"Hi." I shook it and sat. We were quiet for a few minutes. It was an awkward silence, a not-normal silence actually. Not just because I was sitting there in a bulletproof vest about to have lunch with a man I vowed never to speak with again. But the street seemed strangely clear, almost staged. There were no buses. This was Market Street, a one-way street city buses took to get to the Downtown hub.

I smiled as I remembered the first day and only day I had been on a city bus. It had been Tate's idea. Part of the black experience, he had called it. *Tate, where are you right now, man?* How would I start over with him? I didn't know for sure, but it had to happen.

I put that out of my head and remembered Agent Blue's instructions: "Make small talk, let us do the rest." Somehow she'd figured out my history with this Judge Hunt.

"Nice restaurant," I said.

"Your mother . . . Um, Chloe and I have been coming here for the past couple of weeks." He shot me a strained look and took a sip of water. "Establish a pattern. That's what the agent told us. It's been so strange knowing that so many people are watching us. And that some of them want to—"

He glanced at me again. "Anyway, the penne with shrimp

sauce is great. Chloe doesn't much like the location. I told her that was part of the charm of eating outdoors Downtown —having a little diesel with your dinner." He chuckled, then winced.

I attempted a smile.

"You've gained weight."

"No, it's the vest underneath," I said.

"Yeah, you're right. He touched his back. "Does wonders on the lower back."

"How have you been?"

"Besides my back, fine. Your mother—" He sighed. "Chloe's not too happy about this arrangement. 'You're a judge, can't you find another way?' she asks me. Forbids me from letting them go ahead with this. We had a big fight just before they came over for me. We're putting you in great danger, Isaac. And I want to apologize for it. Doesn't show the best judgment. And I'm sorry for—"

"Dad." There, I had done it. I had called him Dad. I bit the inside of my lip. *Isaac, man, this is where you say "I'm sorry."*

He stared at me, his hand halfway to his gaping mouth. A white van pulled up beside us. Two big white men got out and walked toward our table. Instead of running like I was supposed to, I watched them like I was watching someone walking their dog or delivering papers. And it didn't strike me as odd until one of them took me by the arm and started pulling me to the van. Needless to say, my mind was on other things. Like finally coming to grips with forgiving Ricky and Chloe Hunt.

"Hey," Dad yelled. He grabbed for my other arm. The other man produced a gun, a small black thing almost lost in his big palm. I leaned back against the big guy with my arm and kicked the arm of the one with the gun. He stumbled one way and somehow I was stumbling the other way, back on Dad.

"Run," I yelled, pulling Dad with me. In our wake we left squealing tires and honking horns. No one was running after us. That was something Agent Blue had hoped for. That would have made the decoy part of this plan work seamlessly.

Operation Scrambled Egg, she called it. She had two pairs of men, who supposedly looked like me and Dad, planted around Downtown near the restaurant. When we took flight they would too, drawing all Highsmith's men and possibly Highsmith himself out into the chase. The plan sounded okay in the wee hours of the morning. At that moment, with the Kevlar vest weighing me down, all I could think of was I didn't like the word "possibly."

We ran to the corner. The light was red. No decoys in sight. And for the life of me I couldn't remember which way was up. So much for Eric's drilling me with Downtown maps.

"This way," Dad yelled. He took off to the right.

"There they are," I said, running behind Dad. Up ahead, at the next corner, I saw two men dressed like us, running toward us. And then I saw another set wearing the same clothes, running along the intersecting street.

The plan was working. My memory was not.

"What's the street, Dad? Where are we supposed to meet Agent Blue?" I was out of breath. What was Dad running on?

"West."

"No, West Street."

"No," he yelled over his shoulder. "We're supposed to go

west down North. Then east on Hornet. There's a little alley-way about five blocks up Hornet."

"You sure?"

He nodded, breathing hard. "Boy, I'm outta shape."

"You!"

I followed him, running through lunchtime foot traffic on North Street, occasionally seeing a decoy pair and hear-ing the sounds of squealing tires echoing off the buildings.

Hornet Street was just about deserted. There were a couple of delivery vans and a man in a wide-brimmed hat eating a sandwich on the sidewalk outside a print shop. We arrived at the alleyway drenched in sweat. No Agent Blue. Just brick wall and concrete on three sides, broken pavement underfoot.

"Where is she?"

Dad stood scratching his head. "I don't know. Wait a minute."

Someone was running down Hornet.

"I don't like this," Dad mumbled, searching his pockets. "Where's my phone? I don't like this. I must have dropped my phone. Do you have a phone?"

I had frozen, straining to remember. Straining to hear Him. *God is in charge.*

"Isaac, do something."

The someone had stopped running. Looking down the other alleys and cut-throughs that we had passed along Hornet, no doubt.

I walked past my dad toward the street.

"Isaac, come back. What are you doing? This isn't the plan. Something's not right. Son!" I heard Dad scramble around behind me. I took another step toward the street.

God is in charge. God is in control. You are in control, Jesus.

The someone appeared. It was just who I suspected.

"Hello, Isaac Ulysses Hunt." He took off his hat and threw it down.

"Hello, Mr. Smith. Or would you rather I call you by your real name, Mr. Highsmith?"

"Hmm. That's clever. Stand back."

"Isaac."

"I'm okay, Dad."

I waved him off. It felt good calling him Dad again. It felt good feeling good again. And knowing deep down that I had Someone else concerned for me even more so than the man behind me. That Someone was in control. I had nothing to fear. Something that Trip had marked in my new Bible came back to me. *Though I walk through the valley . . .*

"Forgive my manners. Good afternoon, Judge Hunt. Your wife sends her regards."

Dad jerked. "My wife!"

I held my breath.

"Would you like to join her?"

"You're crazy. This place will be swarming with cops in a matter of seconds."

"I don't think so." Highsmith pulled out a gun. "Come with me, Isaac."

"No, you're mistaken," Dad said and stepped in front of me. He lunged forward. Something black and round left his hand and went flying for Highsmith's head. Highsmith dodged it and shot toward us.

Tires squealed. A siren blared. Highsmith cursed and took a leaping step toward us.

He raised his gun at me. Dad pushed me down, then fell toward me as the bullet hit his back. I wrapped my arms around him. Highsmith shot again. My dad screamed.

"Dad!"

We fell back. More shots were being fired, though not from Highsmith. He was running, or I should say, attempting to run. Two black-and-whites had cut him off.

"Dad, are you okay?" I slid out from under him and eased him on his back.

He moaned. "Yeah—"

He had been hit in the back of the thigh.

"No you're not." Blood was everywhere.

"So, I lied. But I'm alive. And so are you, thank God." He smiled.

"I'm sorry. I've been a fool. To think I could go on without parents. Somebody to call Mom and Dad."

"Isaac, I'm not dying. Don't get sappy on me."

I blew him off and continued. "Someone to fight with over how I wear my hair. Someone to come back to 'cause they've lived in the same house for forever. Someone to accept me, love me. Can you forgive me?"

"Yes." Tears ran down his face. "Your mother will kill me if you tell her I told you this. But I think you need to know. When we adopted you, we were hoping that it would trigger something in her body. You know, that she would get pregnant within a few years. That she would give birth." He closed his eyes against the tears. "It was foolish of us to play that game with you. But believe me when I tell you this, son. We love you. We really do. It's just been so hard. Can you ever forgive us?"

I wiped my face. "Yes, I can and I do."

"Thank you, son."

Someone walked toward us. I turned to face my grandfather. Agent Blue stood a few paces behind, smiling. She nodded toward me and walked to her car.

"Granddaddy."

"Isaac."

"Dad," my father said, "next time you want me to be in on one of your spy games remind me just how bad it hurts to get shot."

Old Ulysses chuckled, looking down on us with one of his typical granddaddy expressions.

"Granddaddy, I need to ask your—"

"Already accepted, son." He knelt beside my father and took off his suit coat. He balled it up and put it under Dad's head. "Now, let's make old gimpy here more comfortable until the ambulance gets here."

While we were waiting I started telling the story of my painful journey to find the truth about me. Not to make them feel guilty. It wasn't about spreading guilt or punishment. It was about freedom and healing.

I had the truth now. It was a hard thing, that truth, but it was a good thing, without a doubt.

epilogue

my grandfather was on all fours, holding his side. He sat back on his heels and held his stomach with both hands. He blew hard from his mouth and pulled the back of his hand across his eyes.

"This—" he panted, "this is—" He paused again and wiped his eyes with a corner of the bedsheet. "Too much for an old man." He let out a laugh and started pounding the mattress.

My dad threw his head back and laughed. "Isaac, turn the TV up. I can't hear a thing with your grandfather carrying on like that."

I got up and handed my father the remote. "I'd better get going, Dad."

"You don't wanna stay?" He pulled himself up in the bed and winced a little. "He's gonna do the punctuation part soon. You used to love that." He reached down and rubbed his bandaged leg.

I glanced at the TV and saw a rerun of Victor Borge falling off the piano bench again. I couldn't help but smile. I did like Borge, me and my not-quite-black-enough self, but I had other things on my mind.

Part of me wanted to stay, a large part of me, to be honest. But part of me, the less rational part of me, knew I needed to go. Then there was the part of me that didn't know what to do with these new feelings. This new awareness. I longed for a talk with Preacher Trip, of all people. And of course, I longed for my Catty.

Dad let out another laugh and waved me off.

I stepped over my grandfather, the secret agent, and left, closing my parents' bedroom door behind me.

"Isaac."

I turned, with my hand on the knob, to see my mother. Her hair was up in rollers. *When was the last time I saw that?* She returned my smile.

"Will you be back—" Her last word hung between us. Would she wonder every time I left the house? I guess I didn't blame her. "For dinner I mean."

She was a beautiful woman, even in the green and yellow plastic rollers. Even with the frown on her face.

I nodded and looked at the floor, ashamed at my thoughts. "I'll be back."

She and Ricky Hunt would have made some beautiful babies. The beautiful couple. But then there was me. The adopted child.

I cleared my throat and checked my back pocket for my wallet. "I'd better get going."

Before I could turn or move aside, her hand was on my face. Her smooth cool palm was pressed against my cheek, her thumb brushing the left side of my wide nose. She smelled of flowers. I held my breath and clenched my teeth.

She was touching me. It felt good and bad at the same time. I wanted so badly to turn away. I yearned so badly for more.

"Isaac, I—" she bit back the words and stepped back. "I'd better let you go."

I frowned. She frowned. We just stood there frowning at each other for a few seconds. Unspoken words churned inside me.

"Yeah, I'd better get going," was all I could say.

She let me go with a nod. I made it to my car before I realized I couldn't leave. I couldn't carry these words any longer, tumbling around my insides like broken glass. She had to hear them. I needed to say them to her.

She needed to hear how much she'd hurt me. She needed to hear about all the things I'd longed for all these years.

My mother was still there in the hallway when I opened the front door. Her back was turned. She was breathing quickly like she did when she was mad.

"Mom?"

"What is it, Isaac?"

I could barely hear her words but the agitation was unmistakable.

"We . . . we need to talk, Mom."

She spun around. "Talk?" Tears streaked her face. Great long tracks of mascara muddied her cheeks.

I stepped toward her. "Don't cry."

"No. Go. Please, go." She pulled a tissue from her pocket and started wiping at her face. She waved me off with her free hand. "Go, Isaac."

"No. I need to tell you something."

"Tell me what, Isaac? I know I've been a bad mother. I've been selfish and greedy and—"

I stepped closer. She stumbled back.

"Mom," I said, taking her hands in mine. "I love you."

She crumpled in my arms. A few of her rollers fell to the floor, sending soft brown curls around my forearm. I eased my body to the cold tiles beneath us and pulled her in.

"I love you, Mom." All the hateful words I had planned were gone, dying on my tongue with the realization that they had no real purpose at all. They would bear nothing good if spoken. Like the lies that Ulysses had told all these years, in the end my words would have brought nothing but misery. I didn't want the misery to go on any longer. The power to end it lived within me.

She cried more. I lowered my head and smelled of her hair. *Like flowers.* I brushed a tear from her cheek. *Like petals.*

"Please don't cry," I whispered.

She only shook her head and buried her face in my shirt. "I don't deserve you, Isaac." She drew a long breath and told me about how she knew long before she married the young talented lawyer from Richmond that she would have trouble bearing children. She told me about the miscarriages, and of the tens of thousands spent on treatments and procedures. Then she told me about the first time she saw me.

"You were so sweet. And you had those little freckles over your nose. I'm so sorry, Isaac. I thought—" She bit back a sob. "At first, I thought that if we adopted then I'd conceive and I'd carry full-term. We'd heard of that happening to couples. It was stupid. I'm sorry, Isaac. But when I saw you, the way you looked so much like your father, like Ricky, when he was young—"

She smiled up at me. "You really did look like him. We knew about the Bensons and Pettigrew, and Betty. But you see now why we didn't tell—"

I nodded.

"For years I was so scared that someone would just jump out of the bushes and take you away. I didn't want anyone to take you away. Those are lost years, I know that now. Years you needed me to be a mom, not just someone absorbed in her own pain, protecting you from a distance. I'm so sorry. You are precious to me. And it's about time I found a way to get past my own pain and—Oh, Isaac, I'm so sorry."

I nodded again. I tried to say thank you but the words didn't get past the lump in my throat.

She pulled away and looked into my eyes. "I love you."

Tears welled in my eyes. "I forgive you," I whispered and wiped at my eyes.

She laughed. "Well, look at us. Crying on the floor."

"I'd better go." I stood and started backing toward the door, suddenly uncomfortable crying in front of my mother.

She nodded as she turned. "Tell Tate I said hello."

I smiled. She hadn't lost her touch at all. She could still read me like a book.

I didn't go to Tate's right away. I dropped by the grocery store and picked up a few things—milk, butter, bread, and corn chips; lots of corn chips. Cut Tate and you'd find corn chips like sawdust in a scarecrow. I smiled when the cashier made comments about a party.

Deep down I was hoping for a good reception from my old friend, but I was trying to be realistic too. His hateful words still rang in my ears. It would be no party.

Passing for black.

The words still stung. But I had to forgive him. Let it all go. Start over with this man who knew me better than my own family. He was my family.

I sat out in the car fumbling around in my memory for the words of a Psalm to embolden me.

Tate was a reasonable man, after he'd had a chance to cool down. He was pretty hot when I told him good-bye and walked out. I was hoping that two and a half months was enough time for him to cool down. All the same I knew I wasn't ready to cross his path.

I didn't see Tate's car in his spot so I figured I could just go in, put the groceries away, and leave a contrite note. That was my plan. God had another plan.

I barely had time to tear a sheet from the notepad on the fridge before I heard a key turn in the lock.

We stood staring at each other for too many seconds.

He broke the silence. "What are doing here?"

I stammered something about still having an apartment key.

"What are you doing?"

"I . . . uh . . . bought you a few groceries. Milk, bread . . . uh . . . and corn chips! I was always eating your corn chips." I tried to laugh.

"Don't be bringing stuff up in here. I don't need your stuff." He stepped forward and jabbed a finger down the hall. "Matter of fact, go in there and get the rest of your mess." He threw his keys on his old piece of sofa and stepped closer to me. "I don't need—"

"Tate, I didn't come here to fight."

"Well, get on out of here."

"Stop it, man. Listen, I—" I took him by the shoulders. He shrugged me off. I continued. "I'm sorry for how I hurt you, disrespected you, and I want to start over."

He looked down and turned his back to me, started shaking his head. "What is wrong with me? I should be ashamed of myself." He turned to face me. "I'm sorry, Isaac. I had no right talking to you the way I did just now or that day you left. If I had had some sense, I would have been prayed up. But I messed up again. I'm the reason you went off to that crazy town. I'm so—"

"I would've gone off to that crazy town sooner or later. Wait a minute. How did you know?"

"Your granddaddy told me."

"You're talking to General Grant now?" Tate chuckled at

335

my use of his euphemism for my grandfather. The two had never been on good terms.

"He called me earlier today. Said you might come over."

I chuckled. I was an open book to my whole family, I guess.

"He also gave me some things to think about. Confirmed some stuff actually. Things I'd been hearing from the Lord but ignoring. About me and God, my job, and this." He reached in his pocket and pulled out an engagement ring. My heart broke for him.

"I'm sorry, man."

He shrugged. He reached around me, pulled out a kitchen drawer and dropped the ring inside. He took a quick breath and let it out slowly, his shiny head wrinkled like a basset hound.

"Might come in handy one day. When I need some money to get away or something." He punched my arm. "I'm glad you're okay, man. I really am. You've been through a lot." He stared at the drawer for a bit. "And we're brothers for real now, man." He smiled.

I nodded. "For real."

＊

Abraham was snoring on the swing beside me when the letter came. It was in with the regular mail that Crazy Eddie had brought up from the mailbox by the road but it was anything but regular. I could tell that before I saw the stamp with the corner missing or the hand-inked postmark.

Tate and I had spent our share of rainy days playing spy

games, perfecting our signals and code. Deciphering the message had been easy enough but accepting it—that was another matter.

"Message from your other woman?" Crazy Eddie asked from his perch on the bottom step. He had some rocks there in the dust he kept stacking and restacking. "I'm gonna tell Catty." He laughed and slapped his dusty knee.

"Yeah, right. The *other* woman."

I got up, careful not to disturb Abraham, and went to the far end of the porch so I could stand in a patch of sun. The afternoon breezes were getting cooler of late. I leaned on the rail and listened to my Catty humming in the kitchen.

Liver and onions?

"You'll love it," she had promised. Smelled good, but the thought of eating liver almost turned my stomach. I never did develop a taste for pâté.

Trip was coming over too. It would be good to see him again.

"What's wrong, son?"

Abraham stretched and shook himself.

"Letter from the other woman," Crazy Eddie volunteered.

I rolled my eyes. "Letter from an old roommate. We didn't part on the best of terms. Not all that bad, I guess, but it could have been better. He'd just broke up with his fiancée and now he's left his job."

"Is this the Tate you mentioned before?"

I nodded, forgetting that I'd emailed Abraham about Tate a few weeks ago. "It's him. He says he's training for work in a place called the blacklands with my grandfather."

Abraham smirked. "With Old Ulysses, huh?"

I didn't see the humor in it. I'd spoken with Old Ulysses this morning, and he had said nothing about Tate joining up. The secret agent and his secrets was going to drive me insane.

"I'm sure your friend is fine, Isaac."

Catty came out of the house. Smells of biscuits and gravy followed her. She was fragrance for the eyes. Crazy Eddie sprang to his feet.

"Not yet, Crazy Eddie."

The poor man sank to his perch, patting his stomach like it was a sick puppy.

"Where is Trip?" she asked of no one in particular. "Oh, the mail came." She went to retrieve the rest of the letters from the porch swing.

"Where's the blacklands?" I asked, looking at Tate's letter again. When no one answered, I turned around to face them. Catty looked from me to Abraham, a smile on her face.

"What kind of question is that?" Eddie blurted.

Abraham chuckled and got up. "Well, Eddie, hold on. Seems like nobody's explained it to Isaac." He lifted a thick finger and pointed toward the far end of the porch and pulled his arm slowly around, finger extended. There was softness in his eyes, his calloused face, his voice when he spoke to me.

"It's all around you, son, and under you, and in you. You've felt it. Almost as strong as the Spirit Himself, I'm sure.

"Covers over three counties. Nothing but the richest, blackest farmland on the planet. Thick virgin swampland. Alligators. Black bears. And corn. Folks say I own most of it. I know that's a lie. Man can't own something this precious."

I looked out over the dry cornstalks in the distance. The

sheer number of them made a constant hush all around. Crickets chirped. Crows cackled. When the good breeze ruffled by, up came smells of corn and earth. Smells and sounds that completed me.

"But it's more than land, you see. What's here is not all good. But not all bad either." Abraham continued. "If your friend is out there, he's in good hands. He'll be fine."

I couldn't help but laugh out loud at the thought of Tate out there. It was a strange place. Not the kind of place I would have picked to settle in a million years.

And certainly not the kind of place I would have guessed that I would find the real Isaac Hunt.

acknowledgments

Thanks to my God and Light for the many ways He uses me.

Thanks to my mother for her support even though I'm sure she was wondering what her highly educated knee baby was doing with her time.

Thanks to my dear husband for his unwavering support.

Thanks to all my kith and kin (the Leighs, Honablews, Cherrys, Dickersons, Hargroves, and so on). A better family, I could not imagine. Thanks for all your support (and the great material).

Thanks to all my church family (from Creswell to

Raleigh to Greensboro . . . you know who you all are) for your support and prayers.

Thanks to all you ole school Building Together Ministries Supper Club members (and your "boss lady" Reggie Edwards) for the wonderful incentive to write this book.

Thanks to wonderful authors such as Spencer Perkins, Chris Rice, Raleigh Washington, Glen Kehrein, and Dr. John Perkins for paving the way for this work of fiction. Your excellent books on biblical racial reconciliation and Christian community development are my constant inspiration.

Thanks to my agent, Les Stobbe, for believing in this book and its message.

Thanks to Cynthia Ballenger and Moody Publishers for bringing *The Making of Isaac Hunt* to life.

To download a discussion guide for
The Making of Isaac Hunt, please visit
www.LLHargrove.com.

ISBN 0-8024-1166-5
ISBN-13 978-0-8024-1166-2

A generation is under attack . . . who will protect your family?

The war is at home, and the battlefield is in the lives of our young men. In any community, and particularly in the black community, millions of young men feel the void of a role model. For every absent father, complacent leader, and passive bystander, there is someone who will step in and fill the father figure void—whether he is a trustworthy man of God or a dangerous enemy. It's up to us to win this battle and prepare the next generation to join the fight.

"Young men are in desperate need of mentors who model their message. This book challenges the strong among us to become mentors and provides them with the equipment to do so."

~ Rev. William Dwight McKissic, Sr.

Senior Pastor, Cornerstone Baptist Church

by Dr. Harold D. Davis

Find it now at your favorite local or online bookstore.

www.LiftEveryVoiceBooks.com

ISBN 0-8024-8989-3
ISBN-13 978-0-8024-8989-0

This practical, encouraging, and biblically based manual will help trauma survivors
—and their loved ones—move toward healing. Philadelphia-based, licensed
psychologist Collins describes how trauma victims get caught in the trauma zone,
a place they want to escape but can't. Some can't move forward, feeling stuck and vic-
timized by their past. Some can't see, living in denial of what has happened. And others can't learn from the past, repeating the same mistakes over and over.
All of them find they can't cope with the overwhelming emotions that accompany
trauma. Dr. Collins believes there is a way out of the trauma zone and back to emo-
tional health, a path he outlines in this valuable resource.

by Dr. R. Dandridge Collins

Find it now at your favorite local or online bookstore.

www.LiftEveryVoiceBooks.com

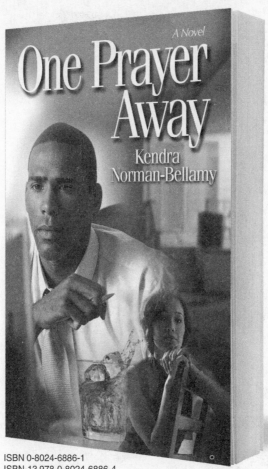

ISBN 0-8024-6886-1
ISBN-13 978-0-8024-6886-4

Seven years ago, Mitchell Andrews made a bad mistake. His alcoholism and angry outbursts drove his wife away—but they also drove Mitchell to find Christ, sobriety, and hope. Now he wants to win back the love of his life, but the past threatens to undo his second chance. Will he come undone at his weakest moment, or will God give him the strength to endure?

Read more about Kendra and her books, including her latest release, at
www.knb-publications.com

by Kendra Norman-Bellamy
Find it now at your favorite local or online bookstore.

www.LiftEveryVoiceBooks.com

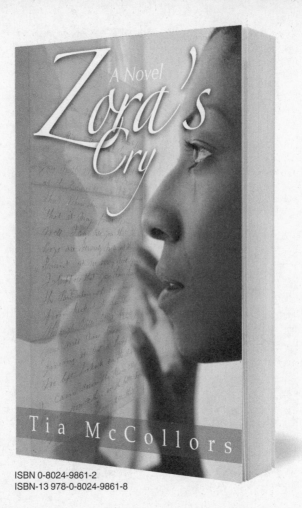

ISBN 0-8024-9861-2
ISBN-13 978-0-8024-9861-8

I'm adopted? Zora Bridgeforth can't believe her eyes. Reeling from the recent deaths of her parents, she uncovers a shocking secret. With her own wedding just months away, Zora feels adrift, unsure of who she is and where she belongs. Then she finds a discipleship group where she and three other women gradually drop their masks, get real, and learn to draw strength from God and one another.

Read more about Tia and her books, including her latest release, at
www.tiamccollors.com.

by Tia McCollors
Find it now at your favorite local or online bookstore.
www.LiftEveryVoiceBooks.com

The Negro National Anthem

Lift every voice and sing
Till earth and heaven ring,
Ring with the harmonies of Liberty;
Let our rejoicing rise
High as the listening skies,
Let it resound loud as the rolling sea.
Sing a song full of the faith that the dark past has taught us,
Sing a song full of the hope that the present has brought us,
Facing the rising sun of our new day begun
Let us march on till victory is won.

LIFT EVERY VOICE

So begins the Black National Anthem, written by James Weldon Johnson in 1900. Lift Every Voice is the name of the joint imprint of The Institute for Black Family Development and Moody Publishers.

Our vision is to advance the cause of Christ through publishing African-American Christians who educate, edify, and disciple Christians in the church community through quality books written for African Americans.

Since 1988, the Institute for Black Family Development, a 501(c)(3) nonprofit Christian organization, has been providing training and technical assistance for churches and Christian organizations. The Institute for Black Family Development's goal is to become a premier trainer in leadership development, management, and strategic planning for pastors, ministers, volunteers, executives, and key staff members of churches and Christian organizations. To learn more about The Institute for Black Family Development, write us at:

The Institute for Black Family Development
15151 Faust
Detroit, MI 48223

We hope you enjoy this book from Moody Publishers. Our goal is to provide high-quality, thought-provoking books and products that connect truth to your real needs and challenges. For more information on other books and products written and produced from a biblical perspective, go to www.moodypublishers.com or write to:

Moody Publishers/LEV
820 N. LaSalle Boulevard
Chicago, IL 60610
www.moodypublishers.com